To Swede and Stella,

Semper Fidelis,
Buena suerte,
And Yea Wildcats!
With all best wishes.

Bud Daub

To Polly and our kids: Debbie, Becky, Doug, Bonnie & Brooke

I gratefully would like to acknowledge permission to republish portions of articles written by the author which appeared in the following newspapers and journals:

Harper's Magazine:	"Colorado Football's Galloping Disaster," October, 1965.
Incredible Idaho:	"Bagdad on the Portneuf," Spring, 1972.
NASPA Journal:	"Vulgarly Called a Dean," October, 1966.
Pharos:	"An Intimate Discussion of Kidney Stones," October, 1971.
Phi Delta Kappan:	"Nobody Calls Me Doctor," May, 1965. "Stamp Out Commencement Speakers," June, 1969.
Liberal Education:	"A Day in the Life of a College President," October, 1971.

Empire Magazine of the Denver Post:

"My Adventures as a Whistler," Dec. 5, 1965.

"I Was No Football Hero," Oct. 6, 1968.

"Cheers for Dear Old Mom and Dad," Nov. 9, 1969.

"I Tried to be an Understanding Dad," March 1, 1970.

"The Year Debbie Made the Drill Team," July 5, 1970.

"Quick Kicks and Quick Quips," Sept. 13, 1970.

"The Education of Doug-'loss'," Oct. 25, 1970.

"Whiskers on the Last Frontier," March 21, 1971.

"Teen-Age Daughters and God's Infinite Wisdom," June 6, 1971.

"My Lonely, Losing Battle Against Co-Education in the Dorms," Oct. 17, 1971.

"Sweet Little Gladiator on the Gridiron," Nov. 14, 1971.

NOBODY CALLS ME DOCTOR

by

WILLIAM E. (BUD) DAVIS

Anecdotes and accounts of the family life
and wanderings of an itinerant educator
through college, the Marine Corps, teaching
and coaching to the humorous adventures of
a university president in the remote and
primitive regions of the high mountain West.

ISBN: 0-87108-065-6

First Edition

Pruett Publishing Company
Boulder, Colorado 80302

Printed in the United States of America
by
Pruett Press, Incorporated

TABLE OF CONTENTS

PROLOGUE

When my appointment as President of Idaho State University was first announced back in the summer of 1965, the news came as quite a shock to some—my mother-in-law, my old classmates at the University of Colorado, Marine Corps buddies scattered around the world, the Idaho State faculty. It was apparent that to many, I didn't fit the image of what a college president should be.

But while the suddenly acquired dignity and decorum of my new position was to be subjected to other onslaughts of outraged opinion, perhaps the unkindest thrust was the day I came upon a letter to my long suffering wife, Polly, from an old admirer of hers. (Since their courtship in junior high days he had gone on to fame and fortune as a surgeon.)

After having admonished her for marrying me in the first place, his tone turned to abject sympathy as he began to deal with my continuing employment problems. He wrote: "I keep hoping for the sake of you and the children that perhaps one day, Bud will be able to hold a job for more than a couple of years, and then perhaps his employer would kind of get to know him and be able to see through those more obvious shortcomings and glimpse the value deep within, whatever that is. Poor Polly, lashed up, after all these years, to an itinerant, seasonal worker."

I was all set to reply with some devastating missal to the effect that while he was in med school all those years carving cadavers, I at least, was bringing in the sheaves. Then I paused to total up the score. In the fourteen years between our marriage in 1951, and my appointment to Idaho State University in 1965, I *had* had twelve different jobs—we had moved fourteen times—and Debbie, our eldest daughter who would enter the seventh grade that fall, had attended seven different schools. Throughout, my professional career had had more ups and downs than a yo-yo, and more changes in direction than a weather vane in a tornado. Poor Polly, indeed, had lashed up to an itinerant, seasonal worker.

These frequent shifts and shuffles seldom went smoothly. Characteristically, the announcement of my appointment to a new job was greeted less by fanfare than alarm. The furors usually stemmed from my lack of acceptable credentials or experience to do whatever I was appointed to do, or my frustrations in seeing personal goals go frittering off on unexpected or uncharted paths.

For example, my college football coach had in me a potential All-American who for four years remained anonymous. After graduation from college, I tried to enlist in the Army, only to be rejected and then drafted as a private in the Marine Corps. I never won a footrace in my life and detested the tedium of running, but my first head coaching job was as a track coach.

Later, as a high school English teacher and football coach, I was constantly confusing split ends with dangling participles. On the football field, my teams alternately were criticized for scoring too few touchdowns or too many.

Upon entering college administration as an alumni director, there were those who pointed out I had had no experience in higher education. When, in the long history of intercollegiate football, I became the first alumni director to be appointed as a head football coach, I was greeted by a threatened player revolt. They protested against being coached by an "unknown, alumni glad-hander."

Upon departing from the ranks of coaches, I was to find that my brief six-month tenure had tagged me with the label of "Super-jock" (which must have been a laugher to my old coaches and teammates familiar with my true athletic prowess). No matter what academic or administrative road I might choose, I was greeted with the sometimes open, sometimes whispered aside, "This guy was a college football coach." Personally, I have been kind of proud of the fact, but learned that in some academic circles, having been a coach was not always considered a gilt-edged credential—more like a blight on the ivy.

If, in retrospect, I ever suggest that I overcame all the obstacles, reservations, criticisms, and inadequacies with stoic fortitude and patience, it would be misleading. More often it depended upon luck and the chance opening of one door which led to the opening of another door, or sometimes just walking over a trap door and plain falling in.

But, throughout, I always recalled an old admonition from Harry Carlson, Dean of Men at the University of Colorado during my undergraduate days, who used to say, "Bud, never take yourself too darned seriously."

Bob Newhart, the great comedian, once philosophised that crisis plus time equals humor. I've had my share of crises—as a student, a Marine, a teacher and coach, a college administrator, and, entwined throughout, as the father of a lusty family. Sometimes the crises overlapped, probably because of the confusion and impossibility of separating my different careers and roles. The challenge remained constant—letting time do its part and then trying to find the humor, wherever it might be.

4

CAMELOT

In a way, I suppose I took my first big step toward becoming a college president when I entered the University of Colorado as a wide-eyed freshman in the fall of 1947. The physical beauty of the campus created a mood as well as a setting and called forth all of those domantic freshman notions of what a college should be. The spires of Camelot could not have impressed me more than did those red-tiled roofs of the University buildings silhouetted in sharp relief against the backdrop of glaciered peaks and brilliant Colorado sky. For me, going to college was like stepping into a new and mystical world.

Not that I was a stranger to Boulder and the University of Colorado. I had been there often, usually for football games when I had hitch-hiked down from my home town of Loveland, less than forty crow-flying miles to the north and east. It was on such trips that I had fallen in love with the Colorado campus and planned for the day I would enroll as a student.

My planning was based more on faith than science. I arrived on campus a few days before registration to participate in "Rush Week." An obliging fraternity, Alpha Tau Omega, welcomed me as a house guest and provided a bunk for the pre-school fraternity festivities. Beyond that, my planning had been sketchy indeed.

I had with me $200, an academic scholarship for my tuition, and one suit—but no permanent room and no job. Other things I had none of were: any concept of what college really might be like; any idea of what I would do if my $200 ran out or I didn't get a job; any lack of confidence that everything was going to turn out fine. I had faith that someone always took care of the wayward scholar.

The "someone" in my case turned out to be the young men in the Alpha Tau Omega fraternity, who took pity on my plight, pledged me, and gave me a job for my board and room. They also took half the $200 for initiation fees and the other half for monthly dues, but I had the best of the bargain as I ate up that much in peanut butter sandwiches alone.

While standing in block-long lines the next week for my first registration as a collegian, the full impact of having neither a job, nor a *room* began to dawn upon me. The wave of returning veterans from World War II had hit the campus, and where 6,200 students had been expected for the fall quarter, more than 10,000 showed up. Six men sleeping in triple bunks in one small room was not uncommon, either at the dorms or in the fraternity houses. Surprisingly, there was little griping about the crowded conditions.

The combination of grizzled veterans back from the wars mingling with smooth-cheeked freshmen who shaved only every third day (I was in the latter group) provided a strange mixture in that freshman class. One of my fraternity pledge brothers had been a major in the Army Air Corps; another had been with the Marines for three years in the South Pacific; better than half were veterans, but they accepted the hazing and horseplay with good humor.

In fact, there seemed to be a good-humored acceptance of life in general, a kind of relief from the pressures of the war years and a gratitude for the luxuries of peace. When a coal strike caused a shortage of fuel during the first big snow storm to hit the campus, a veteran wrote in the school paper:

> *There's no reason classes can't keep going—coal or no coal. A lecture sounds just as good—or bad—whether the speaker is wearing an overcoat or a sport shirt.*
> *. . . An awful lot of these "poor students" got constitutions like polar bears.*
> *These guys have been weaned in the winter resorts of Northern Italy, Attu, Kiska, and the Ardennes. If they were in the Air Force or Colonels, maybe they had a pyramid tent complete with one of those tin-can stoves— the kind that develop about as much good solid heat as the blush of a virgin.*

These guys always seemed to be looking for a reason to laugh. Take, for example, the time the Library was undergoing a face-lifting. The inscription over the center doorway of the building read: "Enter here the timeless fellowship of the Human Spirit." A small sign across the doors proper stated: "Use Side Doors." That seemed to fit the mood of the campus.

They called themselves "the Old Breed." Those of us as yet uninitiated into the rituals of manhood were called the "New Breed." And yet there was a spirit of comradeship that spanned the gap of years. In our fraternity we shared the pangs of near-poverty as money seemed scarce to all, the experience of being "first generation" college students because most of our folks had not been to college, and the togetherness of a crowded campus.

Perhaps it was this sense of togetherness that was the most meaningful of all. At any rate, I, for one, was acutely aware that going to college was something special in life, and I wanted it to go on forever. It was a wonderful year to be a freshman.

8

CHEERS AND TEARS

Climbing the ivied walls of academe was not always a case of scaling a well-charted ladder of success. The footholds were sometimes shaky, the handgrips elusive. Part of my frustration no doubt stemmed from what I had envisioned as a two-fold mission in my intercollegiate life—success as a scholar and a position on the varsity basketball team. I approached the first goal with systematic enthusiasm, the second with the modest assurance that I was one of the world's gifted athletes.

I got some of my early academic inspiration from Gene Fowler, one of the University's favorite sons who had made good in the bigtime as a journalist and author. Just as the ATO's had befriended me, the fraternity had taken in Fowler in a similar fashion a half-century earlier. Later, he wrote the fraternity a letter of thanks, which the ATO's proudly framed and hung in the chapter room. They also had a collection of his books, which I read voraciously, because several were filled with his colorful tales of Colorado, and particularly, his life as a student at CU.

Most of all, I loved his *Solo in Tom-Toms*, where he told of his hashing job and life at the ATO house, his wanderings in the Foothills Cemetery, and his aspirations and preparations for a career in journalism. Fowler had a cavalier attitude toward grades, writing:

> *I had had no difficulty in respect to college grades, but somehow I never was able to regard marks as a true revelation of a man's potentialities. It seemed to me that anyone could get good marks if he set out to do so. But can you eat marks? Can you keep warm with them? Can you make love to them?*[1]

I soon discovered, however, that complete adherence to the Fowler philosophy of grades promised little in the way of con-

[1] Gene Fowler, *A Solo in Tom-Toms*, New York, Viking Press, 1946, p. 268.

tinuing membership in the university community. In no time at all, I became a conformist intent upon those arbitrary evaluations that passed for academic currency—grades.

I also learned that even the greenest freshman never had to go it entirely alone. Generations of students experienced in the game of "reading" the professors passed down an informal formula for "getting" grades. If ever formalized, this organization might fall under the heading of the Student Protective Society, which indirectly sets forth a set of ground rules for maintaining one's relations with fellow students while managing to pass the various courses. As a student, I found these rules, while simple, were practical. They went as follows:

1. Know your professor.
2. Quote your professor.
3. Use the professor's terminology.
4. Cite sources, even if you have to make them up.
5. Don't offend by talking too much.
6. Avoid letting the professor single you out.
7. Hand in thick term papers.
8. Never ask a question at the end of a period.
9. Don't undermine the morale of other students.
10. Don't be too damned smart.

For one who violated these basic principles, the embarrassment could be excruciating.

Despite good coaching from fraternity brothers and other seasoned veterans, I almost became an early academic casualty. I was writing a mid-term exam in a freshman journalism class, when, pausing to stretch, I glanced at my neighboring student. This was a very attractive young lady who had an abundance of everything. She had, I noted, thoughtfully copied her crib notes on her thigh.

The longer the test lasted, the higher her skirt rose. This was most disconcerting. Try as I would, I could not keep my eyes from her exposed notes. Nervously, I looked around. The graduate student who was proctoring the test was having the same trouble as I. Bug-eyed, he was observing in detail this flagrant cheating, but seemed transfixed. Soon, it was apparent to every member of the male population in the room just what was going on (or up). The busy scratching on the exam booklets stopped, and an uneasy calm prevailed.

We were snapped from our stupor by the harsh clanking of the bell. The immodest coed smiled demurely, handed in her test, and passed from the scene, while I, for the rest of the term, scrambled to pass the course.

I chalked this one up to experience, but soon realized that under the pressure of exams and grades, students often would go to great lengths to beat the test. Occasionally, I had to marvel at the artistry and ingenuity involved, and the usual inevitable consequences.

I well recall the time a fraternity brother spent the better part of a week making detailed crib notes for a mid-term exam in geology. He took his notes to class, wrote the test, and returned to the frat house in a state of satisfied exhaustion. While in this mood of happy relaxation, he suddenly recalled that he had left his crib notes in the exam booklet. The following week he mustered the courage to attend the class, whereupon he received the results on the test—an "A" on the crib notes and an "F" on the exam. Justice sometimes triumphed.

I am sure that he was impressed by the old cliche, "Honesty is the best policy." So, too, was one of my struggling roommates, who in complete frustration at the conclusion of an exam once handed in a blank paper with only his name. The professor gave him 20% credit on the test—10% for neatness and 10% for brevity.

As I gained more sophistication in matters academic, I also discovered that the course content and the route to a good grade were nothing if you failed in the classroom diplomacy so important in that polite warfare between professors and students. This covered the little niceties, like knowing when to laugh. For example, I learned that when the professor stated, "I shall now illustrate what I have on my mind," and then proceeded to erase the blackboard, it was no time to laugh.

But if he were acutely sensitive about the fact that he had been teaching for years without a single scholarly publication accredited to his name and dragged out that tired old tale of the two Roman soldiers standing at the foot of the cross, one listened patiently. Allegedly, the first soldier said, "I hear he was truly a great teacher." The other responded, "Oh, sure, but what has he published?" *That* was the time to laugh.

My early academic goals and athletic aspirations began to wither under the pressure of that freshman year. Whereas (like Fowler) I had visions of majoring in journalism as a prelude to becoming a great newspaperman, I tired of reading and rereading Milton's *Aeropagitica* and started casting about for a new major.

At about the same time, I also was forced to reassess my athletic talents. As a high school basketball player, I had sported a ten-point a game scoring average over my junior and senior years. Naturally, I reasoned that with such prolific scoring potential, the University of Colorado basketball team needed me.

More than a hundred candidates reported for the try-outs for the freshman basketball squad. Those showing up in swimming trunks and street socks were quickly eliminated. I wore the appropriate uniform and survived the first cut. But shortly before the Christmas break, I arrived at my locker to discover my gear had been removed.

It was easily the darkest moment of my life, at least up to then. I went back to the fraternity house, packed my bags, and hitchhiked home to Loveland in a soggy snowstorm that matched my mood of self-pity.

Later that night, three fraternity brothers arrived at my home to fetch me back, arguing that if my obvious skills in basketball weren't appreciated, I could always play football. After all, no coach ever cut a man from the football squad.

I bit the bullet, swallowed my wounded pride, and returned— but with new goals and aspirations. What strange mechanisms of the mind accounted for my settling on a career as a teacher and a coach at the time, I will never know. But when one door closed, another opened.

I WAS NO FOOTBALL HERO

The obvious direction for this Horatio Alger account to take would have been for me to turn out as the greatest football player at the University of Colorado since the days of Byron "Whizzer" White. I kept waiting for it to happen. But, the fact is that among the fans watching Colorado football from 1948 to 1950, those who even knew I was in a game included only my girl friend, my parents, and a few loyal fraternity brothers. After three years of varsity service, my jersey, number twenty-five, was untouched, unsoiled, and unknown—probably the only jersey in almost eighty years of football at my alma mater that never had to be cleaned.

In the spring of my freshman year, 1948, I joined an eager group of perspiring candidates for the varsity football squad. It was Dal Ward's first year as head coach at CU, and every former high school football star with the dream of making the varsity turned out with high expectations. It must have been indicative of things to come that of the thirteen teams organized that first week, I was on the thirteenth. I was confident I had a lot going for me, however. I was little, but I was slow.

I well remember my first interview with Coach Ward. Frustrated that the full potential of my 145 pounds of dynamite and enthusiasm was flagrantly unnoticed, I cornered him one day after practice. "Coach Ward," I said with dignity, "I'm not sure whether I should be playing fullback or quarterback."

He looked me up and down critically before replying, "Frankly, I don't think it makes a hell of a lot of difference."

I survived the spring massacres and the gleeful bloodletting of early September and looked forward to my first college game. From the safety of the bench, I enjoyed a close-range view of the mayhem on the field. But it was during the half-time that I first began to appreciate the true spirit of collegiate football.

We were trailing by a touchdown as we trooped into the dressing room. I fully expected Coach Ward to enter and in

Rockne-like fashion plead for us to get out there and win one for the "Gipper." Of course, this was a litle far-fetched because Colorado had no "Gipper." But, we had had a "Whizzer" White. He was, however, far from dead. In fact, he was probably sitting in his law office somewhere listening to the game and wondering why the coach wasn't doing something sensational and Rockne-like to pull this game out of the fire.

But there were no tears, no fiery orations—just cigar smoke as the staff had a high-level meeting to determine second half strategy.

While the players flopped in various attitudes of exhaustion, the trainer walked around with a bucket of iced orange slices. Initially, I was slow at taking advantage of this refreshment. But, after the first few games I soon became adept at getting my share. Toward the end of the season, I was high point man among the subs with an average of 6.8 orange slices per half. This provided some outlet for my natural competitive instincts and soon became the highlight of every game.

Offensively, the coaching staff could never decide what to do with me. I finally ended up as a "T" formation quarterback. Now that was fine, except for the fact that Colorado was running a single wing. For three years, I quarterbacked the scouting team. One week I would be the Kansas quarterback, the next week, the Missouri quarterback, then the Iowa State quarterback, and so on through the season. Annually, I ran ten different offenses, but never our own.

Once in awhile, however, I did get into a ball game. The coach used a rule of thumb for inserting me at crucial times. Whenever we got fifty points ahead or fifty points behind, he called on me.

I shall never forget my first action as a varsity player. We were playing Kansas State at Homecoming in '48, and things were going well. In the fourth quarter we were enjoying a 50 point lead, and Coach Ward was clearing the bench. As players would come out of the game, he would have them move to the south end of the bench. Finally, I was sitting all alone on the north end, wondering when I would get my chance. With 51 seconds on the clock, Ward walked up, looked at me, studied the scoreboard clock, shook his head and started to walk away.

At that moment, my fraternity brothers up in the stands began chanting, "We want Davis! We want Davis!" Since there was a time-out on the field and the crowd had long since lulled into apathy by the one-sided score, the idea suddenly appealed to the whole stadium. Soon the place was roaring with the plea, "We want Davis! We want Davis!" They really didn't know who Davis was, but suddenly, everybody wanted him.

All of this yelling obviously embarrassed Coach Ward. He turned to me again, studied the scoreboard and the clock once more and barked, "Okay, Davis, get in there at defensive half-back. And for God's sake, don't blow our lead!"

I dashed onto the field. Then I went back and got my helmet. As I was adjusting my chin strap, a Kansas State back ran around end for forty yards. I bent down to pull up my socks, and the opponents completed a pass in my territory. I looked over to see how the coach was taking all this, and they completed another pass for a touchdown.

This sterling performance no doubt accounted for the fact that during my junior year (in addition to my scouting team quarter-backing) I became a defensive specialist. I got to hold a dummy in the defensive secondary. It is a demanding task that requires great skill, a firm knee to brace the dummy, and the ability to stand for hours without freezing to death.

With maturity, I learned that training rules are essential for disciplined, well-conditioned teams. My training rules, however, were always a little different from the rest of the squad's. While most of the football players went to bed early on Friday night so as to be in good shape for Saturday's game, I always went to bed early on Sunday so as to be at my peak when the varsity tail-enders scrimmaged the freshmen on Monday. I helped discover some of Colorado's most promising freshmen.

On Saturdays, I never worried much about my pre-game diet. Game weekends, the coach always took the rest of the squad up in the mountains to hide them from overly enthusiastic fans and admirers. He never had to hide me. Besides, I was hashing at the Gamma house at the time and enjoyed their usual nutritious Saturday lunch—hamburgers, onions, potato chips, and pickles. That diet worked fine up until the Missouri game of my junior year.

That day I stuffed myself liberally to ward off the chill of another long afternoon on the bench and waddled over to the dressing room as the team came whooping in on the bus from their mountain retreat. I suited up in my usual game uniform, which consisted of only those items most comfortable on the bench. I wore shoulder pads to fill out my jersey, but dispensed with those usual protective devices, such as thigh pads, hip pads, rib pads, and knee pads.

Leisurely, I picked up my chewing gum ration from the trainer and stretched out on the mat for the pre-game pep talk.

Coach Ward walked briskly in, picked up the chalk, and said, "Starting on the defensive unit today will be . . ." I lay there day-dreaming until he said, "Davis will start at defensive right half."

I thought he was out of his mind. One look at the horrified expressions on the faces of the other coaches and my teammates confirmed that I was not alone in my thoughts. Madly, I scrambled to put on my pads, wiped burnt cork under my eyes, and, as my lunch settled like a wad of gravel in the pit of my stomach, followed the varsity out on the field.

All through the pre-game warmup, I had this stabbing pain in my groin. Just prior to kickoff time, I discovered the trouble: in my frenzied dressing, I had inadvertently put my thigh pads in backwards, and the long projections were stabbing me in a tender spot. Quickly and unobtrusively, I ducked into the team ambulance to make an adjustment.

Thus, I missed the kickoff. As the coaches frantically looked up and down the sidelines to find why we had only ten men on the field, I hurdled the bench and rushed to glory.

The Missouri quarterback scanned our defense and spotted a weakness. On the first play, he threw a hook pass to an end so tall I could chin myself on his navel. Trying for an interception, I rushed by him like a nervous gazelle and missed the ball. With only sixty yards between him and a touchdown, he tripped and fell.

I didn't wait for my substitute. I anticipated him. As inconspicuously as possible, I slunk to the anonymity of the bench.

The following Monday, my varsity football career took a turn for the worse when we reviewed the pictures of the game. As there had always been some element of the "ham" in me, I could hardly wait to see myself in action. It was not an academy award winning performance.

When the crucial play unfolded, I could see the back of my big number "25" go flashing by the Missouri end and sprawl ignominiously on the turf. My thrill of ecstacy at seeing myself in the movies soon turned into a nightmare as Coach Ward shouted, "Great Ceasar's Ghost! (or words to that effect). Who was that? Run that picture back!" They ran it back.

I slithered further and further into my chair as the film went back and forth, back and forth. I was praying the heat from the projector lamp would burn the damned thing up.

Ward again broke the awful silence, "For heaven's sake, will someone get a program so we can find out who number '25' was?"

Then some unknown benefactor in the back of the room whispered mercifully, "Hey, Coach. That was Davis."

There was a brief silence, and then Ward grunted, "Oh . . . All right, let's go on."

But the coaches hadn't entirely given up on me. My senior year, they made a kamikaze specialist of me. I was on the kick-off team, the kick-off receiving team, the point-after-touchdown team, and the point-after-touchdown defensive team. They were doing their best to help me earn a letter, and I was determined not to embarrass them.

It was in the final game of the year against Colorado Aggies that my fondest hopes were realized. I got to go in as offensive quarterback. To show how far the coach had progressed in these three years, as the game went into the waning moments, he called me off the bench. We had only a 25 point lead, so I regarded this as a real vote of confidence.

"Davis," he said, "go in there and call 88P."

I got in there, all right, and I called 88P just like he asked. That "P" behind the "88" meant the play was pass-run option. The reverse unfolded like a chalk-talk diagram with the wingback swinging wide and waving the ball high in the air. I broke into the flat all alone. I could just picture myself catching a nice, easy lob pass which I could field on the dead run and turn twisting and driving and stiff-arming and cross-stepping up the field to explode into the end zone while the cheer leaders were going crazy on the sidelines. I looked at the wingback and waved frantically, meaning for him to throw me the ball. But he, too, could see himself twisting, driving, and stiff-arming and cross-stepping into the end zone while the cheer leaders went crazy. He gave me a contemptuous glance, tucked the ball under his arm, and headed goalward.

Undaunted, I, too, turned upfield, looking for someone to block. Three Aggies loomed in the vicinity of the goal line. I charged after them, fully expecting to steamroller them into the end zone and clear the path for the ball carrier.

I attacked!

There was a great crash, and it seemed as if the whole stadium had dropped on my head:then blackness. I thought I was blind until I realized that the suspension straps in my helmet had broken and it had come down over my eyes. Peeling the headgear from the bridge of my nose, I could see our wingback lying there toes up while a big fat Aggie gleefully cuddled the fumbled ball.

The defensive team came in, I went out, and barring my unlikely entry into the professional ranks, my football-playing days were through. To paraphrase those words of Winston Churchill: "Never in the history of the intercollegiate football has one man sat so long to play so little." I doubt if my old jersey—number "25"—will ever find its way into the University's trophy case. I do hope, however, that sometime in the long history of Colorado football, it will be appropriately adorned with blood, sweat, and grass stain.

Time later mellowed the pangs of frustration—but just barely. Much as I admired and respected Coach Dallas Ward, I could never understand how he could have had a potential All-American right under his nose for four years and never discover him.

THE SINK AND I

Meanwhile, throughout these turbulent undergraduate years when my academic and athletic careers were taking on new dimensions, I also was learning first-hand the values of working one's way through college.

There are those who are enamoured with the notion that there is something glamorous about working your way through college. Supposedly, it has a kind of purifying effect upon the struggling student and impresses him with the worthiness and meaningfulness of his efforts. The most purifying effect it had on me was to get my hands cleaner than they have ever been before or since because I washed dishes in those waning days preceding the electric dishwasher.

After observing the formalities of rush week, I received my ATO pledge pin and disappeared into the kitchen. The work was challenging (I got challenged every time I dripped hot coffee down an active's back); the diet was ample (you can fill up on peanut butter sandwiches); and the life was invigorating (fraternities still used paddles in those days). I managed all of this well enough until the hot fudge sundae episode.

The actives had been laying it on us pledges with zest and enthusiasm, and our patience and our bottoms were wearing thin. A fellow pledge, John Chontos, the pot and pan man, scanned the menu one Friday and noted that hot fudge sundaes were scheduled for dessert. That stirred our creative instincts.

A hasty trip to the drug store produced an ample supply of chocolate ex-lax bars, which we gleefully mixed with the simmering fudge. Then we heaped bountiful helpings of the laxative on the ice cream and with blank expressions served the desserts.

While they were lapping it up and pounding on the table asking for more, we removed all the toilet seats in the house and hid them in the attic. About ten o'clock that evening, our little surprise got through to the actives, and soon they were literally standing in line (first on one foot and then the other) to use the facilities—such as they were.

The next quarter in school, I was looking for a new job. A benevolent house mother at the Alpha Phi sorority took pity on my hungry face and offered me a position as dishwasher. "Ah-hah," I thought, "at last I will be exposed to the glamour of working my way through college." But whatever glamour there might have been quickly wore off as day after day I saw these campus queens wander downstairs for breakfast looking like death warmed-over.

In general, life was good living with the Alpha Phis until their houseboard appointed a new house mother. She took a strong dislike to me, and I got blamed for every prank that took place in the sorority—the horse that wandered onto the third floor, the episode of the bricking up of the doorway, the panties and bra flying on the flag pole. But when she caught me kissing one of the girls in the back hall (a fringe benefit considered to be well within the domain of hashers and dishwashers), I got fired.

This time it was the Gammas who kept me in school. (They weren't really the Gammas, but out of gratitude, I'm disguising the name). Having decided I had about used up my luck and my jobs, I was a model of good behavior. It was while washing dishes for the Gammas, however, that I had a first hand observation of inter-sorority warfare.

It seems the Gammas had a long-standing feud with the Pi Beta Phis, whose large house casually was referred to by Gammas as the Pi Phi Hilton. This irritated the Pi Phis no end, and they were determined to get back at their foe at any cost.

Thus, the Pi Phis coaxed a talented campus actor (who went by the name of Marion) into going through rush week disguised as a girl. They improvised and forged a very impressive high school record, complete with outstanding scholarship and a long list of activities. They also provided glowing letters of recommendation from alleged Gamma alumni, and Marion was greeted by the girls with open, loving arms. He was charming.

I shall never forget that final pledging ceremony. We were peeking through the dining room doors as the Gammas assembled on the stairs, candles held high, and sang their sacred songs. One by one, the neophytes descended. Then came Marion. With radiant face he reached the bottom of the stairs, jerked off his wig, and happily proclaimed, "Thank God! At last I'm a Gamma!"

Thank God I had nothing to do with that, or the near riot and wake that followed.

By the end of my junior year, I decided that I had best escape from the kitchen lest I go through life with permanent scars of my trade—namely, dishpan hands. Thus, I entered campus politics as a candidate for student body president.

My opponent ran as an intellectual on the slogan—"To buddy together is to study together." This was the concept of the older scholar leading the younger scholar as hand in hand they ascended the ladder of knowledge.

I knew that if I were to win, I had to unite all the other factions on the campus, so my platform was all-encompassing. I appealed to the hashers with a program that would prohibit coeds from coming to breakfast in curlers. I made my pitch to the lovers by promising more privacy for back-hall courting. I conned the drivers on the campus with a proposed revised policy wherein parking spaces would be provided in the proximity of their classes. This tied in well with my physical fitness program for the faculty urging them to walk to get in shape. And, as for the administration, I promised that if elected, I would crack down on campus vandalism. Needless to say, I had the solid endorsement of all these groups and won by a twenty-vote margin in an election where 5,000 votes were cast.

I was to discover, however, that the student body presidency was a non-paying job—lots of glory, but no chow. So I soon was back in the kitchen arm deep in luke-warm suds.

By the end of the fall quarter of my senior year, my academic career was jeopardized by a financial crisis. I was flat broke. Even the dishwashing job and the scholarship did not appear to be enough to keep me going. I owed $200 on a loan, which to me looked like the national debt, so was chary about going that route. In desperation, I went to the Dean of Men, Harry Carlson, to plead my case. I needed a job—*any* job.

Luck and timing were on my side. The Assistant Dean of Men had just resigned, and Dean Carlson needed a part-time replacement to finish out the school year. Would I be interested?

My appointment as Assistant to the Dean of Men, however, was almost disastrous to my campus political career. I was in the final month of completing my term as Student Body President, and the loyal opposition introduced impeachment proceedings charging that I had sold out to the administration. By a strictly party-line vote on the Student Council, I survived this alleged conflict of interests, and expired normally. And coincidentally, almost by chance, I was officially launched into my first *paying* job in higher education.

22

A WHIRLWIND COURTSHIP

The new job as Assistant to the Dean of Men paid $112.50 per month. I not only had enough money to pay my personal expenses until graduation, at long last I could afford to get married. I say at long last because I had been courting the same girl for seven years.

In retrospect, I gave fate its due. Had my dad not been an itinerate linotype operator, I might still be a bachelor somewhere in southeast Kansas. But in the summer of 1944, he had quit his job in Parsons, Kansas, and moved the family west to Loveland, Colorado. I was fifteen at the time and regarded this relocation of our clan in much the same way I would have welcomed our banishment to Antarctica—merely as the greatest tragedy of my life.

All of this was soon dispelled, however, as the family drove down one of Loveland's broad, cottonwood-lined streets to our new home. We passed this attractive girl peddling furiously on her bicycle. I eyed her long golden hair flowing in the breeze, and in near-record time, became acclimated to the Colorado scenery.

We pulled into the driveway of our new home, while two doors down she skidded to a stop and looked my way. Without even so much as removing a suitcase, I rushed over to get acquainted.

This, I discovered, was Pollyanne Peterson—a blue-eyed, apple-cheeked descendant of what I was to learn was a long line of stubborn Swedes. The first conversation was brief as my impatient mother kept pestering me to unload the car. It was significant, however, in that from the very first moment, I was smitten. The feeling, for some time, was not mutual.

I did my best to protect her from high-school adventurers, usually sophisticated seniors much too old for her. When other gentlemen callers occupied her evenings, I used to stand out in front of her house honking the horns of their respective auto-mobiles, hoping to coax one of them into a fight.

The most annoying nuisance of my early courting days was a large light on the front porch of the Peterson home—a veritable beacon that burned constantly and illuminated the scene for a hundred yards in every direction. The first time I kissed her good-night the whole block knew.

In those waning days of World War II when gas was rationed and an automobile for a date was a rare luxury, boys often walked their dates to the movies or high school functions. This wasn't too bad on balmy summer nights, but in the winter of Colorado, it got cold. I well remember one such evening. Polly and I had been feuding and fussing for several weeks, but had finally made up. Having enjoyed an evening at the movie and a brisk walk home in zero weather, I was reluctant to let the moment and mood end so quickly. At the Peterson's, the light was burning brightly on the front porch. So, we saw no harm in slipping into the garage and sitting in the back seat of the car while we more or less talked things over and reconciled our differences. Time passed. The next thing we heard was the opening of the garage doors, then the opening of the car door as her father got in. He slammed the gears into reverse, and we were roaring out the driveway. At that point, Polly spoke up and in a meek voice said, "Daddy, here I am."

There was more crunching of gears as we roared back into the garage, followed by the slam of the car door, the slam of the garage door, and the slam of the house door—but nary a word from an irate father.

I beat a hasty and strategic retreat. Two weeks later, when I gathered courage to appear on the Peterson threshold, I was invited in for doughnuts and hot chocolate. From that time on, I did my courting in the living room and away from that illuminating search light.

It wasn't that her parents were opposed to me, as I was so often reminded—it was just that they were opposed to *her* going *steady*. Consequently, throughout those high school years, I often was going steady with her while she was going steady with a lot of other guys, too.

Polly's folks had attended Colorado U., so there was never much question about her college plans. For awhile, I thought about going to Colorado Aggies, where I had been offered a scholarship to play basketball. But, the more I thought of those fraternity boys at Boulder with their flashy cars and polished ways, the more reluctant I became to expose her to their wily charms and take a chance on losing her. So, I, too, went to CU. (At least, this is how I always explained my choice of college to Polly.)

It was a good thing I did. Very quickly some smart upper-classmen on the campus observed that she was loaded with talent. She was appointed Secretary for Student Spirit and Morale, which did a lot for hers, but little for mine. She made a big impression on one of the campus wheels. He was an aspiring attorney—one of those guys with greasy hair and an oily line—and she an innocent, impressionable freshman. I soon found myself cooling my heels in the girls' dorm waiting for him to walk her home from committee meetings. I never knew of a committee that had so many meetings.

It was clear to me that if I were to compete at all, I had better get active in campus politics. That led to my filing for the office of president of the freshman class. My fraternity brothers all put on green freshman beanies and voted in the frosh election, and by that narrow margin, I won. So, once again, I was back in the running.

The harsh winters of Colorado were not conducive to court-ing—at least for a guy with no car. A simple thing like going to a movie was comparable to a short hike on the Yukon Trail (without sled or dogs). If one's ardor were sufficient to withstand the cold, the hard climb from downtown up the hill to the campus left a guy too short-winded to kiss his date goodnight. Unless you were resourceful, one was faced with the miserable alternative of not kissing her from fall until the spring thaw.

The only solution to this problem seemed to be a kind of community kissing program conducted in the back halls, the front halls, and the lounges of the sorority house each night about closing time. This worked fine. There wasn't much chance to get too intimate in this fish-bowl atmosphere.

The summer before our senior year of college, Polly began to take me seriously. I seized upon this opportunity to invest a portion of my summer's savings in a ring. (That was why I was so broke in the fall.)

What with this formal engagement in August, one would hardly think that an actual proposal in December would cause much of a shock. So armed with the good news of my forthcoming job as Assistant to the Dean of Men, I felt the time had come—at long last.

Over the Christmas holidays, Polly and I made our plans for the wedding, but decided to break the news to her parents at a strategic moment. We waited until her folks were driving us back to Boulder from Loveland. Just as we left the city limits, Polly said, "Daddy, we have decided to get married during spring vaca-tion."

This was greeted by amiable silence. There was not a grunt, a cough, or a sigh for forty miles. Then, as the Petersons deposited me at the door of my fraternity house, her father broke the anxious stillness. He said, "Good night."

Polly and I were married in a Swedish church on an Irishman's holiday, March 17, 1951.

(It was another eleven years, however, before I was really accepted by her family. The occasion coincided with my appointment as Colorado's head football coach. From this lofty position, I was able to use my influence to get their season tickets moved from the end zone to the twenty yard line.)

During our last quarter in school, I juggled my duties in assistant deaning with those of a new husband and lame-duck politician. June couldn't come too soon.

On commencement day, as we clutched our diplomas to our bosoms (to protect them from the thunder shower that darned near drowned out the graduation exercises), I was acutely aware that during my undergraduate years, the extra-curricular often had overshadowed the curricular. I also recalled that when I had first arrived on the campus and looked forward to those four bright college years, the stretch ahead had seemed interminable. As Polly and I wandered out of the stadium with the rain warping our mortar boards, I wondered where all that time had gone.

But eagerly, we looked forward to the next great adventure.

ONCE A MARINE

The old adage, "Once a Marine, always a Marine," holds true. There are nights I close my eyes and swear I can still hear the sounds of boots on the drill field at San Diego and the husky voice of my Drill Instructor calling: "Reep, reep, reep fo' yo' left! One, hut, three, fo'! Heels! Heels! Heels! Heels!"

I almost can feel his hot breath on my face as eye-balls glued on the horizon, Gung-Ho cap crushed down upon my sagging ears, and rigid at attention, I hear him growl: "Remember, Private Davis, nobody made you volunteer."

At the time, I would liked to have corrected him, but thought better of it. I had a hunch he wasn't soliciting my opinion.

Actually, I *had* tried to volunteer, but nobody had seemed interested. When I graduated from college in June, 1951, the Korean War was in its second year. Eagerly, I tried to enter the Naval officer program. Because of a deformity in my right elbow, I failed to pass the physical. I then tried to enlist in the Army, but was told it had no use for a man who couldn't turn his right hand over or straighten out his arm. Thus, in the fall when I reported to my draft board and proceeded to the induction center for my physical, I was confident *they would never take me.* As I sat in the barber's chair at the Marine Corps Recruit Depot in San Diego getting my head shaved, I was still wondering what had happened.

I learned early in my days at boot camp that my college education put me in good standing with my Drill Instructor. Instead of being an ordinary "Ethiopian, junk-eating, paddy-hopping, rice-coolie," I was an "educated idiot."

I well recall one of our first interviews. The Drill Instructor, exasperated because I had fumbled my rifle, politely asked, "Davis, what *did* you do as a civilian?"

"I was an assistant dean of men, sir."

"And just what does an assistant dean of men do?" he continued patiently.

28

"He's in charge of campus discipline, sir."

The Drill Instructor got this evil glint in his eye. "The hell you say!"

The weeks passed and my shaved head began to fur out again. And when the D.I. shouted, "Count, cadence, count!"—and the platoon swinging along in perfect rhythm would roar back: "One, hut, reep, four, I love the Marine Corps!"—I really meant it. I liked its style, its arrogance, and its pride.

I well remember one of the few times I ever saw an officer in boot camp. He was a young first lieutenant just returned from Korea, and he talked to our platoon about the Marines coming out of the Chosin Reservoir. He quoted from a book called *The New Breed*, written by a Marine officer, Andrew Gear.

> *Marines have a cynical approach to war. They believe in three things—liberty, payday and that when two Marines are together in a fight, one is being wasted. Being a minority group militarily, Marines are snobs. They are proud, sensitive, and haughty to the point of boorishness with other military organizations. A Marine's concept of a perfect battle is to have other Marines on the right and left flanks, Marine aircraft overhead and Marine artillery and Naval gunfire backing them up.*[1]

The Marines did such a fine job of inculcating in me their *espirit de corps* that after a year as an enlisted man, when I had an opportunity to go to the officer's school at Quantico, Virginia, I jumped at the chance.

As an enlisted man, my pay as a PFC and later Corporal hardly sufficed to support a wife near the base. So Polly had remained in Boulder, teaching in an elementary school. But when I was commissioned as a second lieutenant, she was able to join me at Quantico. We lived in nearby Fredericksburg, Virginia, and by getting up at four a.m. each morning, I could commute the seventy miles to Camp Upshur, the site of the Basic Officer's School. But if the nights were short and the days long, the weekends were one series of honeymoons as we visited the historic shrines from the Shenandoah to the Lincoln Memorial. By Christmas, 1952, however, it was apparent the honeymoon was over. Polly was pregnant.

My first duty station as an officer was Camp Pendelton, California. The duty was invigorating, and daily I rushed from the hills of mock battle to hit the beach at San Clemente, where my

[1]Andrew Geer, *The New Breed*, Harper and Brothers, New York, 1952, p. 8.

melloning wife and I lived just a block from the ocean. With a loaf of bread, a hunk of cheese, and a jug of wine, we dined in style, watching the breakers roll in, the moonlight dancing on the ocean, or the lanterns of the fishing boats bobbing up and down where they anchored just off the pier. On the weekends, she would burrow a hole in the sand for her blossoming stomach, lie face down, and bask in the sun. She looked like a lobster—a pregnant lobster.

But as the time approached for the baby's arriving, I was leaving. In the early days of August, 1953, the Third Marine Division on short notice was ordered to the Far East. Frantic phone calls to my mother-in-law brought her to California on the first plane heading west out of Denver. After giving her careful instructions as to how to get in touch with me overseas, I soon joined my trusty comrades at San Diego, and we were shoving off for parts then unknown.

Two weeks at sea passed, and no word. We disembarked at Kobe, Japan, took a narrow-guaged train to Nara and finally settled down to regimental routine in this ancient city that had been the religious capital of Japan some 800 years before the birth of Christ.

Still no word.

Toward the last of August, I was attending a meeting of officers of the regiment. The Colonel was in the midst of a discussion on the perils of liberty in the domain of the oriental when he was interrupted by a messenger. The Colonel scanned the note, frowned, and in a crisp voice asked, "Is there a Lieutenant Davis here?"

I snapped to attention.

"You have an urgent message, Lieutenant."

With bated breath I dashed to the nearest telephone.

"Davis," the voice on the other end of the line said.

"Yes, sir!" I replied.

"This is the adjutant. I have a cablegram for you. Shall I read it?"

"Yes, sir!"

"Baby arrived 0100, 25 August. Weight, eight pounds, four ounces. Wife and baby doing fine."

"That's wonderful!" I said. "That's great. But what is it?"

There was a fiendish laugh at the other end. "He, eeee," the adjutant chuckled. "It doesn't say, does it?" My mother-in-law had included all the details except the baby's sex.

Communication being what it was, there was nothing to do but wait. So, for more than a week, I walked around proudly announcing my wife had had a baby, but never knowing whether I was a father or a mother.

Finally, a letter arrived from Polly extolling the virtues of my new daughter, Deborah Sue. I calculated she would be almost a year old before I got to hold her. It seemed like a long time. (It would be even a longer time before Debbie adjusted to the Marine Corps influence in her life. She was in the second grade before she learned that the National Anthem was not the Marine Corps Hymn.)

Meanwhile, my regiment, the Fourth Marines, was engaged in a series of training maneuvers which often took us deep into the interior of Japan. One of the maneuvers was conducted at a place called Aebano, formerly a training area for Japanese armored units during World War II. It was there that the pedagogue in me popped out and called my talents to the attention of the Regimental C.O.

The elephant grass hid my platoon from the rest of the regiment, but we could still hear the occasional popping of blank cartridges as other units went through the phases of the mock battle. My platoon, having just completed a series of squad and fire team maneuvers, was waiting to see what would happen next. My academic instincts took over. To relieve the monotony and to broaden the sometimes neglected intellectual horizons of the troops, I decided to deliver an extemporaneous lecture on the merits of the British square and its effectiveness at Waterloo. This led to a discussion of fire by volley, and I organized the platoon for a practical demonstration.

The first rank was to fire from the prone position, the second from the kneeling, and the third from the offhand. With raised swagger stick, I barked the order: "First rank, fire! Second rank, fire! Third rank, fire!"

At that moment I noticed a heavy hand on my shoulder. I turned around and was looking into the bloodshot eyes of my regimental commander. Obviously, the Colonel was distressed about something.

"Lieutenant," he said in a clipped tone, "Where in the hell were you educated? Sandhurst?"

I snapped to attention. "No, sir! Quantico, sir!"

He looked skeptical. "Just *how* did you get into the Marine Corps?"

Well, I could have told him it hadn't been easy.

(The Colonel evidently decided to give me a little direct experience in fire by volley, because I soon was on my way to the First Marine Division in Korea. I returned to the States in July 1954, and was released to inactive duty in the reserves. But the pride in the Corps is something that will be with me always.

For example, as an ex-Marine now turned college administrator, every time I see an academic procession, I cringe. No one is in step, the files are a mess, and there is much talking in the ranks. Clearly, whatever allegiance these academicians have to their respective disciplines, it has nothing to do with close order drill.

Or, take commencement time, always a period of great internal struggle. When the moment arrives for the academic procession, I have to restrain myself to say, "Shall we commence?" rather than barking out in my best parade ground manner, "PASS IN REVIEW!"

But, as the unwieldy, undisciplined scholars shuffle along, there is some satisfaction in knowing that cloaked beneath those academic gowns are the patriotic veterans of many branches of the nation's armed forces—some Navy, some Army, some Air Force, and, by the grace of God, a few Marines.)

YOU CAN'T GO HOME AGAIN

I had read Thomas Wolfe's book, *You Can't Go Home Again,* but I ignored his advice. When the Marine Corps shipped me home from Korea in the summer of 1954, I was desperate to find a job before school opened that fall. Relieved when I was appointed as an English teacher and coach at my old high school in Loveland, I never questioned the salary. I just took it for granted that Polly, Debbie, and I could live on $245 a month.

My teaching load consisted of three classes of sophomore English and two classes of ninth grade phys. ed. The coaching assignment also was varied. I was to assist in football and basketball and take over the reins as head track coach.

The school had changed but little since I had departed seven years earlier. The halls still echoed with the familiar clanging of lockers; the stale odors of the gym lingered on. My former teachers were now colleagues, and my old principal had been elevated to superintendent. It was a constant challenge to keep from being mistaken for one of the students.

One thing had changed, however. Loveland High had appointed a new football coach in my absence—Bob Beckett. (I called him "Old Beck"—not because he was really old, but because I regarded anyone over thirty as being on the down-hill run.) Old Beck had played end on Bowden Wyatt's Wyoming University juggernauts in the late Forties. Beckett and Wyatt both used the Tennessee single wing offense in the manner of General Bob Neyland (the legendary coach at Tennessee), and I soon found it took a personal dispensation from the General or Bowden Wyatt to change even one blocking assignment.

Beck, however, was a master teacher, and I soon picked up a lot of good coaching tips from him. For example, in demonstrating a particular blocking technique, Beck would say: "Get down in your stance and wait until the boy gets down in his. At first, he will be coiled and poised, waiting for you to strike. Then start talking to the rest of the squad. Watch him out of the corner of your eye. When he starts to relax, unload on him. Then step aside and let someone else take the brunt of his wrath."

One of the things I most admired about Beck was that he was never off-balance. One afternoon at practice, he was becoming increasingly disgusted at the frequent fumbles occurring in an exchange between his fullback and wingback on a spinner series. Finally, he stopped practice, called the wingback aside, and color-fully explained just what the wingback and fullback were doing wrong and how it should be done right. Then, like the good coach he was, he jumped into the wingback's spot and ran the play. Beckett fumbled. There was a great deal of snickering and guf-fawing until he strode up to the fullback and said, "Now, son, I'm not going to jump down your throat or berate you for that lousy handoff on the last play. After all, I know that you just aren't used to such blinding speed."

In the heat of a game he was an inspirational strategist with a flair for the dramatic. I well recall the opening game of that season against Greeley High. We quickly scored three touchdowns, but our place-kicker muffed all three extra points. Then we sat back and let them play catch up. We even let them go ahead as with less than a minute to play Greeley took the lead, 19 to 18.

Beck clapped his hands and yelled, "All right, men, let's put it out of reach!" Whereupon our safety fumbled the kickoff and finally fell on the ball on our three yard line. With the clock running out, our tailback got off a frantic pass to our end, and he ran to the Greeley twenty yard line. With three seconds re-maining, Beck walked over to a shivering sophomore sitting on the bench, lifted him by the ears, and said, "Son, get in there and kick a field goal!" He did.

The following week we traveled to Fort Morgan. Trailing 7 to 0 late in the fourth quarter, we stopped a Fort Morgan drive on our five yard line. Then we proceeded to mount our only sus-tained offense of the game, culminating in a score in the final minute. We kicked the point and the game was tied.

I was elated. Beck froze me with a withering stare. "General Neyland and Bowden Wyatt say a tie is like kissing your sister," he grumbled.

Following the kickoff, on the next play the Fort Morgan quarterback faded back for a pass. As he was about to throw, our left end blind-sided him and the ball popped into the air. Our right end caught it in full stride and raced into the end zone.

I cheered again. Beck growled, "We've got 'em on the ropes,

We kicked off again. Once more the Fort Morgan quarter-back dropped back to pass. This time he fired it straight up the middle, right into the hands of our safety who sprinted down the sideline and into the end zone for our third touchdown in less than a minute.

After the game, Beck put his arm around me as we walked into the dressing room. "You know, Bud," he said in a fatherly manner, "had we scored those three touchdowns in the first minute of play, a lot of the fair-weather fans would have gone home by half-time. This way we kept them in their seats the whole game."

As the season progressed, Beck began to take advantage of my talents and experience. Exasperated that none of the scrub quarterbacks was able to handle the T formation plays in any manner resembling our opponent's offense, he ordered me into the slot. My nifty footwork and deft ball handling did wonders for the morale of the scrubs but little for the confidence of the varsity defense. Finally, however, on one crucial play, my pass protection broke down and an irate lineman clouted me in the nose.

As I bent over trying to stop the stream of blood and squint through my rapidly swelling eyes, I could feel Beck's fatherly arm around my shoulders. He was overflowing with concern. I was touched. "Gee," he said, "that's a tough break, Bud. We can't have that." Then he yelled at the manager, "Get Coach Davis a helmet. He can't play without a headgear." As I fumbled with the chin strap, I could hear him exhorting the varsity, "Now, *that's* the way to break up a passing game. Intimidate the quarterback."

For the rest of the season, I suited up daily and ran the scouting team's plays. I rationalized that my college football experience had been valuable indeed.

As the academic year progressed, both in my English classes and with my freshman basketball team which never won a game, I was struggling. The transition from Marine to teacher and coach was not without its problems. I cleaned up my language tolerably well, but the civilian disorganization of the public school system troubled me greatly.

With the approach of spring and my responsibilities as head track coach, the pressure mounted. The only race I had ever won in my life was the basketball dribble back in the fourth grade. As a high school track man I had run the mile in about five minutes, the 880 in 2:10, and could broad jump about 18 feet—none of which earned me more than a place on the bus for an occasional dual meet. And there I was, of all things, a track coach.

To add to this dilemma, the previous year Loveland had won the state track championship, mostly on the strength of two weight men who copped first and second in the shot and discus. Both had graduated, and the leftover weight men could get neither the shot nor the discus beyond their big toes.

I was blessed, however, with three fine hurdlers, a sprinter, a pole vaulter, and a versatile young man who doubled in the unlikely events of the high jump and 880. I figured that if we could utilize the hurdlers and the sprinter on the 880 and mile relay teams, we might have a good season. But it would call for a regimen of hard work and total effort by all concerned—mostly the boys because they were doing the running. I just held the stop watch.

Sometime in March, and before our first meet, I was called into the office of the superintendent. He informed me that Loveland had always taken great pride in its track program, but my disciplinary expectations were not conducive to good morale and performance on the part of high school boys. He topped this off by telling me that I had better look for another job, adding that if I were *ever* to succeed as an educator, I had best quit acting like a Marine Corp Drill Instructor and running my classes and track program like a Marine Corps Boot Camp.

As April mellowed into May, our track team picked up momentum, tying for the Colorado Relays championship and winning the Northern Conference championship. We had a good shot at the state championship if all went well.

Then, the day before the State meet, my star sprinter turned up missing. The principal had notified me of his absence in class early in the morning, and the rest of the day I frantically searched for him. After a brief workout with the track squad, I went over to his house. At that moment he drove up with his girl friend.

"Where have you been?" I gasped.

"Coach," he beamed. "We just got married!"

"Congratulations," I said, taking him by the arm and shoving him into my car. He spent his honeymoon sleeping on the couch in my living room—alone.

The next day we drove to Boulder for the State Track Meet at another old familiar homesite—Folsom Stadium of the University of Colorado. Between the pre-lims in the morning and the final events in the afternoon, I bumped into an old friend, Dr. John Little, Director of Admissions at the University.

He gave me a warm welcome and remarked, "I've just been talking to the Superintendent of Schools from Rapid City, South Dakota. He's looking for a head football coach, and I told him about you. Would you be interested in the job?"

I acknowledged as to how I indeed was looking for a job. I didn't add *any* job. So with great anticipation I accompanied him to a spot high in the stands where I met the Rapid City superintendent, Paul Stevens.

Mr. Stevens and I visited for awhile, my attention being divided between his questions and what was going on down on the track. Finally, he said, "I've enjoyed meeting you. But frankly, we're looking for an older man and someone with more experience."

I must have turned pale as I fought back the nausea. He noticed. Apprehensively, he asked, "I hope I haven't offended you. It's just that you're so young." He didn't know it, but I was aging rapidly right before his eyes. The officials had just kicked my star sprinter out of the hundred yard dash for two false starts.

In a daze I wandered down to the track. After some searching, I found the boy sobbing his heart out down at the corner of the stadium. We talked awhile. He came back and ran well, anchoring the winning mile relay team in the final event of the day as Loveland squeaked through to the state championship.

A week later I flew to Rapid City for an interview and subsequently was appointed as head football coach at Rapid City High School.

SUMMER SCHOOL WHERE SUMMER'S COOL

Between the time of my appointment and my actual departure for Rapid City, I enrolled for my first summer session of graduate work. From my year of experience at Loveland High School, I knew that I had a lot to learn about the art of teaching. Also, at the tender age of twenty-six, I had no yen to tiptoe again on the brink of failure. It was clear that in public education, one's survival and promotion often depended upon professional growth. Calculating that for nine months of each year my days would be filled with teaching and coaching and my evenings with grading themes or diagraming plays, I determined to do my growing at summer school at Colorado State College in Greeley—a short eighteen miles east of Loveland.

One course in particular appealed to my competitive spirit— Philosophy of Education. The College had brought a distinguished visiting professor of philosophy to the campus all the way from Ohio State University for the sole purpose of freeing our thinking, and with the zeal of an evangelist, he soon was liberating it all over the place.

Imagine us suffering graduate students sitting there in a stuffy classroom on a hot, humid, Colorado morning. It was the last class before noon, and the cooing of the doves outside the open windows could scarcely be heard above the rumbling of hungry stomachs. Into this sweatbox would bounce this professor—dapper, distinguishedly grey, and suspiciously enthusiastic for such a hot day. He would take off his coat, drape it carefully over the back of a chair, seat himself on the edge of his desk, and look out the window. After thus setting the stage, he would turn back to the class, cock an eyebrow, wink lewdly at a good-looking girl in the first row, and say, "All right, you bums. We have an hour to kill and only the dullest of instruments with which to execute it—the human mind."

Right from the start, I knew he recognized something outstanding in my attitude. I was sitting by a buxom blonde in the fourth row, and the prof was always looking in our direction.

There was something fresh and challenging in his contempt for the mad quest for inert knowledge that seems to characterize modern education. He was a man who was teaching that the purpose of teaching was to provoke thought, and he provoked our thoughts with such weighty tidbits as "your mind is where your sitting down was after you've stood up."

Ah, the sweet virtue of free thinking! No mention of tests, no hint of term papers—and one could just see those greedy grade-seeking graduate students being lulled into a sense of security theretofore unknown in summer school. One by one, we began putting our pencils down and closing our notebooks. And those symbols of the indoctrinated mind—the parading around in caps and gowns, the official transcripts of credits and grades that had passed for knowledge, that striving to memorize abstract facts in the language of the professor so that they could be faithfully reproduced on tests, those symbols of education with a capital "E"—all those things began to lose significance. We, who had been so madly scrambling for that advanced degree which meant $200 a year more to our struggling families, began to feel like mercenary, money-grabbing, intellectual grubbers whose attitudes toward higher education were entirely out of perspective.

In keeping with his scorn for the traditional, the professor's grading system was a masterpiece of progressive thinking in the field of evaluation and marking. Actually, it was so basic and logical, it is amazing that no one had stumbled upon it before. Here's how it worked. Those students who possessed a throbbing enthusiasm for the course but did not burn the midnight oil received "B's". Those students who burned the midnight oil but did not possess a throbbing enthusiasm would also be given "B's". And those who were both throbbing and burning would receive the "A's".

After listening to this learned professor for several days, I suddenly discovered that I had been teaching and coaching with no clear-cut philosophy that seemed to fit his lofty ideals of education. Mine had been a hodge-podge of disorganized thinking that involved some elements of pragmatism, dogmatism, idealism, and realism. What a mess! And yet, it was a plain, blunt, unadulterated fact—I had no philosophy. I felt naked. I looked around cautiously, hoping no one would notice. And what did I see? I saw other students in the class looking around cautiously.

In desperation, I decided to become a throbber and a burner. So, this is how I came to embrace the professor's "Phlegmatic Philosophy of Liberating the Intellect." In short, this philosophy stressed that the teacher should teach in such a manner as to make each child feel completely free to discuss anything from birth control to bubble gum. It also emphasized that all decisions arrived at within the school should represent a consensus of democratic majority action. This philosophy, I believed, was a sure-fire guarantee for producing students who were "emotionally stabillized," "socially aggravated," "academically terminated," "frustration free," and "citizenship prone"—or, in a catch-all phrase, "Intellectually liberated."

I could envision the Phlegmatic Philosophy sweeping across the western states like a howling blizzard—and I, as its advocate or disciple, would surely become notorious. Clearly, this professor and this philosophy course had changed my life.

They would have changed my life even more had not the miserable bastard given us a final exam in that Philosophy class that would have wrung tears from Socrates and put John Dewey into orbit.

Disillusioned and confused, I drove the eighteen miles back to Loveland for the last time that summer, chagrined at the thought that it would take three more summer sessions to complete my Masters and all the summers for the rest of my life to get a Doctorate degree.

My melancholy quickly changed to apprehension as I walked into the house. Polly, ripely pregnant, announced she had had a pain. We made it to the hospital moments before my second daughter, Rebecca Lynn made her entree into the world. "Good sport, Polly," I thought. "She timed it perfectly."

The next day I kissed Polly, two-year-old Debbie, and that sweet new Becky good-bye, knowing it would be more than a month before I saw them again. Throwing my bags into our well-traveled old Buick, I headed north for Rapid City and a new job and a new adventure. Football practice began the next day.

BUILDING CHARACTERS

The Black Hills region of western South Dakota is truly one of America's last frontiers. It is Pahasapa, the medicine land of the Sioux, the ice box for tribes of nomadic Indians who wintered at the foot of the brooding mountains. It is the scene of the great gold rush in the days of '76. It is the area explored by George Armsrong Custer just two years before he underestimated the odds at the Little Big Horn. It is the locale where in a Deadwood saloon Jack McCall, having taken offense, took matters into his own hands and placed a bullet in the back of Wild Bill Hickok's head. It is a place where not too long ago they hanged horse thieves, and, as I later learned, unpopular coaches and referees. It also is a vast land where it is one hell of a long way between civilized communities. Rapid City proudly stands as the Gateway to these Black Hills, which, in the derisive terms of jealous flat-landers in eastern South Dakota, is regarded as a one-way entry to nowhere.

Legend has it that football in the region began sometime back in the primitive period when savages kicked dried skulls around the prairie for rest and relaxation. As the new football coach at Rapid City High School in the fall of 1955, I was to supervise an updated version of the sport. But the nomadic characteristics of the old tradition lingered on.

To schedule games with other schools our size, we often had to travel vast distances. Over the years, the itinerary included such far away places as Sheridan and Capser, Wyoming; Billings, Montana; Scottsbluff, Nebraska; Sioux City, Iowa; Fort Morgan, Colorado; and Minot, North Dakota. Even staying within the confines of the state, trips to Aberdeen or Sioux Falls involved journeys of from four to five hundred miles (one way). Thus, a football coach and his team covered a lot of yardage not confined to the playing field.

We even had to travel to get to the practice field, which was located some five miles from the high school. When I arrived in Rapid, we were hard pressed for funds for the athletic program, so the Athletic Director thought we could save money if the coaches also served as bus drivers.

The buses provided hadn't been used since World War I, and mechanical failures were common. Business men and lady shoppers soon became accustomed to the sight of our padded gladiators pushing the buses through the downtown traffic while robustly singing the song of the Volga Boatmen.

I soon learned that I would get no sympathy from our veteran athletic director, Euclid Cobb. Heeding the advice of Horace Greeley, he had come west to Rapid City in 1920 from Monmouth College, in Illinois, bringing with him most of his hair and a crisp new diploma. He kept the diploma, but lost all of the hair as for the next four decades he guided the athletic fortunes of Rapid City High, serving at times as combined football, basketball, and track coach. The high school varsity was nicknamed the Cobblers, such was his impact on the community and school.

As with all great characters in Black Hills history, time has a way of confusing fact with legend. For example, it is only legend that Cobb rode with Custer and was scalped at the Battle of the Little Big Horn. But it is fact that during World War I he rode with "Black Jack" Pershing as a member of the U.S. Cavalry chasing Pancho Villa up and down the Mexican border.

Likewise, it is legend that in the early days when Cobb took his teams to the eastern part of the state for basketball tournaments and track meets, travel was performed via ox cart. It is fact, however, that the trip had to be timed so as to reach Pierre before sundown as the ferry did not cross the Missouri River after dark.

It is also legend that he knew every mile of the east-west trail so well because he was on the initial surveying crew with Lewis and Clark. But it is fact that he had made the trip so many times that he knew the exact mileage from every fence post to the bridge at Pierre or the city limits of Sioux Falls. Some claim that he utilized this knowledge to build his fortune by winning dimes on bets from "rookies" driving with him on athletic trips through the years.

So there was no use whining to him about the rigors of travel. I calculated that if B.C. in Rapid City meant "Before Cobb," I had best see to it that A.D. meant "After Davis."

On our first jaunt out of state that year, the bus was rolling merrily through the sage brush of northern Nebraska when the radiator boiled over. For two hours we sat waiting in vain for a passing car or pony express rider. None came. In desperation, I sent the first team out on the flats to run plays while I organized the subs into a line to tote water from a nearby creek. We'd fill the radiator, drive five miles, boil over, and repeat the process. All the while, the antelope looked on in bemused silence.

We later dressed on the bus and arrived in Scottsbluff just in time to kick off. Our left end had misplaced his shoes and had to play the whole game barefooted. All the way home we regaled ourselves with funny stories as we tried to forget the score.

Arriving intact for a ball game often became a greater challenge than the contest itself. On one trip to Sioux Falls, my nearsighted star halfback forgot his glasses, so I loaned him mine. I heard he dropped the opening kick-off and four punts. Meanwhile, I had to play the game by ear because I couldn't see the field.

Keeping the morale of the troops high was always a rough task, but especially so after a defeat. One night after being clobbered by a rough team from Sheridan, Wyoming, some of our stalwarts asked if they could go to the high school dance. I agreed, but only after stressing our strict curfew rules.

A twelve-o'clock bed check later revealed that two of our heroes were missing. In outraged indignation, the assistant coach and I waited at the head of the hotel stairs. Along about 1:00 a.m., we caught them tip-toeing up the stairs, shoes in hand.

Not trusting myself in the heat of the moment, I ordered the guilty culprits to bed and announced I would talk to them when we got back to Rapid.

The long ride home was a trip of frosty silence.

The following Monday, I called the two into my office. Their story was a classic. The quarterback, who was never at a loss for words, served as spokesman while his partner in crime looked on in nodding argeement. The QB said, "Coach, you're never going to believe this . . ."

I acknowledged that this was probably true.

He continued: "We met these two good-looking Wyoming girls at this dance. They were sisters. The more we danced, the friendlier they got. Finally, they asked us if we would like to drive out to their house for some hot chocolate and cake. We were hungry, so we agreed, but only on the condition that they get us back by curfew."

He paused, took a breath, and plunged on. "Well, we got out on this dark country road about ten miles from town. And, Coach, you'd never believe this, but hot chocolate and cake wasn't what they had on their minds at all."

I looked at the ceiling as my star quarterback continued: "We argued, but they were persistent. Finally, they said, 'Kiss us or walk.' And, Coach, knowing what you would do in that situation, and knowing that the school expected us to act like gentlemen, we got out and walked."

At this point his buddy chipped in, "Yeah, Coach, and it was *ten* miles."

Well, we won a few and lost a few, and in between, I could rationalize that I was building a lot of characters indeed.

SPLIT ENDS AND DANGLING PARTICIPLES

Teaching high school English and coaching football is an unholy alliance which works its hardships on both the individual concerned and the school system which has to absorb him. I found that in this competitive and demanding environment, one must not only possess a passing familiarity with his subjects, he must also develop the acting ability of a poker player with a pat hand, be good to his family, abstain from drinking hard "likker" in public, confine his smoking to the boiler room, remain free from financial encumbrances which might clutter up the school with too many bill collectors, and see that the superintendent's son plays in enough games to earn his letter.

I might have managed all this tolerably well had I not turned into an enlightened crusader after that session in summer school. I resolved that in my new job at Rapid City High, I would forego the traditional forced transition of an adolescent's reading diet from comic books to Shakespeare (which to me was like converting him from pablum to beefsteak). I reasoned that the English curriculum had gotten locked into a rut sometime about the era of Alfred Lord Tennyson, and decided to change all this.

With my competitive instincts whetted, I launched into a campaign wherein I took more emotional baths than the Lady of the Lake. But, like a run-away halfback eyeing the goal line, I set my sights on freeing the intellects of the steeley-eyed students in my charge.

When school opened that fall, I found my ideas were as welcome as a Marine Corps PFC in the non-commissioned officer's club.

Take our English department, for instance, where the high point of our meetings was the serving of tea—an old English custom for old English teachers. This was usually followed by stimulating reports on such subjects as: "The Split Infinitive and Its Relation to Sputnik," or "The Immorality of the Double Negative."

At the first meeting of the school year I leaped joyfully to my feet and moved that we liberate the sophomore students by revising the curriculum—substituting *Catcher in the Rye* for *Evangeline*. This went over like a grasshopper in the punch bowl (or a rip in the old tea bag). Pouncing ferociously, these good ladies (I was the only man in the department) told me where to go and prescribed the locomotion whereby I could get there the fastest.

Bloody, but unbowed, I next decided to apply my philosophy of freeing the intellect to the classroom. I had an early opportunity to instigate this policy when I thought I detected some cheating in one of my classes. The whole affair revolved around Prudence Eveningstar, a well-put-together blonde who was very mature for her age and repeating the course for the third time. Alvin Apple, who sat behind her, also was repeating the course for the third time. During a test I thought I saw Alvin whispering the answers to Prudence. Closer investigation proved I was wrong. He was merely nibbling on her ear. But this incident focused my attention upon Prudence—for here was a student who obviously needed liberating.

I then noticed that Prudence was concealing a paper-backed book behind her copy of "Idyls of the King." The paperback just happened to be a sensational best seller on the lack of morals and the over-exaggeration of the sex life in a small New England town. "Prudence," says I, "would you like to read some selected passages from your book to the class?"

Would she? Brother! Prudence had that whole book dog-eared to mark certain spicy excerpts which she gleefully read to the class with gusto and enthusiasm. The response was tremendous —almost overwhelming. This definitely established Prudence as an "outgoing" personality.

A day or so later, Prudence's mother visited me in my classroom after school. Built like Paul Bunyan's Babe, the Blue Ox, she made an awesome impression as she squeezed through the doorway. "Sir," she snarled, "my daughter says you discussed that awful book (she didn't mention its name, but I knew) right here in your classroom."

"Yes, ma'am," I replied, enthusiastically. "In fact, Prudence led the discussion on that very book."

"I'll have you know I burned that book at our house."

"Before or after *you* read it?" I replied slyly with a suggestive wink, kidding her along and giving out with the old tact and diplomacy.

"Young man," she snorted derisively, "don't you know that reading that book might give Prudence bad ideas?"

Remembering that when dealing with parents the teacher always should use the positive approach and say something flattering about their child, I decided to stress Prudence's creative talents and unwittedly stated, "Madame, your daughter might well have written that book."

As I later pleaded with my superintendent, I had no intention of being "fresh" with the lady, particularly *that* lady.

Almost in despair, I thought back upon my philosophy professor of the preceding summer, dwelling upon his casual debonair rapport with his class. I thought by imitating him I could break through the barriers and free intellects. So I, too, began each class period by sitting on the edge of my desk, winking lewdly at a pretty girl in the first row, and saying, "All right, you bums. We have an hour to kill and only the dullest of instruments with which to execute it—the human mind . . ." And I would go on from there.

But again I had a visitation—not just one parent, but a whole delegation. One big, raw-boned father (who I later learned was a professional steer wrestler), was their spokesman.

Gruffly, he asked, "Don't my kid wear clean clothes every day?"

"Yes," I replied cheerfully.

"Don't he comb his hair and wash his teeth?"

I acknowledged as to how this was so.

"Ain't he got no good manners?"

I was at loss as to how to answer that one, and, feeling it was not time to point out his use of a double negative, I merely nodded.

"Then how come you say to him each day—'All right, you bum, I'm gonna kill the next hour with you!' "

Outwardly, I was rapidly becoming a battle-scarred veteran. Inwardly, I was looking for a way out. But these experiences in the unplowed furrows of liberated education sufficed to make a philosopher of me. I immediately philosophized that it was easier to coach split ends than dangling participles.

DON'T SPLASH ME!

Meanwhile, all this time I was asserting my authority on the football field and in the classroom, my family was getting out of hand. Admittedly, I didn't have too much trouble with Becky. She wasn't talking yet. But, Debbie—well, she was something else.

It is understandable that Debbie should take after her mother. For the first year of her life, I was chasing around the Far East with the Marines, and for the subsequent years, I was herding athletes around various playing fields, thus, leaving the bulk of the disciplining and training to my good spouse.

By the time Debbie was three, it was apparent that she already was reflecting her mother's influence in at least two respects—her driving habits and her steadfast refusal to be taken advantage of. This message came home with a vengeance the morning of Debbie's baptism (long delayed because of my prolonged absences).

Debbie was up and dressed for the occasion by the time I arrived sleepy-eyed for breakfast. I ignored her urging to hurry, and paused to read the basketball results in the Sunday paper as I sipped a last cup of coffee. But the child was persistent. Finally, I said, "Debbie, go get in the car and we'll leave in a minute." She raced for the garage.

Minutes later, I subconsciously noted that a car engine was starting. I was unprepared, however for the roar and crash that followed. Bursting out the door, I saw our car protruding through the front of the garage. A quick dash, and I opened the car door to find Debbie, wide-eyed and disheveled, heaped on the floor beneath the steering wheel. Snatching her up and relieved to find her in one piece, I asked, "Debbie, what have you done?"

What she had done was turn on the key, step on the starter, shift into forward, tromp on the foot-feed, and plow through the front of the garage. After paddling her behind, I sternly lectured her on the dangers of messing around with the car.

She was impressed. Dry-eyed and poker-faced, she marched into the house to tell her mother, "Daddy says I can't drive the car until I learn how to back and have a license."

Later that morning, at the First Methodist Church, Polly and I proudly led her down the aisle to the altar for the baptismal ceremony. Debbie was struggling and balking all the way. Things went well, however, until the minister dipped into the bowl for the symbolic sprinkling of the water on her head. Debbie glared at him and in a loud, clear voice, cried: "Don't splash me!"

At that point, Polly tightened her grip on Debbie's arm. Debbie jerked free and howled, "You're pinching my arm!"

I grabbed her by both arms and held her up while the minister warily dabbed her with water before jumping back out of reach of her swinging foot. Then I tucked her under my arm and beat a hasty retreat with Debbie screaming to high heaven.

It was then that I resolved to spend more time at home—further, that all future Davis infants would be baptized before they could talk—further, that however this child turned out, I was going to give my wife all the credit.

BIG STAN

My first football season at Rapid City High had been some-thing of a disaster as we won three while losing six. I knew that the material had been better than the performance and recalled that old adage of Napoleon's, "There are no bad soldiers, just bad generals." I spent the winter and spring reading everything I could get my hands on concerning football, changed my offense from the single wing to the split T, and simplified the plays and defenses to the lowest common denominator. I had learned that on a football team if even one individual does not perform up to his capabilities, the coach has been guilty of a "teaching" failure.

With the opening of fall practice I was pleased with the progress of the offense. We used a version of the belly series that stressed good faking and ball handling, and were blessed with backs fast enough to explode for the long touchdown. But the defense was so lacking in ferocity that it looked like the Union army at the Battle of Bull Run. It couldn't stop Shirley Temple on a quarterback sneak.

Then, four days before the opening game, I met Stan.

He wandered into the coach's office just before we were leaving for practice and wanted to check out some gear. I checked him out carefully, noting not only his long sideburns (which were a novelty in those days), but also a lengthy frame that looked as hard as re-inforced concrete. I asked him why, if he were interested in football, he hadn't reported for the pre-school practice two weeks ago. He replied he had been working on a farm, then clammed up. Obviously, he wasn't the talkative kind.

I had the manager fix him up with some gear. Later that afternoon, we lined the teams up for a scrimmage. I wanted to polish the offense without getting anyone hurt, so picked a group of sophomores for the defensive team. On a hunch, I put Stan in at left end.

On the first play, our fullback roared off-tackle. Stan met him head-on and darned near killed him. Back in the huddle the fullback shook his head and asked, "Who the hell was that? Give me the ball again!" We did. Stan smashed through a double-team block and pole-axed the fullback once more.

By the end of the week, I was playing him on the first defensive unit. We were opening the season with the Lead Golddiggers, a long-standing Black Hills rival. They had a big strong quarterback who ran the split-T option with a lot of power. My directions to Stan were simple—"Just step across the line of scrimmage, then come down the line as hard as you can and blast the quarterback. Make him pitch that ball on every play."

On Lead's first offensive series, the quarterback faked the hand-off and slid down the line. The quarterback and Stan met nose-to-nose. Stan nearly ripped his head off as the quarterback pitched the ball twenty yards toward his own goal line. For the rest of the game, Stan looked like Beowulf on a good day.

The following week, he performed in the classroom with the same intensity. He was as handy to have around school as a fox terrier in a cat show. For example, on entering a room, it was not uncommon for him to grab the top of the door and swing, all the time yelling like Tarzan. Assignments and recitations made him sullen and uncommunicative. If someone mistakenly used his towel in the locker room, he would cold-cock him on the spot. I soon had a parade of concerned teachers trooping into the faculty lounge asking, "What's with this Stan kid?"

I decided I had better find out. The story went back quite a ways. When Stan had been in about the third or fourth grade, he and his brother and sister had been abandoned. They spent the winter living in a packing crate behind one of the hotels and the summer sleeping under the bridge over Rapid Creek. For food, they took milk from doorsteps in the early mornings. For money, they grabbed the daily papers and resold them on the street. Finally, the welfare agency found them and shipped them off to Plankington and the State Training School.

He had been there ever since, going to school and working in the laundry. The summer he came to Rapid City High, he had been sent to Yankton to work and live on the farm. But with the crop harvested, he had left and hitchhiked the 400 miles across the state to Rapid City, where he enrolled in school. He also found his mother and was living with her in two small rooms above a store in the downtown district.

Learning this, I checked with the officials at the school in Plankington. They were upset that he had left the farm and had been trying to locate him, but after considerable discussion, it was agreed that he could remain at Rapid City High.

Meanwhile, when appraised of the circumstances, his teachers pitched in with real enthusiasm to help him bridge the gap in his schooling. God bless them, they tackled the job with patience and understanding. His English teacher particularly was superb. Ethel Wood was then in her early sixties, had raised a family of her own, and gave Stan a lot of tender, loving, academic care.

He responded in kind, but not without occasional outbursts. There was so much unharnessed energy and strength in the young man that it was difficult to believe. I recall walking into a physical education class where the students were working on "dips." A "dip" is a hand-stand with one's feet braced against the wall. In this position you do a push-up, the chief difference between this and a regular push-up being that you are lifting your entire weight. I was impressed as I saw Stan do thirty in a row. It was all I could muster to do one.

His prowess on the football field continued as we chalked up an unbroken series of wins. But when the weekly academic eligibility sheets came out, I always held my breath as I checked Stan's. He had a solid string of "D's", but was never ineligible.

All went well until the next-to-the-last game on our schedule. We were meeting the Sturgis Scoopers, a Black Hills neighbor, who had one of their best teams in years. Both ball clubs were going into the game undefeated, and spirits were running high.

Late in the afternoon as we were loading the bus, I missed Stan. Finally, he arrived, dressed in a white T shirt and jeans. We had a rule on the squad that when we traveled the players dressed in slacks, sport coats, and ties. Stan had stopped off at the pool hall after school, and had been goaded into a bet that I would take him on the trip regardless of the rule.

I talked to him and explained that we would wait ten minutes for him to go home and dress. He walked away and didn't come back, so we left without him.

Later that night at the game, I could see him across the field prowling the sideline, still in T-shirt and jeans and wearing a thin satin athletic warm-up he had brought with him from Plankington. He looked lonely and miserable. I felt the same way. I knew somehow I had blown this.

We missed him in other ways, too. We scored three times, but without him on defense, so did our opponents. With 35 seconds left in the game, our half-back popped for an eighty yard run which broke a 21 to 21 tie. But it was a quiet ride home.

Early the next morning, a Saturday, Stan knocked on my door. It was the first time he had come to our home. I invited him in for breakfast and was amazed as he attacked the bacon and eggs.

"What do you usually eat for breakfast?" Polly asked.

"Bread and jelly," he replied, "same as I have for lunch."

And I thought, "Probably the same for supper."

Later we drove out to the practice field at Sioux Park. It was a crisp, late October day, and I can still recall the yellow leaves on the cottonwoods were almost gone. The turf on the field had lost its green and was taking on the brown mantle of fall. Above, the geese in giant V's dotted the sky. Stan and I sat on the side of the hill and talked.

For the first time he really opened up. He told me about going to Plankington—how great it had been to have a clean, warm place to sleep and good meals. He commented on how well he had been treated there and about going to Yankton to work on the farm. He also told me about when he was a little kid he used to sneak into the Rapid City football games, and over all these years how much he had thought about coming back to Rapid City and playing football.

I asked, "Do you still want to play football for Rapid City?"

He nodded.

"The guys on the squad are sore as hell," I explained. "They feel you let them down. You'll have to make your peace with them."

"I know," he said. "I will."

On Monday we had a squad meeting. I don't know what Stan said. I left. But ten minutes later when they all walked out, there wasn't a dry eye in the place. Stan was back on the squad.

That Saturday we played our final game in the season at Sioux Falls for what amounted to the mythical state championship. Our team played as well as it could, but lost. Stan was superb, making tackle after tackle. When with two minutes to go, I took him out of the game, the partisan Sioux Falls crowd gave him a standing ovation.

When we got back to Rapid, I took Stan over to meet a good friend, who gave him a job working in his warehouse and took him under his wing. Since that day, the two have been like father and son.

Other businessmen also took an interest in Stan. One of the clothing stores outfitted him completely, including a heavy winter coat. Stan became one of the snappiest dressers in school. He later told me that this marked the first time in his life that he had ever picked out such things as socks, underwear, shirts, or a suit.

Stan's next two years at Rapid added to the legend. For three consecutive years he was selected on the All-State football team and was also picked as a high school All-American. Likewise, he excelled in basketball with his ferocious rebounding, and made the All-Tournament team at the state meet where they described him as "having the touch of an elephant but the heart of a lion." In school his grades climbed steadily until by his senior years he was making "A's" and "B's."

Following a hitch in the Marine Corps, Stan went to college, graduated, and now is teaching and coaching in the Midwest. I hear from him a couple of times a year and treasure the pictures of his growing family.

I learned a lot of things from Stan, and now I think how true it was when the late Charley Caldwell, Princeton's great coach, once wrote that in coaching ". . . it is the men, not the scores, you remember."

58

TOO TIMID TO TOOT

With Stan and a host of other good players, over the next two years at Rapid City, we continued to have winning seasons. But I never learned to relax. I soon became aware that it wasn't the quality of my coaching that kept me awake nights. It was my off-season activity as a basketball referee.

Basketball is played with a passion in the Black Hills where winter sets in early, and it might be more accurate to refer to the intensely partisan fans as combatants rather than spectators.

When I first arrived as a stranger in this land lying between the Cheyenne and Belle Fourche rivers, I was considered somewhat of a neutral. For that reason, I was invited to referee the traditional game between two blood rivals—Black Hills Teachers College (BHTC) and South Dakota School of Mines (Tech). I was flattered that a rather inexperienced young official should be called upon to referee such an important game. With good intentions, I accepted.

Some clue as to the disposition of the crowd that night was revealed in the fact that the fun-loving Miners hung from the balcony of the gym and playfully kicked the balls out of the basket as BHTC players went through their warm-up drills.

From the very beginning, the game was wilder than a Deadwood casino on pay-day. The teams exchanged baskets and elbows on even terms, and the pressure mounted. In the final minutes, a Miner cleared a rebound and heaved a long pass down the floor. His teammate gathered it in, and in full stride slammed it through the net. I signaled two points as the BHTC contingent howled, "Traveling! Traveling!" I ignored their protests and turned to follow the play back down the court. From the corner of my eye, I saw a civilian rush onto the playing area. Unable to alter my course, I slammed into him full tilt, caromed off, and continued down the flood. Over my shoulder, I saw two policemen dragging him out of the gym as he vigorously announced, "You can't throw me out. I'm the coach!"

He re-entered just as the gun went off with Mines winning a narrow two-point victory. The coach (popularly known as Billie the Bullet) injudiciously ran up to the biggest, meanest Miner on the court and took a wild swing. Whereupon this Miner promptly knocked him over the scorer's table. The battle was on. The bleachers emptied onto the flood from both sides and the student bodies merged in the middle in a wild-swinging melee. Looking around anxiously to find my fellow referee, I discovered him on his hands and knees crawling off the floor. Not one to stand on ceremony, I wisely followed his example, hoping that in this manner I might live to referee another day.

It was extremely embarrassing to open up the *Rapid City Journal* the following afternoon and find a picture of the massacre spread across the front page. Conspicuous in their striped shirts were the two officials creeping for cover.

Not long afterward, I was refereeing a game at a town that served as a stage stop some hundred miles east of Rapid. My fellow official was Pev Evans, a solid 250-pounder who once had been a lot of tackle at the University of Nebraska. The game was played in the community building, which was distinguished by one of those overhead running tracks once common in Y.M.C.A. gyms.

At a critical point late in the ball game, Pev called a rather obvious foul on one of the local players. As the teams lined up for the free throw, a spectator came racing onto the floor and grabbed Pev by the arm. Pev, who towered over this courageous soul by a good foot, picked him up by the lapels of his coat and threw him bodily into the stands. Once more this individual rushed onto the floor, shouting that he couldn't be treated that way—he was the superintendent of schools, which, in his opinion, entitled him to some sort of diplomatic immunity. Having patiently listened to this bit of information, Pev called a technical foul on the home team bench.

He stepped up to wave the players back from the free throw line, then turned to hand the ball to the shooter. At that moment, a heavy desk came crashing down from the balcony above. It missed Pev by mere inches and smashed into the floor. It darned near went right on through to the basement. The rest of the game was played with caution as players and officials maneuvered carefully to step around the gaping hole.

I doubt that I would have survived long in such a hostile environment had I not met Happy Whistle. (I am using an alias to protect what remains of his reputation as one of the veteran officials in the Hills.) Hap stood only five feet tall and weighed but 115 pounds, so I suspected his long tenure as an official was not because he intimidated irate fans with his size. Rather, I believe his long and flamboyant career can be attributed to a fortunate blending of many personal and physical ingredients— namely, the finesse of a ham actor to play to the crowd, the hide of an elephant to endure its insults—the cockiness of a banty rooster to instill confidence—the caution of an unkissed coed to discourage over-aggressiveness—the quick moves of a pick-pocket to cover the court—the wind of a politician to sustain long blasts on his whistle to cover his own mistakes. Above all, he possessed an uncanny instinct for self-preservation.

I got my first lesson from Happy Whistle when I worked a game with him at Belle Fourche, where the stocky cowboys were meeting a bitter rival—the Sturgis Scoopers. Late in the game, I blew my whistle lustily and called what would have been the fifth foul on the Belle Fourche center. The crowd booed and began throwing debris on the floor—programs, chewing gum, knives. I repeated, "Foul on number 23 from Belle Fourche!" At that point Hap grabbed the ball and shouted, "No! No!" In more moderate tones, he whispered to me, "You're mistaken. *Belle* is the *home* team. The Sturgis player traveled *before* the foul was committed." Taking the ball, he stepped out of bounds, handed it to the Belle Fourche player, and peace and harmony were restored. The Sturgis coach didn't speak to us for weeks—or at least until we were refereeing a home game for Sturgis.

Even Hap, however, had his problems at times. Usually, this occurred at tournaments where it was impossible to identify the home team. Thus, I well recall working my first tournament with him—a class B regional in a small town lying between two Indian reservations. Things went well until the final night when two Indian teams from the rival reservations met for the championship. The game was played in the State Armory, which was all right except for the fact that the V.F.W. and American Legion clubs had a bar right next door. The firewater did little for the temperament of the crowd. Likewise, the temperament of the crowd did little for my *espirit de referee*. Fortunately, a light moment preceded the hostilities.

Prior to the game, I was standing near the scorer's table when the teams were introduced. As the announcer called out the name of Sam Crow-That-Flies, a young Indian from the opposing team grunted and smiled—the latter a rare occurrence for a Sioux in such a serious moment. I turned to him and asked, "What's the matter?"

He replied, "Who ever heard of a name like Crow-That-Flies?"

I thought nothing more of this until this warrior, in turn, was introduced. He went by the appropriate name of Joe Bear-Comes-Out.

The gym was packed. Folding chairs were added to increase the seating capacity. Row upon row of stoic, somber Sioux sat there, blankets wrapped tightly around them, toes of their moccasins defiantly on the out-of-bounds line. I could well understand how Custer had felt at the Little Big Horn, trying to bring the white man's culture and law to a tribe of unwilling warriors. These were the grandchildren of the winners of that fracas.

It was strangely quiet during the first half of the game. Then, as the tempo picked up and the teams (contemptuous of defense) raced from one end of the floor to the other, the fans began rocking and chanting in a guttural rhythm, "Hi-ya, hi-ya, hi-ya." It made the hair rise on the back of my neck.

After a particularly wild scramble, the ball went out of bounds in the proximity of a large Indian lady planted solidly on the sideline. Hap gestured and shouted, "Blue out." At this point, the woman broke her silence and spat vehemently, "Blue out! Blue out! No-good white man all time call Blue out!" Hap carefully retrieved the ball, wiped it off with the sleeve of his striped shirt, handed it to a lad in blue, and off it sailed down the court where it was flipped into the basket.

Back came the white team (merely the color of their jerseys). I scrambled to get ahead of the play and turned in time to see the following scene unfold.

As Hap came tearing down the court following the play, the irate squaw rose majestically to her feet, folded up her chair, cocked it in the same fashion of one wielding a baseball bat, and, as Hap went by, let him have it square in the choppers. Hap flipped in the air, hit the floor on his back and lay there toes up, his coveted whistle shoved far into his bleeding mouth. Without changing her expression, the lady unfolded her chair, placed it on the floor, and with great dignity, sat down and gazed at the supine official. Hap sat up, blinked, tenderly removed his whistle, got to his feet, looked neither right nor left, and followed the play. His calmness in this moment of crisis undoubtedly saved our scalps.

A year later, Happy Whistle and I once more were working a class B tournament—this time at the Sturgis Armory. This appeared to be a patsy compared to our previous experiences. Deadwood had a fine team and waltzed into the finals against Newell, where they once again won by a margin of some 40 points.

Following the game, we went to our dressing room in the basement of the armory. Hap was in the corner smoking a cigarette, and I was pulling off my shoes, when we were startled by a loud pounding on the door. I opened it and was confronted by two guys whose most distinguishing characteristic was that their knuckles dragged the floor, and they were standing erect. The biggest one tapped me on the chest with a hairy finger, and in breath that reeked of bourbon, asked, "You ever play basketball?"

"No," I replied in a joking mood, "I was a tennis player in college. Did you ever play basketball?"

"I'll have you know I lettered for four years at Newell High School."

"Well, bully for you," I said, foolishly.

The other one tapped me gently on the shoulder in a playful fashion that almost dropped me to my knees. He growled, "You guys ever referee before?"

Trying to get into the spirit of the thing, I answered, "A couple of times. Did you ever referee?"

"I," he said proudly, "referee in the Newell City League."

"Well," I smiled feebly, "then you can sympathize with our problems."

"Sympathize, hell!" he roared. "The only people I sympathize with is those poor kids from Newell. They'd have won that game if it hadn't been for you."

Considering the 40-point spread, I thought that last statement rather exaggerated, but saw that they were in no mood for debate. Deciding to take the bull (or bulls) by the horn, I said in my firmest manner, "Listen here. We don't have to put up with this kind of abuse from you. You get out of here or I'll call the cops." That caught them by surprise, and taking advantage of their confusion, I slammed the door in their faces and bolted it.

Again there was a pounding on the door.

"What do you want?" I yelled.

'What's your name?" came the reply.

"Davis," I answered. "What's your?"

"Tuff," he shouted. "We're the Tuff brothers." The name seemed appropriate.

Behind me I heard a groan, and looked around at Hap. "Lordy," he whispered. "You know who those guys are?"

I shook my head.

"Those Tuff brothers are the two guys who stood outside the American Legion Club here in Sturgis last week and fought toe to toe from midnight until dawn." Hap was always full of this cheerful kind of information.

"You'd better get out of here," I yelled through the door, "or someone's going to get in trouble."

"You can say that again," one of them volunteered. "We're leaving. But we'll be waiting outside for you."

At this point, Hap, his eyes bulging, shouted in a high thin voice, "You'll have to stand in line. There's eight ahead of you."

I applauded his bravado, but a little prematurely. Three hours later, I still couldn't get him to leave. The building was closed, the heat was turned off, and it was twenty below zero outside. Finally, it was either leave or freeze to death. I decided to take my chances with the Tuffs. I took out my false teeth, placed them carefully in my gym bag, and instructed Hap that once outdoors, he was to run for help while I attempted to slow them up.

Then, in the frigid darkness, we tiptoed through the halls, edging cautiously around each corner. Once at the door, we scanned the street in all directions. Nothing was moving in the sub-zero weather. Heaving sighs of relief, we sprinted to our car. It was so cold that the air in the tires had decompressed, and they had frozen square on the bottom. In a gay mood, we bumped out of Sturgis on those square tires, happy as two horse-thieves who had just escaped the hangman's noose.

I was to watch Happy Whistle work one more tournament before I left the Hills. Again it was in Sturgis. Once more Deadwood met Newell in the finals. This time, however, Newell nipped Deadwood in what was considered a major upset. I was watching from the safety of the stands. If the Newell crowd had been rough the preceding year, the Deadwood crowd made them look like a bunch of elderly maiden teachers at P.T.A. This crew was hairier than hardrock miners on Saturday night.

Hap's timing was perfect. When the final gun went off, he was near the dressing room door. Even at that, he had some trouble crawling off the floor, having become wedged between a fat lady's legs as she enthuiastically pounded him on the head with her purse. Finally, however, he bucked her off, scrambled to safety, and bolted the door behind him. I had to admire his artistry.

His fellow official, though, did not fare so well. After beating a path through a belligerent crowd, he finally clawed his way to the door. There, he pounded furiously—shouted vigorously—pleaded plaintively. The door did not open. I later learned that Hap was leaning against it on the far side and refused to open it until he heard the password from his beleaguered colleague. The word never came. In horror, from my vantage point in the balcony, I saw the desperate man in the striped shirt go under like a Christian fed to the lions.

I was shocked—not just because I had seen a brave man succumb to a bloodthirsty crowd. After all, it could have been worse. It could have been me. I was shocked because I had seen an idol fall—an ideal shattered.

Happy Whistle had betrayed the sacred trust—"Never bolt the door on a fellow official."

At that moment I decided I had refereed my last game. Trembling, I vowed never to harass another official—unless, of course, he committed some unpardonable crime such as calling a foul or a violation on the *home* team.

EVERY MAN A WILDCAT!

In the spring of 1959, which marked my fourth year at Rapid City High School, I received a letter from my in-laws enclosing a clipping which announced the resignation of the head football coach at Greeley High School. They suggested I apply.

I could see their point. For four summers they had experienced the annual invasion as Polly and the children and I moved to Loveland to live with her folks while I commuted to summer school at near-by Greeley. Inasmuch as I had completed my master's degree and had determined to begin a doctoral program, they thought it might be handier (and quieter, for them) if I had a job in Greeley.

So, I applied for and got the job. Thus, the first week in June we bade farewell to Rapid City, loaded our meager belongings in a U-Haul, and moved—again.

At first, it was hard to adjust to Greeley. True, the fragrant whiff of beet pulp on a balmy night brought back nostalgic memories of my youth, but when a neighboring community that has been a blood-rival most of one's life suddenly becomes home, it is a whole new ball game. I almost choked on the words those first times I led the cheer—"Every man a Wildcat!"

As a high school player and later as coach at Loveland High, I had learned at an early age to hate the two chief villains of the Northern Colorado Athletic Conference, namely basketball coach Jim Baggot and baseball coach Pete D'Amato.

Sunny Jim Baggot's Greeley Wildcast basketball teams had so completely dominated the Colorado high school tournaments in the era from Franklin Roosevelt to Lyndon Johnson that when they failed to win a championship, it was considered a major upset. And if there were those who questioned whether he was in fact the greatest coach since Naismith first nailed a hoop on the barn, they tip-toed through Greeley and talked in soft whispers.

Pete D'Amato had been just as impressive with his baseball program, winning the Northern Conference championship with monotonous regularity and always in contention for the state crown. At a Greeley High baseball game, the student spectators had to sit on the ground because the bleachers were always jammed with pro scouts.

Where Sunny Jim bubbled, D'Amato growled. While one oozed with loquacious charm, the other could explode in a vocabulary that would make a Marine Corps sergeant sick with envy. But both had two endearing characteristics—their teams almost always won and neither ever had a thought he didn't utter. Preaching the Wildcat gospel that athletics should be fun, they stressed that those who had the most fun were those who were winning. Kids on their teams had a lot of fun.

Upon actually arriving in Greeley that summer, I quickly discovered that my problems were not confined to burying the hatchet with former rivals now turned *compadres.* The community was uneasy about its new coach. My predecessor, Bob Kula, had been a popular winner and had left behind the nucleus for an excellent team. And, whereas for years the Greeley Wildcats had enjoyed considerable success with a single-wing offense, my introduction of the split-T was viewed with some alarm by these sports-minded fans who took great pride in hardnosed football. The players, their parents, and the "towncats" had been honed on the philosophy that a "T" was for sissies, and why fake a man out when you could run over him?

As we took the field for the first game, my new friend and assistant coach, Pete D'Amato, gravely informed me that the town also was impressed with a rugged defense. He went on to add that in the preceding season, the Greeley Wildcats had shut out their opponents five times. We started the game by kicking off into the end zone. On the first play from scrimmage, the opposition ran a double reverse, and the ball carrier sprinted eighty yards for a touchdown. With the season only fifteen seconds old, a banner unfolded that read: "Good-bye, Bud!"

When the team rallied and roared back from this devastating blow, I could see that as a coach I had been blessed with an abundance of talent. There was shifty Ted Somerville, an all-state halfback who had more moves than the navel on an Egyptian belly-dancer. There, too, was Rambling Ralph Cowan, the fullback who hit with the force of a tank and the nimbleness of a prima ballerina. On the wing was Manny Ortiz with the great speed and fine hands. And towering above our center was Big Jim McKay, a red-headed, freckled-faced quarterback who was so tall that if he stood on the hood of a car, he could see into four states. In front of these four fine backs was a fast, aggresive line. All the characteristics for a great team were there. These young men were mobile and agile if I could only make them hostile.

At first, my biggest challenge was my quarerback, McKay. He was so relaxed that I was afraid to take him out of a game for fear he would fall asleep on the bench or wander off to visit with the cheerleaders. Worse, when the game got boring, he liked to make up plays in the huddle.

I had a little huddle with Big Jim and firmly announced that if he didn't pay attention and follow my instructions to the letter, the only Greeley Wildcats he would be leading would be in the band. Solemnly, he agreed.

The next game was a cliff-hanger throughout the first half. Pacing the sidelines, I was relieved when our defense stopped a drive and we took possession of the ball on our own six-yard line.

I put my arm around Big Jim and gave him his orders. "Run the triple option play and see if we can break it for a touchdown. It might surprise someone."

McKay dutifully followed my instructions. He faked to the halfback, faked to the fullback, and then made a blind pitch to the trailing back. The latter had stumbled and fallen down, and the ball bounced crazily to our one-yard line, where our opponents recovered.

Stunned, I greeted McKay as he trotted to the bench. "Jim," I moaned, "just what were you thinking of out there?"

He shrugged his shoulders and wistfully replied, "I was thinking I sure did have a *dumb* coach."

Raw talent, however, soon offset my coaching, and the Wildcats racked up a steady stream of victories. The scores were so lopsided that I began to fear overconfidence and complacency, problems that were new to my coaching experience.

That Friday night, we played in Loveland against my old alma mater and hometown. The troops were in a merry mood on the bus ride over, and I had visions of a real fiasco and embarrassment in front of my old friends and relatives. (In one respect, I was relieved, however. My old friend, Bob Beckett, was no longer coaching at Loveland. He had departed that fall for a job in Phoenix. At least I would not have to put up with his last-minute, game-saving theatrics.)

But the pre-game ceremony did little to ease my tension and uneasiness. The Loveland band had dedicated a special number, "My Buddy," to its visiting alum, and I had been honored with an introduction in the middle of the field. I was touched, but worried. Were they softening us up for the kill?

As the team sat in the locker room prior to the kickoff, I launched into my most impassioned pre-game oratory. I raved about how in the previous game against Ft. Morgan we had given them an early lead with foolish mistakes, come back to take the lead ourselves, and then eased off to let them play catch-up at the end. I accused them of keeping the game close just so the crowd would stay in the stands, then climaxed my talk by saying: "You don't have the mental attitude to be champions. You lack the killer instinct to take advantage of an opponent when you've got him down. You refuse to concentrate on doing your best on every play. You have no pride. Tonight, I want to see an uncaged band of hungry, angry wildcats looking for someone to hit on every play!"

They practically tore the door off getting out on the field, but I sighed as I wondered how long it would last.

I didn't have to wonder long. The first time we touched the ball, it was like a bomb going off. Our fullback went the distance on the first play. The same thing happened the next time we took possession, and the next.

By the start of the second quarter, the score was out of sight and the first team was on the bench. But the second team carried on with the same "killer instinct." So did the third.

At the end of the game, only a handful of spectators was in the stands as the score read 66 to 0.

Somewhat dazed by the enormity of the overkill, I wandered into the gym, wondering whether it was worse to be a whining loser or an arrogant winner.

When at the end of the season Greeley High's football team had finished with an unbeaten record and won the state championship playoffs, I felt very proud—that is, until I went to put the hardware in the trophy case and found there wasn't room. Baggot's string of championship basketball teams and D'Amato's baseball teams had collected such an assortment of pot metal over the years that the trophy case was packed tight. As I grumpily placed the trophy in an obscure corner of the coaches' dressing room behind a row of smelly sweat shirts, Baggot and D'Amato yawned. "Remember," they admonished, "every man a Wildcat!"

ALUMNI TOGETHERNESS

Shortly after Greeley High School won the state championship game in late November, 1959, the news broke that I had been offered the position of Director of Alumni Relations at my alma mater, the University of Colorado. I requested that the Greeley Board of Education release me from my contract for the spring semester in order that I might accept. This created a lively furor in the community. The Greeley Board accused the University of raiding its faculty, and the issue was only finally resolved when the Colorado University President, Quigg Newton, met with them to smooth it over. For a change, I was flattered that someone was concerned about my departure rather than my arrival.

While delighted with the prospects of returning to the University, intrigued with the excitement and challenge of the new job, and encouraged that the President had provided that I might continue work on a doctoral program as time would permit, I, nonetheless, had real regrets in leaving a career of high school teaching and coaching.

My taking the Alumni Director's job meant another separation from Polly and the kids. Polly was teaching the first grade in one of the Greeley elementary schools and felt obliged to finish out her contract even if I had been relieved of mine. Besides, we needed the money. So, from the first of February until the first of June, 1960, I rented a room in Boulder and commuted on weekends to Greeley.

It was an exciting time to be an Alumni Director at my old alma mater. Only nine years had passed since Polly and I had graduated, but Boulder and the University had literally exploded in the interim. Where the football stadium had once marked the eastern boundary of the town and rolling hills and farmland had abutted the campus, sprawling housing developments now reached as far as the eye could see. Civilization was everywhere and was reflected in the fact that Boulder had jumped from a population of less than 20,000 to over 60,000 since last we were students.

In my role of Alumni Director I had a ringside seat to the fast-moving action as the University entered the decade of the Sixties. I was privy to Regent's meetings, budget hearings, Administrative Council briefings, and the whole elaborate mechanism of what in western terms was considered a "big" university.

The job of interpreting the internal developments of a progressive and liberal university to its most conservative constituency took me to virtually every community in the state. I shook more hands than a gubernatorial candidate and could cry about the University's needs or extoll its virtues all in the same breath.

Mostly I addressed friendly, partisan audiences where the question-and-answer period dwelt on such weighty topics as to when we were going to beat Oklahoma in football or why we had extended closing hours in the women's dorms. Occasionally, the footing got sticky.

Take the night in Cortez, for example, when the mood got downright hostile. Located so deep in the southwest corner of the state that they called themselves the "disenfranchised taxpayers," they were ready to pin me to the wall. I had just elaborated on developments in the language department and the excellence in the program in Russian when a disgruntled alumnus rose to his feet. With fervor he protested that they had had enough of this teaching of Communism in a state university, but teaching it in the Russian language was just too much.

Campus speakers, "liberal" professors, the student newspaper, relaxed housing regulations, internal battles within the Board of Regents—all served as heady desserts after heavy meals of roast beef and potatoes.

On the lighter side of the Alumni Director's menu were the reunions, homecomings, commencements, alumni institutes, and alumni board meetings. At such times the controversies revolved around whether we should serve cornish hen under glass (sponsored by the women) or steak and potatoes (endorsed by the men) at the class reunion of 1910.

Although no longer in coaching, I nonetheless still had an affiliation with the football program. To some I represented the "last chance" as desperate alumni sought last-minute tickets for extravaganzas such as the Oklahoma or Missouri game. Arrangements for anything outside of the forty yard lines were interpreted as personal insults. Reserved seats in the "prestige" section became so precious that they were included in wills and even in court cases on divorce settlements. I envisioned the perfect football stadium as extending from forty-yard line to forty-yard line ten stories high.

Repeated protests that I was not the ticket manager were to no avail. The alum from Cortez once gave me hell for fifteen minutes via long distance for his seats in the end zone. With real bitterness he pointed out that the Ute Indians from the reservation had seats on the fifty yard line. No rhetoric on my part could convince him that the Denver bank which carried the Indians' account had more seats on the fifty yard line than I did as Alumni Director.

I did enjoy accompanying the football team on many of the trips and the alumni meetings held in conjunction with the away games. On such occasions, I sometimes helped entertain the V.I.P.'s. The worst debacle occurred when we played Baylor in Waco, Texas.

The team had left for the stadium and I was winding up an alumni dinner when the phone rang. It was the Governor of Colorado calling from Houston where he had been attending a meeting. He wanted tickets for the game and asked if I would make arrangements.

I jumped at the chance to do my bit for the Governor, called the Highway Patrol to arrange for an escort from the airport to the stadium, and reserved a room at the hotel for his Nibs. The room turned out to be one of a suite housing several other Colorado boosters who had accompanied the team.

The Governor arrived, and, after a dismal game and a post-mortem wake, retired to his room. Several members of our party, however, did not return to the hotel until the dawn. One disoriented member of the hoary crew mistook the Governor's bedroom for his own. Dismayed at finding his bed occupied, he jerked down the covers. "Who are you?" he roared.

"I'm the Governor of Colorado," came the startled reply.

"The hell you say!" With that, he threw him out of bed.

Aside from the football trips, most of my help in Alumni Directing came in the shapely form of Miss Peggy Tague, a red-haired, blue-eyed doll who specialized in menus, grumps, reunions, and gossip. Under her efficient eye and management things usually went tolerably well. She could sweet-talk a stone dog into wagging his tail. But even she could do little about the enforced "together-ness" that characterized our office.

While no one ever complained about being too cozy with Peggy, it was Wiley Will Fowler, the Development Director, who bugged me—and I who bugged him. We shared an office, and the brilliant afternoon sunshine bounced off his bald pate creating a glare that made it impossible to check Peggy's imaginative spelling. He, in turn, constantly complained about the clatter of my type-writer as I churned out messages of state, maintaining that it garbled his dictation.

Frantically, we determined to take our problem to the top— or as near to the top as two neophyte directors could get, namely, the Executive Assistant to the President, Don Saunders, who served as chief trouble shooter and our father confessor. We drafted a desperate and inspired letter.

August 11, 1960

Mr. Don Saunders
Executive Assistant to the President
University of Colorado
Dear Mr. Saunders,
The purpose of this letter is to call to your attention the present limitations of the space assigned to the Alumni and Development Offices and to outline present and projected needs for suitable office space based on an expanding program over the next ten years.

At the present time, both programs (entailing a staff of two directors, one assistant director, and nine secretaries and clerks) jointly occupy a 22 by 28 foot office on the third floor of the University Memorial Center. There are no private quarters, per se, in that we two Directors (Alumni and Development) share a glass encased cubicle—a veritable fish bowl where one can neither rub his nose, wind his watch, nor scratch his fanny without being placed under the scrutiny of the entire staff.

Further, there is no place to hide. Either Director is completely at the mercy of wandering insurance agents, itinerant peddlers, or aggressive creditors without the recourse of his secretary being able to say, "I'm sorry, but the Director is in conference." While we are firm advocates of the "open door" policy, this philosophy can go too far. Intimate, private conversations (either in person or via telephone) are impossible. Our business is everybody's business in that every conversation is monitored with enthusiasm. This encourages a wholesome democratic atmosphere wherein everything is shared and there are no secrets. It does, however, have its limitations. We not only share the secrets, we share the germs. No one can suffer the miseries of a common head cold all alone —the whole office must share.

As for space for our secretarial and clerical staff, again the emphasis is on intimate relations. We have people stacked on people. Nine clattering typewriters, two blaring dictaphones, and five ringing telephones give our staff more color and clamor than a Chinese fire drill, and just about the same degree of organization.

Alumni who somehow manage to wriggle their way into the inner sanctum often spend the bulk of their time gazing furtively for an easy way out. One elderly and wealthy widow once became so bewildered and confused that she was trapped in the office the better part of a week. (We finally discovered her in back of a filing case wildly licking stamps—her only nourishment for several days. We attacked this problem by giving her a sponge and some unsealed envelopes and putting her on the payroll.)

As for filing space, we are hard-pressed to find employees who can effectively fulfill the job. With filing cases stacked from floor to ceiling, we desperately need girls who are seven feet tall for the "A" through "D" records or three feet tall to handle the "X" through "U" categories. And our fireproof vault is a real menace. We have to call the roll every time we shut the door. (One girl got locked in with the Class of 1905 and has never been quite the same.)

To further complicate matters, our staff recently was augmented by the addition of an Assistant Development Director—a six foot, four inch, two-hundred and forty pound former football player who tiptoes around our constricted quarters with all the finesse of a General Sherman tank. When both of his size fourteen shoes are planted firmly on the floor, there literally is no place to walk. Thus, all travel must be performed by swinging from the light fixtures or hopping from desk to desk. While this does a great deal for the physical development of the staff, it plays hob with the over-all dignity and decorum of the office.

The situation is becoming tight. In fact, if it becomes any tighter, the two Directors will soon be moving out the west window and sharing office space with the pigeons.

We sincerely beseech you to give our situation your immediate attention.

> *Respectfully submitted,*
> *William E. Davis,*
> *Director, Alumni Relations*
> *Will Fowler*
> *Director, Development Foundation*

Our plea got an immediate sympathetic response from the President's Executive Assistant.

August 17, 1960

Prof. W. E. Davis
Prof. Will Fowler
UMC
Colleagues:

This will acknowledge receipt of your able joint study on Claustrophobia in UMC *in which you document the results of your experiments in intimate living. I can see that such close association might lead to touching situations. However, as a confirmed optimist, I like to think that an atmosphere of "Togetherness" can be conducive to good feeling. May I venture, also, that I think you will be better men for this experience. Life, after all, is a prolonged test of character. As Confucious said, "Look not, scratch not, pinch not—and you will be a frustrated man."*

If you are irrevocably committed to joining the pigeons, I can commend to you the loft immediately above this office in the administration building, a spacious, cool, quiet spot, with some choice squabs available.

My advice to you is to hold tight, dig in, bite down hard, look neither to the right or left. Better days will come.

> *Regards,*
> */s/ Don*
> *Don Saunders*
> *Executive Assistant to the President*

In retrospect, it appears that the President's Assistant was putting us on—or off. But that was not the case. Action *was* forthcoming. He moved the editor of the alumni publication and his secretary in with us.

Eight years later the Alumni and Development offices were relocated in their new home, but both Will and I were long gone from the scene.

FOOTBALL COACHES FATHER GIRLS

For some mystical reason, football coaches tend to father girls. This accounts for those six-foot-four lassies with shoulders like Paul Bunyan and thighs like a Russian weightlifter who prowl the corridors of our high schools frustrated because they can't turn out for the varsity. Meanwhile, the accountants and the lawyers get all the quarterbacks.

As long as I was an active coach, I suffered this fate. But, philosophically, I adjusted to our two daughters, Debbie and Becky, reasoning that with girls one need not be concerned whether they were too small for the line or too slow for the backfield. Besides, they had a charm all their own, but, like their mother, were impossible to discipline.

During my temporary retirement from coaching to serve as Alumni Director for the University of Colorado, my wife greeted me with the news that *we* were expecting again. But for nine months I could never quite bring myself to thinking in terms of a son. Once again, we selected girls' names, and I envisioned myself engulfed with *more* petticoats, *more* dolls, *more* of the trimmings and trapping that accompany precious little girls.

The year 1960 was drawing rapidly to a close, and the bowl games were in full swing. On December 31st, I was sitting in front of my television set watching the Gator Bowl game between Baylor and Florida. My wife was out shoveling the walks, as there had been a heavy snow the preceding night. Slowly, she waddled in huffing and puffing so loudly I was forced to get up and turn up the volume.

"I think it's time," she said cheerfully.

"It's time Baylor opened up its passing game," I agreed, "or they'll get blown clear out of the stadium."

"No," she replied gently. "I meant I think it's time to go to the hospital."

Upon hearing that bit of news, I offered her my chair and stated, "Why don't you wait awhile and be sure? We can take you to the hospital at the half."

By halftime, she was sure, so off we went. We checked her into the delivery room during the third quarter; and, by the time the fourth quarter had begun, I had mosied down to the waiting room for expectant fathers. Turning on the TV, I was soon engrossed in the closing plays of the game.

With only minutes to play, Baylor scored a TD, and trailed Florida 13 to 14. A one-point conversion would tie; a two-point conversion would win. At that climatic moment, a harried-looking individual (obviously another expectant father) came rushing down the corridor.

"How long's your wife been in the delivery room?" he asked breathlessly.

"Oh, about a quarter and a half," I replied.

"Well," he went on, "someone down there just had a big baby boy."

"Wait till I see how this extra point comes out," I answered. Baylor failed at the two-point conversion, so I flicked off the set and started down the hallway. I was soon greeted by a nurse coming out of the delivery room holding a red, wrinkled baby. Proudly, she announced he was a boy. Proudly, I checked him carefully; and, sure enough, he was a boy—*my* boy!

A very accommodating young chap, he had more or less paid his own way into the world from the very beginning, having been born some seven hours before New Years. I thought at that magic moment I saw him for the first time that in years to come, he would think the whole world was celebrating his birthday. There was no denying the fact that son number one had come in like a Chinese New Year.

"Have you chosen a name for him?" the nurse interrupted.

"Yup," I replied. "His name is T. Douglas Davis."

"T?" she asked, with a puzzled look on her face.

"Un-huh," I said, poking him with my finger. "That's so his initials will be T. D. Davis."

"I suppose the T.D. stands for Tax Deduction," she suggested amiably.

"Yeah," I replied, "or Touchdown. Would you look at the size of those hands!"

THE GATHERING STORM

When Polly and I accompanied the football team and University officials to Miami, Florida, in the waning days of 1961, to organize the Colorado alumni activities in conjunction with the Orange Bowl game, neither of us suspected that this was but the prelude to an amazing series of events probably unmatched in the history of intercollegiate athletics. In contrast to the holiday season, there was a sense of foreboding in the air. Throughout the festive gaiety that adorned the balls and banquets and parades of the Orange Bowl Classic, there also was the gloom of the gathering storm that clouded the Colorado football scene.

While Colorado boasted of its first Big Eight football championship and national ranking, it also was laboring under the public announcement that the University was being investigated by the National Collegiate Athletic Association (NCAA) for alleged illegal recruiting practices. Suspicion hung heavy over the cocktail parties, and there was as much speculation on the outcome of the investigation as there was on the score on the New Year's Day game with Louisiana State.

It may have been some ill omen that it rained on the day of the game for the first time in Orange Bowl history. The proud Colorado Buffs were clobbered and showed little of the finesse and power that had carried them to the championship. A sad and gloomy party returned to Boulder.

For the next two and a half months, the campus and the state were rocked with almost daily accounts of the Colorado football situation. Internally, the University conducted an investigation of its own. Coaches, players, and boosters were interviewed and cross-examined, and the rumors flew. Finally, on March 17, 1962, the Regents met to hear the final report, which acknowledged that there had, indeed, been irregularities. After heated and bitter debate, the Regents dismissed the head football coach by a vote of five to one.

For a week the news focused on the aftermath of the firing, then predictably changed to speculation on nominees for the vacated head coaching position. One of the former assistants was a popular candidate.

From the sideline I had witnessed these proceedings, having attended the meeting of the Regents and various administrative sessions. I was unprepared, however, for the phone call the following Saturday summoning me to the President's office. There I was informed that the University definitely was not going to hire one of the former assistants as head coach. The President asked if I would consider taking the job and try to stabilize the football program, thus allowing the administration time to study the situation and formulate long-range plans. On Sunday I met with the President and the Faculty Athletic Committee, and all agreed that if I were appointed, I could have a free hand in selecting my assistants, including the retention of existing members of the staff if they chose to stay on.

That evening I was asked by one of the Regents to meet with him and two of the assistant coaches, one of whom had been the leading candidate for the job. In this session I was advised by the Regent not to accept the position. (He later was the only Regent to vote against my appointment.) The two coaches stated that if I were appointed, they would not serve under a former high school coach.

By Monday morning, the news had leaked to the press, and I awoke to find my picture on the front page of the *Rocky Mountain News* with the banner headline: "Bud Davis Looming as New C.U. Coach." The rest of that day was pure hell, culminating in a demonstration that night by some 400 students and members of the football team in which they hung the President and me in effigy.

Forty-five members of the football squad signed an open letter which was read on the late TV news and subsequently was published in the papers. It went as follows:

> *Open letter to the board of regents of the University of Colorado and the public:*
>
> *Just what political moves can switch the minds of intelligent men from one of the best proven coaches in the country to one unknown, inexperienced and unqualified handshaker? How can these minds justify the switch from . . . to Bud Davis?*
>
> *(Following a review of the qualifications of the former coach contrasted to mine, the letter continued:)*
>
> *After looking at these unbalanced qualifications how can Athletic Director Harry Carlson recommend this man when he has stated at a meeting of the football*

team last week that some of the most qualified football coaches throughout the country have expressed their desire to coach at CU?

. . . The players are not really against Mr. Davis personally, but we question his qualifications as head football coach and recruiter for a major college, competing against the best in the nation.

What do the people of Colorado want? A team that can continue in the winning tradition or shall we flood Folsom Field and use it for an ice hockey rink to challenge Denver University?

I didn't sleep that night. I don't think the President did either. He called about 5:00 a.m. and wanted to know if I would still take the job. I told him I couldn't back out at that point and would accept if the Regents appointed me.

The Regents met in Denver. Also in attendance were four representatives of the football squad, including the captain. When the Regents approved the appointment 5 to 1, the captain angrily stated: "You have yourself a coach—now get yourself a football team."

Except for two new arrivals on the former staff, none of the assistant coaches elected to stay on. Newspaper accounts reported rumors of a threatened player walk-out.

Late Tuesday afternoon, I met with the football squad. I acknowledged that the existing situation was in chaos, but that we would have to do our best. I outlined the immediate plans for the program. Then I announced that if anyone wanted to leave or transfer to another school, I would understand and do my best to help him get relocated. No one quit. (One player did transfer at the end of the semester.)

Later that day I officially accepted the appointment as Colorado's head football coach. There was no sense of elation. I thought of Abe Lincoln's remark about the man who stubbed his toe: "It hurts too much to laugh, and I'm too big to cry."

COLORADO FOOTBALL'S GALLOPING
DISASTER

With the perspective of time, I can now look back and find *some* humor in that grim football season of 1962. For example, I surely must be the first coach in the history of intercollegiate athletics to be hung in effigy *before* he got the job.

Also, I must have been the first Alumni Director to move directly to a head coaching position in a major institution. In some ways, one might rationalize that alumni and their directors had had so much to say about the football program over the years that it was high time someone gave them the ultimate responsibility—a kind of poetic justice.

As the new football coach, I was given a one-year appointment. I was tempted to ask for a definite contract covering a longer period, then remembered the coach who insisted upon and was given a life-time contract. After two miserable seasons, the president of his university called him in and said: "I now officially pronounce you dead." Also, I rationalized that history favored my future. In 71 years of intercollegiate football, Colorado had never fired a *losing* coach.

In this predicament, I began casting about for someone who had had some experience in college coaching, and managed to persuade my former coach, Dal Ward, to return as my assistant. (Ward had been ousted from the head coaching job at Colorado U. in 1958, after an eleven year tenure in which he compiled a winning percentage of over .600. The emotional circumstances of his dismissal seemed to focus upon his practice of kicking on third down.)

He promised to return only on the condition I assume the responsibility for punting on third down. I told him that with my offense, I didn't think we would ever need to punt. He replied that with my offense, we had better have multiple punt formations.

Dal also gave me some good advice about handling alumni. He quoted Herman Hickman as saying, "Don't win all the time. That makes them angry. Just win often enough to keep them sullen, but not mutinous."

With spring practice only a week away, there was not much time to assemble a coaching staff. Two assistants, Ed Farhat and Don Stimack, had just joined the previous coaching staff when the head coach was fired. Both elected to stay. Jim Smith, a former Marine Corps buddy who had coached high school football and obtained his doctorate before becoming C.U.'s assistant Dean of Men, was enlisted. Phil Cantwell, a successful high school coach at Bishop Amat in southern California, came as end coach. And finally, my old head mentor at Loveland, Bob Beckett, arrived on the scene. With the exception of Ward, all were ex-high school coaches. As Ed Farhat equipped, "This will either open the door for high school coaches into the college ranks or slam it shut forever."

While we were pulling together a coaching staff, we also began losing players faster than we could coach them. Several players were declared ineligible following the NCAA and Big Eight Conference meetings, and academic ineligibilities took another heavy toll later. Each night I anxiously read the newspapers to see whom we were losing next; between spring practice and our first game we lost thirty-five key players.

Newspapers quit referring to us as "the Golden Buffaloes" and substituted "the Vanishing Herd." When signing the contract for a weekly TV program that fall, I started to name it, "Where's My Line?"

As we prepared for the opening game against Utah, a non-conference opponent, I knew we were in for a long season. When we boarded the plane for Salt Lake City, we had three juniors and three seniors on the squad—and only two of the latter shaved. The rest were sophomores who had never heard a shot fired in anger in the college wars. For that matter, neither had I.

In the pre-game warm-up drill, I was acutely sensitive of the fact that when our center bent down to snap the ball, he was thinner through the shoulders than our quarterback was broad across the hips. We dropped the Utah game 37 to 21.

At a meeting on Sunday morning I tried to cheer up a dejected staff, saying brightly, "Don't worry. The University administration is behind us all the way." To which one of the assistant coaches replied, "So were the Utah pass receivers."

The following week we appeared before the home crowd for the first time as Kansas State came to Boulder. We scored early and hung on to a 6 to 0 lead. Early in the fourth quarter, our only center got hurt, so we moved a language major to this key position. His scholarship was excellent, but his snaps to the punter left something to be desired. In that agonizing final period, we had four punts blocked. Dal Ward, who by this time had turned philosopher, mused, "Some teams punt out of trouble. We punt into trouble." The game became one long goal-line stand, ending with Kansas State one foot away from the goal; and for one week we were leading the conference standings—undefeated, untied, and unscored upon.

We hit the road for three long weekends with games against Kansas, Oklahoma State, and Iowa State. The scores were so lopsided that it was clear that what had started out as a bad situation had begun to deteriorate.

After a 57 to 19 drubbing by Iowa State, we returned home to Boulder. Standing there in the drizzling rain, waiting to meet the bus, was my family. Little Becky, my seven-year-old daughter, greeted me with a big hug, exclaiming, "Daddy, we won! We won!" I felt obliged to tell her the truth—that we had really lost. "Oh, I know that," she replied, "But it's lots more fun to pretend we won."

The alumni, however, had lost none of their sense of humor. At a luncheon in Denver, the emcee quipped, "Coach Davis is a big success. No one expected him to do much with his material this year—and he hasn't." But the worst was yet to come. The soft part of the schedule was behind us. Ahead lay Nebraska, Oklahoma, and Missouri, in that order.

We rallied our forces for the Homecoming game against Nebraska and played a respectable first half, in which we led 6 to 0. That was probably our biggest mistake of the season. In the first five minutes of the second half we had so many casualties that our stretcher-bearers were exhausted. We lost 31-6. That was followed by a humiliating 62 to 0 loss to Oklahoma. It was at this point that the president called me in and informed me that some of the alumni were getting restless. Very politely, but very firmly, he hinted that we had better win the next game or I might be in trouble. "By the way," he added, "whom are you playing?"

"Missouri," I replied cheerfully. They were undefeated at the time and nationally ranked.

We could only get twenty-five able-bodied bodies aboard the plane for the trip, and when we landed at Columbia only twenty-three would get off.

I learned the full measure of humility that Saturday. I stood on a hostile sideline with the score 57 to 0 while some 40,000 Homecoming fans beseeched their team to "Hit 'em again, harder, harder!"

In those four weeks, we had had more than 200 points scored against us. Each time our opponents scored, a cannon was fired. Our coaches and players had reached a stage of shell-shock when we visited Texas Tech.

We started the game in typical fashion by giving up an early score, and, as was our custom, anticipated the dreaded report of the cannon. I kept waiting for it to go off, and, hearing nothing, glanced down at the end zone where the ROTC boys were furiously jerking at a balky laniard on their howitzer. As the ball was dropping into the outstretched arms of our sophomore halfback, the cannon fired. He left the ground about eight feet as the ball caromed off his chest and into the loving grasp of a Texas Tech lineman. Tech soon added another score.

Texas Tech had a tradition in which a masked rider, the Red Raider, rode a black stallion around the field after every touchdown while the crowd cheered. With my attention diverted by the trouble over the cannon, I didn't see the horse that second time around. I was probably the only college football coach ever run down by a horse on the sidelines.

We almost got back into that ball game. Driving for what might have been the tying touchdown in the fourth quarter, we threw a sideline pass from the five yard line. A Texas Tech end picked it off at the goal line and returned 100 yards for what proved to be the winning touchdown.

On the plane back to Colorado I asked our quarterback how he had happened to pick that particular man to throw to. He wistfully replied, "Coach, he was the only man open." I had heard this old story before, but had never believed it until then.

We limped into the final week of a sad season—a season which the sportswriters daily reminded the public was the worst in the history of Colorado University. The ball players eagerly rushed home from practice to read the evening papers and find out whether I had been fired, or whether authorities would wait until the final game to announce the decision.

I vividly remember those quiet moments before we went out to play the Air Force Academy. There was an awful silence, broken only by steady dripping of a leaky faucet. As the trainer passed among the players handing out chewing gum and daubing their cheeks with burnt cork, they were remote, almost grim.

I was all choked up as I launched into my final speech to that squad. "Lads," I said. "If you beat the Air Force today, I'll resign after the game."

They went out and fought like hell. The final score was Colorado 34, Air Force Academy 10.

But the memory of that season continues to haunt me. I still wake up nights hearing not the solid sound of toe against leather as a punter gets off a high spiral, but the double thud of toe hitting leather hitting opponent, followed by the vision of twenty-two players chasing the ball toward *our* goal line.

THE AFTERMATH

After the Air Force game I buried myself in the stacks at Norlin Library or in my basement at home typing the final drafts of my thesis which remained as the final obstacle to my doctor's degree. I had no desire to appear in public. I could still hear the chant of the Iowa State crowd when with us trailing 59 to 20 they taunted, "Go back to Greeley High."

In thinking back on the season, I knew I hadn't done a very good job of coaching. The personnel problems had so over-shadowed the game-to-game preparation that there were times I doubted if we even could score a touchdown on the blackboard. But I could never fault the courage of the young men on that team.

Rocked by one emotional upheaval after another as we lost man after man to eligibility rulings and later injuries, they never quit. The captain who had said, "You have yourself a coach, now get yourself a football team," was Ken Blair. His leadership was nothing less than heroic, and his loyalty was never lacking after that memorable meeting of the football squad. It was a thrill to see him honored on the All-Big Eight team for his inspired play. Every game, he gave everything he had. (He later became an assistant coach at Colorado U.)

People later asked if my being an Alumni Director aroused the antagonism of other coaches in the conference and if they purposely ran up the scores. If so, I was never aware of it. Dan Devine of Missouri played everyone on the squad including the manager who kicked extra points. Bud Wilkinson's Oklahoma squad had a hot day and there was no holding them back. A coach just can't tell a team to go out and hit someone "half-hard." Un-happily, we played that Oklahoma game at home and Wilkinson couldn't dip any lower than the third team. Bob Devaney's Nebraska crew simply hamburgered us after we led at halftime. These are men I admire and respect—gentlemen and great coaches in every way. I had to restrain myself from asking for their auto-graphs when we shook hands after the game.

One of the finest men in the game has to be Ben Martin of the Air Force Academy. As poised in defeat as he is in victory, he couldn't have been more gracious after that final game. Some years later, when rocked by two cheating scandals at the Air Force Academy which decimated his squads, he had the courage to stick it out and rebuild the program to where his teams once more are in the national rankings.

And, of course, one of the guys I got to meet that tumultuous year was Eddie Crowder, then an assistant on the Oklahoma staff. I cheered when he was appointed as my successor and have been cheering ever since as he has reorganized and built a solid program where the Golden Buffs once more are a perennial power.

Time dims the pangs of frustration and memories of defeat. Bright and clear are those moments of ecstacy. Shining through is that glorious locker room scene after the Air Force game when players and coaches stood around bawling their heads off as Captain Kenny Blair held the game ball over his head.

Adversity can often sharpen the appreciation of victory. A long time ago when I was still an undergraduate, Dean Harry Carlson, the University's Athletic Director, gave me a short quotation from a speech by Theodore Roosevelt. It goes like this:

> *In the battle of life it is not the critic who counts, not the man who points out how the strong man stumbled or the doer of the deed could have done better. The credit belongs to the man who is actually in the arena; whose face is marred by dust and sweat and blood; who strives valiantly, who errs and comes short again and again because there is no effort without error and shortcomings; who does actually strive to do the deeds; who knows the great enthusiasms, the great devotions, spends himself in a worthy cause; who at the best knows in the end the triumph of high achievement; and who at the worst, if he fails, at least fails while daring greatly, so that his place shall never be with those timid souls who have never tasted neither victory nor defeat.*

I like that.

VULGARLY CALLED A DEAN

While no student demonstrations or hangings in effigy surrounded my appointment as Dean of Men at the University of Colorado, the event was not without trauma or incident. Sometime in January 1963, President Quigg Newton and Dean of Students, Art Kiendl, called me into the adminstrative inner sanctum. By that time these little invitations were enough to get me as jumpy as a pheasant who has been shot at forty-nine times. I was informed that the position of Dean of Men had been vacant since September and was asked if I would be interested in being a candidate for the job.

Since my coaching appointment ran out in March (and along with it my pay check), I can honestly say I again was a candidate for just about *any* job. The next thing I knew, however, the rumor mill had cranked up and the news had leaked that without the screening committees, interviews, and the whole appointive procedure I was to be shoved down the collective throats of the Student Personnel Division. This was alleged to be some kind of "pay-off" for my having undertaken the coaching job.

I met with Art Kiendl, a man whom I admire a great deal and with whom one can be bluntly frank, and told him to forget it. I was tired of being the illegitimate son at the family reunion. Art replied that there had never been any intention of directly appointing me; that they had just wanted to know if I wanted to be a candidate. If I were interested, he continued, I could submit my application to the screening committee and take my chances through the regular channels.

I hope no arm twisting went on behind the scenes, but when finally appointed to the position, I was warmly welcomed into the bosom of the Student Personnel Services staff and never heard another word about the alleged "pay-off."

As Dean of Men I soon settled into the life of the administrator in charge of demonstrations, confrontations, riots and panty-raids. Contrary to my coaching problems where I labored to get the students fired up to commit acts of violence, as Dean I ran around urging patience and restraint. It was like switching from stoking a furnace to pouring water on each smoldering ember.

Despite my outwardly calm appearance, my sensitivity threshold was running high. While I accepted the heavy mantle of maintaing the peace on campus and realized it was my duty to avert the crisis rather than create one, nonetheless, I almost came to blows with a distinguished professor from the English Department.

It all began at this cocktail party which was attended by the usual faculty free-loaders, including me. And being a wet evening, tongues unlimbered with rapidity as the world's most outspoken collection of experts fired volleys on all topics. Searching for a conversation wherein I, too, might qualify as an expert, my antennae picked up a dialogue (a popular academic term) in a crowded corner. Elbowing my way through the masses, I got within earshot. What I had mistaken as a dialogue really turned out to be a monologue; but since one of the University's renowned English professors was holding forth, I listened.

This learned academician was among those members of the faculty who approached criticism of administrators with a missionary zeal. His lecture for the night was on the fragmentation of the job of the president of the university. I smiled as he referred to the titular president as one who dealt with such vital matters as fund-raising, football scandals, and the hiring of new coaches. I was amused at his tolerance of the vice-president in charge of budget, for even an academician knows what side his bread is buttered on and who butters it. I openly laughed when he referred to the vice-president in charge of academic affairs as one who was sometimes called a provost when the speaker was in a good mood.

But when he came to the administrator charged with the health, morals, and manners of students, and stated that this person often was *vulgarly* called a dean, my mellow and charitable mood quickly changed. It was at this point I felt like slapping him on the cheek with a pair of white gloves and challenging him to a duel.

Fortunately, I had a martini in one hand and a sandwich in the other—not to mention the restraining influence of my wife, who, noting my baleful countenance, had pinned both arms to my sides. Under such circumstances, it was easy to maintain some semblance of self-control. But inside, a tempest was raging. *Vulgarly called a dean, indeed!* A raw, jangling nerve had been twanged.

The evening passed, but not so the anger. Reaching the protective shelter of my home, I was still churning. I crawled grumpily into bed, where I lay awake like a wall-eyed pike, staring at the ceiling and rehashing the events of the evening. Clearly, that rigorous academician numbered himself among those who resented the title of dean being conferred upon any but the administrators of the academic programs of the university.

That took a lot of gall, considering the origin of the term "dean" in academic circles and the nature of the position since its inception. Inasmuch as I had researched the subject carefully upon my recent appointment, I was well acquainted with the details. These included such weighty tidbits as the fact that the word "dean" could be traced back to the Latin word "decanus," meaning a head, chief, or commander of a division of ten. Later its meanings ranged from "a chief of ten men," or "a head over ten monks in a monastery," to "a resident fellow at an English university charged with the discipline rather than the instruction of undergraduates." Only in its most recent context had it referred to an academic administrator in a collegiate institution.

Historically, the "dean" appeared on the Oxford scene in 1274. In American colleges, Harvard's President Eliot appointed the first dean in 1869. Most of his duties pertained to student relations, discipline, and record keeping. It was not until 1890 that Eliot divided this position and in addition to his dean for extra-instructional matters created the post of Dean of Arts and Sciences.

So, there was no call for the academician to get uppity on who deserved the title of dean. In a larger sense, however, the English prof's narrow-minded attitude probably extended beyond nit-picking terminology and reflected on an older and colder war in the academic community—namely, the English versus the German philosophy of higher education.

At one end of the log was the English dedication to the university's responsibility for the education of the whole man. On the other was the German attitude that the university should only be concerned with what transpired in the actual classroom—the student's out-of-class activities, such as dueling, drinking (to the rollicking strains of the Student Prince), and whoring were his own damned business. A modern summation would be the policy of *en loco parentis* as opposed to "hands off." (In one sense, the universities which cling to the *en loco parentis* concept have one thing in common with the parents of the students—they probably exercise as little control over their emotions and activities as do their own blood and kin.)

The nature of the duties of the Dean of Men changed as the influences of foreign philosphies ebbed and waned on the stormy seas of academe. A century ago, rules and regulations pertaining to student conduct were quite stringent. In the 1800's the student was forbidden to lie, steal, curse, duel, play at cards or dice, get drunk, fornicate, associate with persons of bad reputation, fight cocks, or be disrespectful or tardy or disorderly.

By 1960, the rules had been modified somewhat—at least to the effect that they prohibited these student activities *only* in the classroom. And movements already were under way to the effect that if enforced at all, such rules would constitute an infringement upon the constitutional rights of the student and abridge his freedom of expression and action.

Rolling over in bed for the hundredth time, I rationalized that the Sixties indeed were harrowing times to be a Dean of Men—times which called for unusual qualifications for the job. I reflected on the statement of Glenn Leggett (President of Grinnell College of Iowa) who said that to succeed as a dean, a man must develop the qualities of frankness and elusiveness, of vacillation and rigidity, and, above all, a kind of low animal cunning.

Chuckling in the darkness, I also thought he needed some sort of crutch. For me, it had been my pipe. When things got hairy, I could light up my trusty briar and appear to be reflective when I really was desperate. Or, when pinned to the wall by unreasonable, countermanding forces, I could search for matches while I scratched for answers. If all else failed, I might throw up a smoke-screen and dive through the nearest window.

But a good dean should do more than react to emergencies and crises, I mused. He should lead.

In the kaleidoscope fashion of half-sleep, my mind flipped back through the events of the week. The chief problem had focused on what to do with the navels in the Indian Grill. A delegation of students had approached the Student Union Board with a major grievance and lengthy petition protesting the academic dishonesty of the large mural which covered the walls of the main dining area in the campus center. The mural was disarming enough, depicting the romanticized Indian peacefully plowing his fields, roasting wieners, and smoking his pipe (probably peyote.) The artist, not doubt trying to protect and preserve the innocence of the undergraduates, had portrayed the Indians in their state of half-nakedness as having no navels.

Not content with their role as art critics, the student protestors insisted upon showing the West as it really was and agitated for changing the name of the dining area to the Alfred Packer Grill. (Packer was the resourceful guide, who, when he and five members of a prospecting party got lost in the wilds of the Uncompahgre peaks in the winter of 1874, survived by murdering and eating his companions. When caught and sentenced nine years later, the Judge allegedly pointed his finger at Packer and said, "They was siven Dimmycrats in Hinsdale County, but you, yah voracious, man-eatin' son of a bitch, yah et five of thim! I sentence ye t' be hanged by th' neck ontil y're dead, dead, dead!'')

All things considered, it was kind of a gristly fare for students to mix with their hamburgers at the grill. As Dean of Men, I stalled for time by volunteering to find an artist to paint navels on the Indians. (The stalling paid off for several years, but when the Student Union dining area was remodeled in 1967, it was renamed the Alfred Packer Grill.)

Dawn came, and my bloodshot eyes were still unclosed. Albeit, my mood had mellowed. While I no longer had the appetite for a duel with my esteemed colleague, neither could I completely forgive him for his pious smugness. Thus, as I shaved, dressed, and went whistling off to the office for another day of devious deanery, I amused myself by contemplating some scheme of diabolical retribution against him and his ilk—like organizing a student "sit-in" in the office of the English department's chairman.

Vulgarly called a dean, indeed!

NOBODY CALLS ME DOCTOR

As I was completing my first semester as Dean of Men, Debbie was winding up her final week in the third grade. One day she was asked by her teacher what her father did. "I don't know. I haven't read the paper today," was Debbie's frank reply.

Her confusion was understandable. Between February, 1960 and June, 1963 (a period of twenty-eight whirlwind months), I had served the University of Colorado in three different capacities as Alumni Director, head Football Coach, and Dean of Men. In my spare time I also had completed the course requirements and examinations for the Doctor of Education degree. By June, all that remained was the defense of my thesis, a 2,000 page history of the University of Colorado covering the period from 1858 to 1963. (Fellow graduate students were greatly amused as I hauled the various copies around the campus in huge cartons to distribute to the long-suffering members of my graduate committee. These irreverent graduate candidates taunted that if weighed by the pound, my thesis was bound to be accepted, barring some unlucky prof dropping it on his foot.)

At long last the day arrived when I was to complete the final chapter on my formal education. I heard the chairman mouth the magic words, "Congratulations, Doctor!"

Flushed with victory, I beamed. My graduate adviser, relieved that I had not embarrassed him before his colleagues, grasped my sweaty hand and wrung it gleefully. "Congratulations, Doctor!"

The treasured phrase was repeated again and again as my examining committee passed in review—some smiling, some jesting, some looking as if they had just violated some sacred trust. A lot I cared. I had their respective names on the dotted line. It was too late for them to renege. No more devious tests with no correct answers. No more tiresome lectures wherein I had to assume an air of awe and wonder. No more term papers on such worthy topics as "A Guidance Program for Maladajusted Guidance Directors" or "A Comparison of Driver Training Manuals for Third Grade Students." No more legalized plagiarism on that interminable thesis. No more sitting in that oral exam in a hot sweat while my professors were in a cold funk. I had survived.

It has been said that a new doctor feels like an eagle that has gone through a threshing machine. The old eagles want to see that the young eagles do not forget too soon, so they flail them to shape them up. Somehow, I lacked the nobility of the eagle. I felt more like a plucked pheasant. But, I chuckled to myself as I contemplated what I would do to the first new eagle I had a chance to flail.

"Congratulations, Doctor!"

I caressed the words. "Doctor Davis." What a grand sound! What alliteration! What dignity! What pomp! I repeated it again and again, much as a new bride surely must repeat her newly acquired last name. I strolled home, leaping easily from cloud to cloud and chanting again the magic formula, "Doctor Davis, Doctor Davis, Doctor Davis."

I was met at the door by my seven-year-old daughter, Becky, who said, "Hi, Dad." Obviously, she hadn't gotten the word.

Polly, however, caught my victory smile. "Congratulations, Doctor!" she said. I shrugged modestly.

My young daughter looked amazed. "Is Daddy a doctor?"

"Well, almost," my wife explained.

"Barring a volcanic eruption between now and commencement," I joked.

Becky obviously was still puzzled. "Does that mean he can take out my tonsils?"

"No, dear," Polly explained patiently. "He isn't *that* kind of a doctor."

"Then what kind of a doctor is he?"

"He's a doctor of education."

"Oh," my daughter replied, somewhat bored with the whole thing. "Daddy, can I have a nickel?"

Well, what can one expect from a mere child?

In the time between the completion of my oral exams and the actual conferring of the degree, I ambled happily around the campus, aloof and indifferent to those struggling peons shuffling to and from classes unaware of this modern miracle, and smug in my knowledge that on commencement day the whole world would know.

At the graduation exercises, when my name was called I gingerly picked my way to the platform. Conquering my bounding exuberance, I assumed a detached expression of humility as I ducked my head for the hooding.

In the audience, my wife, children, and relatives were assuming the same attitude of humility. I had cautioned them against any outbursts such as standing and cheering with three rahs and a tiger for old Davis. But in spite of my warnings, there *was* an incident.

Two young things receiving their bachelor degrees were sitting in front of my family. Polly overheard one ask the other, "Isn't that the same guy who was fired as football coach here last year?"

To which her colleague replied, "Yes. But I think this is *the least* they could do for him." At that, Polly struggled to restrain herself from splitting the young lady's mortarboard with a well-directed blow with her purse.

Later, I began to wonder why, with all the smart people who had been awarded doctorates, none had come up with some simple method by which we might be identified. For example, like an Army colonel, we could wear some emblem on our shoulders, such as a flailed silver eagle (or a plucked pheasant). Or like an admiral in the Navy, we could wear gold braid on the cuffs of our blue blazers. Like a German Field Marshal, we could carry a baton. Or if that seemed too pretentious, we could carry a swagger stick like a Marine Corps drill instructor. The embroidered letters "Ed.D." on the lapel would be too obvious, but surely some kind of lapel pin like a Rotary button would be appropriate.

Alas, even these moderate gestures were regarded as being in poor taste. I even discovered that it was deemed unthical to sign my correspondence with the illustrious "Dr. W. E. Davis." I learned that it was all right to have the degree, but not all right to let everyone know it. It was enough to make a doctor cry.

Friends still called me by my undistinguished nickname. Athletes still called me "Coach." Bills were still addressed to me as "Mister." The children still called me "Dad."

Even the campus newspaper kept referring to me by my antiquated title. In reviewing a conference, they would state that in attendance were: Dr. Jones, Dr. Smith, Dr. Barnes, and *Mr.* Davis.

It was all very frustrating.

But, by thunder, I decided that at least in one area I would insist upon being called "Doctor." I browbeat the secretaries in our department and informed them in no uncertain terms how I was to be addressed. Cowed into submission, they complied. This went very well for awhile, until one day in my absence, the President of the University called. He asked, "Is Mister Davis there?"

My alert secretary answered, "If you mean *Doctor* Davis, *Doctor* Davis is not in. Whom shall I say is calling?"

"Well, when *Doctor* Davis arrives, will you please tell him that *Mister* Newton called?"

That put an end to that.

I decided to try the subtle approach. I quit referring to myself as "Doctor Davis." Instead, I would make offhand references pertaining to my training. I would drop little hints like, "now when I was writing my doctoral thesis . . ." Or, "I remember that book well. When I was studying for my doctoral exams . . ." This seemed to be working well, until some starry-eyed student asked, "Sir, when do you expect to get your degree?"

I even gave up the battle on the home front. A few weeks after receiving the degree, I was sitting in front of a snapping fire, sipping a scotch and water (a very academic drink), listening to a little Rachmaninoff on the stereo (the cultural touch), and reading a learned publication (the continued pursuit of knowledge). My wife came in looking very fetching and with that come-hither glint in her eye, asked, "Shall we go to bed, Doctor?"

Blushing, I replied, "Aw what the hell! Just call me Bud."

IT WAS HARD TO SAY GOOD-BYE

Coinciding with the final agonies and ecstacies of completing my doctoral program were the negotiations for a new job. A phone call in May had changed my life—again. It came from Dr. Duke Humphrey, President of the University of Wyoming, who invited me to come to Laramie to discuss a position he had in mind in the field of student affairs.

So, on a balmy May Sunday, Polly and I drove northward to Wyoming, not without some misgivings. The last time we had been in Laramie to attend a Colorado-Wyoming freshman football game, the wind had been blowing at about ninety knots while the temperature hovered around zero. But on that day in May the campus was decked out in all its finery and resplendent with spring flowers. The neat, well-kept grounds and magnificent limestone buildings reflected both care and progress.

The most impressive landmark on the Wyoming campus, however, was President Humphrey. In his quiet Mississippi drawl, he reflected both confidence and charm as he discussed the University and its hopes and future. After visiting with him for about two hours, he offered me the job as Executive Assistant to the President for Student Affairs. On the Colorado campus, this would have corresponded to the position of Dean of Students, and entailed the administrative supervision of the areas of Dean of Men, Dean of Women, the Student Health Center, financial aids, counseling and advising programs, and some aspects of housing. I accepted on the spot, pending notification to the administration in Boulder.

Thus, at the June commencement of 1963, I was acutely aware that I would soon be leaving the University of Colorado, the home of my undergraduate years and the scene of so much upheaval and change in my personal life. For many reasons, I therefore viewed the events that day with an acute awareness.

That commencement day was a glorious occasion. The morning was hot and brilliant. The broken skyline of red-tiled buildings basked in sharp relief against the panorama of the Continental Divide. The gleaming white of Arapahoe gracier gleamed in contrast to the fresh-washed blue of the Colorado sky. The President's garden was quiet, shady, almost secluded from the brilliance of the day as seniors, parents, and faculty gathered at the morning reception.

It was the time of the senior and the campus was primed for the event. There were the landmarks of the "old campus"—the towers of Macky reflected in Varsity Lake—flags snapping and popping from the spires of Old Main. Luxurious grass was taken for granted on a campus where grass was everywhere—a far cry from the barren wastes filled with cactus and sagebush that once had surrounded the University's lone building. Trees shaded stone walks; vines covered old buildings. The nakedness was gone. The quad, once the scene of the promenades and song fests, was crowded with graduating seniors in academic costumes posing for pictures against the splendid background of Norlin Library, and proud parents hovered in beaming approval.

But on the eastern fringes of the campus the reverent hush of academic calm was notably lacking. The sounds of hammers and the roar of machinery intruded upon the dignity of the occasion. Great gaping holes and raw framework around the Library served to remind those present that knowledge was doubling every ten years and needed to be accommodated. Construction around the Student Union and new residence halls emphasized that more students were coming and needed to be served.

Now and then, the preening graduates were passed by a bright-eyed, jovial group—the class of 1908, celebrating its fifty-fifth reunion—touring the campus with its glib guide who stated, "On your left is a Dean of Men, an unknown species in your day."

In the afternoon, thunderheads began piling up over the mountains. The Commencement Marshal kept an apprehensive eye on the sky and the other on his watch as the bell in Old Main sent forth its call and the carillon in the towers of the Memorial Center chimed the school fight song, "Glory Colorado." There was the mustering of the faculty—the forming of what was perhaps the most obstinate, most unwieldy, most independent body in the state of Colorado into a "column of groups"—and the academic procession into Folsom Stadium.

Then it was as if the whole pageant passed in review. It was all there—the stirring music of the band, the shuffling of feet as the black-robed lines took shape and mass in the grey stadium. The Marshal's craggy features were outlined against the tableau of faces that represented faculty, graduates, parents, alumni, and friends.

With all assembled, mortar boards were removed and heads were bared for the singing of the National Anthem followed by the invocation.

To me, it seemed that excellence was everywhere. It was there in the more than 1800 graduates who were receiving their degrees—represented in the fresh beauty of the young lady carrying her bouquet of roses as the Outstanding Senior woman—represented in the young manhood of Rhodes scholar and All-American athlete Joe Romig bearing the Senior Cane. It was symbolized by the more than 400 candidates for advanced degrees and the doctors who received their hoods. It was typified by the men and women who had served their fellowman well and were recognized by honorary degrees.

It must have been a moment of high personal triumph for the outgoing President, Quigg Newton, as he presided at his Valedictory Commencement. Despite vicious and repeated personal attacks on him and his administration, he had guided the University with courage and vision through troubled times as it made its bid for greatness. Twice—first when he was presented wtih a gift from the Senior Class, and later at the conclusion of his Commencement address—he was honored by a standing ovation.

Then, for the last time as President of the University of Colorado, Quigg Newton read the charge to the graduates. It was the charge first delivered by the late President George Norlin in 1935 and repeated at Colorado University Commencement exercises ever since:

> *You are now certified to the world at large as alumni of the University. She is your kindly mother and you her cherished sons and daughters.*
>
> *This exercise denotes not your severance from her, but your union with her. Commencement does not mean, as many wrongly think, the breaking of ties and the beginning of a life apart. Rather it marks your initiation in the fullest sense into the fellowship of the University, as bearers of her torch, as centers of her influence, as promoters of her spirit.*
>
> *The University is not the campus, not the buildings on the campus, not the faculties, not the students of any one time—not one of these or all of them. The University consists of all who come into and go forth from her halls, who are touched by her influence and who carry on her spirit. Wherever you go, the University goes with you. Wherever you are at work, there is the University at work.*

What the University purposes to be, what it must always strive to be, is represented on its seal, which is stamped on your diplomas—a lamp in the hands of youth. If its light shines not in you and from you, how great is its darkness! But if it shines in you, several hundred today and twenty-five thousand before you, who can measure its power?

With hope and faith, I welcome you into the fellowship. I bid you farewell only in the sense that I pray you may fare well. You go forth, but not from us. We remain, but not severed from you. God go with you and be with you and us.

It was over. The threatening storm had held off. The One Hundred and Twenty-fifth Commencement was a memory, a part of the past, a moment of history, a discarded program fluttering in the breeze of an empty stadium seat.

It was hard to say good-bye.

FEUDAL LIFE UNDER THE DUKE

Getting acquainted with Wyoming's President, George Duke Humphrey, was an education in itself—a postgraduate course in administrative firmness. In his nineteen years as President of the University of Wyoming, the "Duke" had sat tall in the saddle, and his image was indelibly implanted upon the life and mood of the campus. In all, he was perfectly cast for the feudal role, blending the aggressive nature of an academic king-fish with the practical horse-sense of a southern farmer, the finesse of a diplomat with the hard talk of an irate wrangler.

This appealed to Wyomingites who like their men tough and their talk straight. Though he drove his famed black Buick with reckless abandon and terrorized the casual jay-walkers of Laramie, he steered the University through the rough and tumble of Wyoming politics with a sure grip on the reins. In a crisis he demonstrated the ability to deal with the assurance of a poker player with a pat hand—or, in the words of Mark Twain, "The calm confidence of a Christian holding four aces."

One of his primary tasks was the wooing of those recalcitrant philanthropists, the legislators. On one visit to a legislator who doubled as a sheep rancher in Crook County, the rancher asked, "Duke, how much time do the professors teach over at the University?"

The President replied, "Oh, about twelve hours (meaning twelve hours a week).

The rancher replied, "That's a good day's work for anyone. I've been hearing that the professors aren't doing anything over there, but I know now it isn't true."

Outside the environs of the University, it was not uncommon to hear the President referred to as "Duke," or, more often, "The Duke." Few such liberties were taken in addressing him in that manner on the campus, however, where protocol resided in a place of dignity.

Although Western in location and tradition, there were no cowboys on the faculty under Humphrey—or at least those who were didn't dress that way. A stickler for spit and polish, this former Mississippian had a flair for the southern gentleman's sense of style and taste. He held to the belief that even though a man might have nothing but holes in his pockets, he could comb his hair, shine his shoes, and wear a necktie.

This concern for proper dress is supported by a story that upon the occasion of appointing a new dean for one of the colleges, Humphrey called a prospective candidate in. The latter was neatly, but informally, dressed with a western shirt, a string tie, rancher's trousers, and boots.

The President eye him cooly. "You think we pay enough to our deans around here, Doctor?"

"Why, yes, Mr. President," the anxious candidate replied.

"You think we pay 'em enough to buy a dark suit, a white shirt, a necktie, and some dress shoes?"

The candiate blushed.

"I'll tell you what," the President continued. "You think it over and drop in tomorrow, and we'll talk about the job."

The candidate showed up the next day in appropriate attire and was appointed dean. He never needed to be reminded again.

President Humphrey was just as finicky about time. If a meeting was scheduled to start at four o'clock, it started at four o'clock—come a spring blizzard or a summer flood on the Laramie plains. Late-comers were seldom looked upon in a friendly or tolerant manner. At faculty meetings, as each late arrival slunk in, the "Duke" would stop the meeting and stare him into his seat before proceeding.

He was just as punctual about getting to the office on or before eight o'clock each morning. Rumor has it that around Old Main, where the names of the administrative officers were painted on the curbs, the names were not there so much to reserve parking spaces as to check the roll when the boss drove in.

A perfectionist himself, he, on occasion, was tolerant of error in others—as long as it didn't happen too often. Once in a faculty meeting, considerable confusion arose over a point of order. At this the President graciously acknowledged, "I may be in error on this matter, but I don't see how." No one challenged him.

While demanding of his faculty and assistants, he was not a meddler, holding to the theory of giving a man enough rope either to do the job or hang himself or both. Praise, when forthcoming, was usually well deserved. The same could be said of criticism. All of which led a faculty member, beating a hasty retreat from the President's chambers, to say, "When the Duke wants to pat you on the back, why must he use his foot?"

While he demanded a lot of members of his staff, he also was just as ready to stand behind them in a moment of crisis. Once, during the days when Denver University still played football and the annual Thanksgiving Day game in Denver climaxed the fall festivities, a post-game celebration got out of hand. The head coach and an assistant ran afoul of the law and were hauled into court. The newspapers called President Humphrey and asked if the coaches would be fired because of the incident. The answer appeared in a banner headline on the front page of *The Denver Post*: "HUMPHREY SAYS HELL NO!" The language probably made the preachers wince, but it endeared the President to a constituency that admired a man who stuck by his guns and his people.

Some college presidents take an ostrich-like attitude toward intercollegiate athletics, hiding their heads in the sand, hoping nothing too bad will upset the academic apple cart. Not so the Duke. He let his stand be known in no uncertain terms, stating in a gravelly voice, "When we don't win, I get mean." He smiled when he said it, and one might not know whether he was kidding or not. But it took the courage of a man attacking a grizzley with his bare hands to test him.

As proof, one of the easiest ways to get him riled was to ask him how he liked it in Wyoming. With his sly smile and a bit of grit in his voice, he was apt to reply, "I've been in Wyomng nineteen years. Hell, if I didn't like it, I wouldn't be here."

I was glad he liked it. If he hadn't been there, chances are—neither would I.

Shortly after the opening of the fall semester the year of my arrival the University of Wyoming ROTC cadets staged a review for the Governor. On the sidelines, a bare-footed, bearded heckler marched up and down with a placard that read, "Abolish ROTC." (Wyoming at the time had a compulsory ROTC requirement.)

President Humphrey instructed me to check on the identity of the one-man protest. I did. The following Monday, I reported that the subject in question was a junior who had completed but one semester of ROTC. I then quoted from the college bulletin the section that stipulated that all physically qualified male students must complete their ROTC requirements within their first two years on campus, and that those who were negligent or dilatory in this respect were subject to dismissal from the University. I asked the President, "How tough do you want to be on this?"

He gave me a crooked grin and from the corner of his mouth replied, "He can read, can't he?"

The one-man protest elected to shave, wear shoes, and join the ROTC.

President Humphrey was an easy man to work for once you understood and abided by the rules.

WYOMING WEATHER

Prior to my departure from Colorado, I had heard wild tales pertaining to the harsh climate and semi-isolation of the University of Wyoming and its location in that town straight out of western folklore—Laramie. For example, I had heard that there was no summer in Laramie, just two weks of bad skiing—or that the only way the natives knew it was spring was when they came to the slick pages in the Sears-Roebuck catalogue.

I had listened to fierce stories about the Wyoming wind. It was stated that little children heading north or west walked at an angle, and if the sub-zero zephyrs ever stopped blowing, they would fall on their wind-burnt faces. I'd been told that swings, ropes, and clothes that hung on clotheslines (before electric dryers) dangled at an angle of 45 degrees. I had even heard that the morning paper was printed on native limestone to keep it from blowing away before breakfast. Some said that they called it the *Boomerang* because it blew to Cheyenne for the evening edition, and, with a favorable change in the wind, it would blow back to Laramie the next day.

And cold—I thought surely from the oft-related tall tales that the first week in September the temperature would drop to 50 below and stay there until the next fourth of July. I had been warned that thermo boots, parkas, and cans of sterno should be drug out to fortify the hardy pioneer who dared venture the eight blocks from home to office on a late September or early October morning. I had been told that natives stored huge quantities of alcoholic beverages and referred to it as the white-man's anti-freeze.

And football—I'd heard that any fan foolhardy enough to sit outside in four consecutive home games at Wyoming's War Memorial Stadium traded fervor for frostbite. I'd been belabored by wild tales of games finished in the dark during blinding blizzards—where the headlights of the automobiles had to be turned on to brighten the field in the final quarters of the day.

108

I'd heard of games won on the opening kickoff when the receiver caught the ball and ran straight up the field along the hogback while the opposition slipped and slid trying to climb the banks of ice to tackle him—or of a lonesome end who went out as a flanker, lost his way in the drift, and wasn't discovered until the spring thaw.

But in my first months in Laramie, the howling wind was more like a soft caress than a slap in the face. The anti-freeze served more to enliven the Homecoming activities than to ward off the cold. And I waited impatiently to see a snowflake fall in anger as I sat through four consecutive football games in shirt sleeves. The red glow on the noses of avid, rabid fans was attributed to sunburn rather than anti-weather stimulant.

I put my lawn mower away in September, and the grass was soon knee-high on a tall antelope. In November, flowers were still in bloom, and the marigolds, roses, and carnations were having nervous breakdowns from the anxiety fostered by the long growing season. With all the confusion in the weather, they just kept budding.

Morning after morning I got up to nothing but brilliant blue skies and glorious views of the city resplendent in the golden hues of the cottonwoods. The Snowy Range wasn't snowy. There were no fires in the fireplaces. The wild game was still so high in the hills that the hunters had nothing to shoot but each other.

I asked the friendly natives: "Where is the Laramie winter?" They laughed nervously, and in self-conscious tones replied, "Strangest fall we've ever seen. Never had one like it before. Why, usually, at this time, it has been fifty below and so cold it would freeze the . . ."

I persisted. I wrote a letter to the Laramie *Boomerang.* "Where," I asked, "is the Wyoming winter?"

The next day it arrived, and for seven months it snowed, and it snowed, and it snowed. At Christmas time the natives, instead of singing "I'm Dreaming of a White Christmas," were chanting their own version of that song from *Oklahoma:*

> *"Oh, what a hellova morning,*
> *Oh, what a hellova day.*
> *I've got a hellova feeling,*
> *It's gonna snow all through May."*

One frost-bitten sports writer from Phoenix who accompanied the Arizona State University basketball team on a visit to Wyoming went home and wrote:

> *Young men who come to Laramie to spend school*
> *sessions find that unfortunately this includes one winter*

*each year. One disclosure that always stuns some of the
nation is that people live in Laramie on purpose. It gets
so cold that visiting teams bring enough clothing to outfit Red China and fans who find their way to Wyoming
U's fieldhouse keep the motors of their cars running for
90 minutes or make periodic voyages to the parking lot
to warm engines.*

But, one can forgive his chilling remarks considering the
score. Arizonians seldom thawed out enough to beat the Wyoming
Cowboys in Laramie.

In a similar vein, I recall the visit of the San Jose
basketball team fresh from California's sunny clime. Two of the
players were standing in the foyer of the Wyoming fieldhouse,
gazing with awe through the window at the snow that was howling
by on a horizontal course. One looked at the other and said,
"Do you suppose people live here because they want to?" (Shades
of Arizona!)

His companion shrugged. "What do you suppose the natives
do for entertainment?"

"Oh, I don't know," his buddy replied. "I think there's a
lot to do in Laramie. This morning I walked over to a garage
and watched them grease a car."

I scoffed at these summer patriots and sunshine soldiers,
haughty with my new-found Wyoming pride.

But as April arrived and we laconically viewed the melting
drifts and wistfully looked forward to the blooming of the lilacs
about the fourth of July, I wondered if the endless winter were
not taking its toll on my family. All the signs of "cabin fever"
began to emerge. Doug, age three, was out riding his trike on the
front walk. Suddenly, from the direction of the cement plant came
a terrific explosion. With wide eyes, he ran into the house to
announce hopefully, "Mom! I just heard a rain drop!"

(In those days his mother and I thought he had the makings
of a great Boy Scout. Twice he had wandered from the house into
the hills back of the town on what must have been his fourteen
mile hikes. Each time it had taken a half day to find him. We
kept wondering, however, why a kid that smart and with that
kind of endurance couldn't find his way to the bathroom.)

Debbie, eleven, came home from school that afternoon with
seven books she had checked out from the library—all seven were
horse stories. Concerned that her reading habits were too confined,
I launched into a long lecture on how she should strive for broader
fields rather than concentrating on horses. "Yeah," she replied,
"my teacher says the same thing. She keeps wanting me to read
King Arthur. Last week it was *Jean Lafitte*. I think she keeps

wishing she would be kidnapped by a knight or a pirate." Then she sighed, "But, boy, with all this snow I sure get a lot of reading done. There's nothing else to do!"

About that time, in walked bright-eyed Becky, a chirping nine. Her first observation was to gripe about Doug's hair being too long, whereupon I got out the clippers and proceeded to give him a haircut. To amuse him and divert his attention, Becky read to him from the yellow pages of the phone book. I became so absorbed in her imaginative tales that he ended up looking like a Marine Corps boot.

That night Becky was doing her homework in front of the fireplace while I alternated between reading a book and admiring her casual approach to study. Her immediate task was learning the "6's" in the multiplication table by means of flash cards. She mumbled aloud, "Six times six is thirty-six. Six times seven is forty-four." Pausing with furrowed brow, she checked her card for the correct answer, shrugged her shoulders, and mused, "Oh, well, that's close enough."

I observed that her mother kept the check book the same way, and the warmth of the family circle dissolved into a chilly good-night.

As I banked the fire, I wondered if spring would ever come.

THE NOON-HOUR BASKETBALL LEAGUE

The annals of the University of Wyoming athletic teams and epic games are replete with tales of courage and valor, but notably missing are the unrecorded exploits of the noon-hour basketball league. These informal contests flowered during my two-year tour on that campus from 1963 to 1965 as Exececutive Assistant to the President for Student Affairs. And standing tall amidst its unsung heroes was that fearsome foursome of Moe Radovich, Hardy Rollins, Red Jacoby, and (modestly) myself.

Having reached that turn in life when organized, competitive sports no longer had use of our talents and energies and once thin, trim waistlines were giving way to the middle-age spread, we sought some civilized outlet for our aggressions and skills. Hence, we agreed to forego lunch and play basketball. (Skipping lunch made us even meaner and more irascible.) Occasionally, we were joined in our pickup game by stray students, members of the football coaching staff, and a rare professor or two. But Moe, Hardy, Red, and I always managed to play on the same team.

The rules were simple; Moe made them up. Also, the officiating was casual. We called our own violations (based on the principle, no blood, no foul). Under these guidelines, the games were rigorous. For example, Hardy Rollins and Red Jacoby were the kind of guys who if they saw an elderly grandmother dribbling in for a lay-up would high-low her into the fifth row of seats.

Our games took on an ever-increasing competitive pitch. Elbows would fly with unleashed tempers; sprained ankles and cracked ribs became the accepted course of events. And black eyes and fat lips were regarded as badges of honor. The holocaust became complete one noon, however, when I crouched for a rebound. Unbeknownst to me, Hardy was flying in from a corner. I jumped from the floor just as he came crashing down. I was pole-axed. When I recovered consciousness, Hardy was stretched out on the floor holding his bleeding chin. Moe, in the meantime, was dribbling the ball behind his back gesturing frantically for us to get back in the game so he could shoot again.

I did, and Hardy did, but with all the blood the ball soon was too slick to handle. We had to call the game while Hardy went to the doctor for some 44 stitches in his chin. It was some time before our wives would let us play again.

Hardy, all the while kept protesting that it was just a flesh wound. After all, he proudly proclaimed, *he* was a veteran of Coach Bowden Wyatt's football wars. In those days he was known as "Little Hoss" and famous for leading the single wing's flying wedge with his nose. His chief reward was getting it splattered all over his face where it still remains.

To really understand Hardy's contribution to the Noon-Hour League, I have to point out that he is a physical culture nut. When traveling with the uninitiated (to his quaint customs), it was most embarrassing to stop at a filling station. Hardy took this as a sign to leap out of the car, do twenty-five push-ups, fifteen side-straddle-hops, and run in place until the gas tank was full.

One night he accompanied me to Lusk, Wyoming, where I was scheduled to speak to an athletic banquet. We checked into the hotel and decided to share a room to cut expenses. Hardy immediately observed that the room was too warm—probably an intolerable 70 degrees. With that, he threw open the windows to let in the fresh February air.

Four hours later, after the speech, we returned to find a foot of snow on the floor and the temperature matching the minus twenty degrees below zero outside.

Hardy's aggressiveness on the basketball court, however, made him a pyorrhea at social gatherings. True, hostesses became accustomed to his spending the evening lying prone on the floor arm-wrestling with any challengers. But the night he was demonstrating the lethal qualities of a forearm lift against a kitchen wall and smashed an elbow through the wallboard, he wore out his welcome.

If Hardy added a certain robust freshness and ruggedness to our games, it was Moe who supplied the strategy. It was natural that he served as coach, head official, outside shooter, star, and critic, for, after all, he *was* the assistant varsity basketball coach. (But, for an assistant coach, he got a lot of help, especially from his youngest daughter, Tara. Moe pronounced it "Terror". When asked about the origin of the name, he just shrugged and replied that her mother had sat through too many showings of "Gone With the Wind". Tara had a way of getting to her dad. One night Moe was deeply embroiled in the climax of a freshman game with the Air Force Academy. In the second overtime, the special emergency phone at the timer's table rang. The game was stopped and

Moe was called from the bench. It was Tara, indignantly announcing that it was almost time for the varsity game and when was he coming to pick her up.)

Jacoby, sometimes known as the Red Fox of the High Plains, was the University Athletic Director. His main contribution to our basketball team was as blocking back. At first we argued that there was no such position in basketball, but finally acquiesced. After all, as he pointed out in times of crisis, it was *his* field house and *his* ball. Besides, as blocking back, he never had to shoot. This was good because we were embarrassed to tell him that his two-hand push shot had disappeared with the center jump shortly before the rest of us were born.

What Red lacked finesse, he more than made up in temperament. In all his life he claimed he had never lost an athletic contest—time had just run out on him on a few rare occasions. In our league, this was a decided advantage. He would never quit until we were ahead.

To round out our well-balanced squad, I handled the executive chores (i.e. scheduling, player personnel, protests) and acted as chief spokesman. Occasionally, my experience with the Noon-Hour League carried over into my official duties in the field of Student Affairs, namely, the ability to avert near riots.

This talent gained most prominence during a series of Wyoming games with Brigham Young University and Utah. There was something about a basketball game with these Utah schools that brought out the latent instincts of predatory bears in our normally dormant students. One dreadful night, we were playing Brigham Young University and some unsavory decisions by near-sighted officials brought forth a storm of protest in the form of throwing junk on the court.

The President directed me to put an end to this by talking to the students prior to the game with Utah the following night. Red, Moe, and Hardy skipped a noon-hour workout to help me write the speech, which compared with the Gettysburg Address only in its brevity.

With their moral support and great trepidation, I marched onto the floor before the introduction of the University of Utah basketball team and announced:

> *Ladies and Gentlemen, especially those ladies and gentlemen within throwing distance of the court:*
> *Last Thursday night we had a series of accidents in terms of exuberant student behavior which we would like to request not be repeated again—namely, the throwing of paper cups and other debris on the floor to express displeasure with official decisions. This not only violates*

*the principles of good sportsmanship and Wyoming hos-
pitality, but is highly dangerous to the players, who have
enough obstacles to avoid as it is. It is expected that
our players and coaches will conduct themselves as
gentlemen, even in the heat of the game. Surely those
enjoying the safety of the stands can do likewise.*

*I'd like to remind you that the sap is rising and spring
is just a few days away, and to request that you save your
pitching arms for more appropriate occasions. So, for
now, please refrain from throwing chewing gum, popcorn boxes, paper cups, coins, and knives at the officials.
Support your team with enthusiasm, but also in a way
that typifies Wyoming spirit.*

Then, I ducked. Shortly thereafter, I also began putting out
feelers for a new job.

Moe likewise was looking. But I didn't think it was for real
until he walked into my office one day and asked for a letter of
recommendation. Knowing the threat that this constituted for
the Noon-Hour Basketball League, I cheerfully obliged. I wrote
a letter of recommendation I thought would *keep* him at the
University of Wyoming forever.

Spring, 1965

Dear Mr. Athletic Director:

*Mr. Moe Radovitch has indicated to me that he is
interested in a head basketball position at your school
and would like to git while the gitting is good. While
it is true that a lot of misguided alumni around here
would like to see him go, I am not one of them—in
other words, I am not an alumni. I don't hold to the
theory that a team has to win all the time, but it is
tough making ends meet when our only consistent crowd
is the knothole club, which is admitted free.*

*As to Moe's personal qualifications, I think you might
find him modest, self-effacing, and willing to sacrifice.
He was a whiz as an undergraduate here, and still holds
the school record for most field goals attempted, and
most points per season (an average of 7.2 points per
game for 43 games.) His fall-away jumper has fallen off
with age, but he still has most of his hair.*

*He has a lovely wife who doesn't drink too much too
often, and several of us belong to this keen club that
lives it up every Saturday night after a win. There hasn't
been too much living it up these past years. Moe doesn't
drink. Someone has to drive.*

*His daughters are nice, too. One of them calls him
up on the bench telephone during ball games. That old*

saying about a little child shall lead them sure has applied to Wyoming basketball.

Moe has many interests and is broadminded. For example, he is a great fisherman, and tries to get in a little every day. Of course, this means his working day doesn't begin until about noon, but who can measure the stress and duress and the sleepless nights put in by coaches?

I also should mention that Moe is a natty dresser The Wyoming U. sweat sox and Wyoming U. "T" shirts he wears when speaking to civic groups give the school great free advertising. He would have a neat, clean-cut appearance if he would only shave.

In short, I hope you can see fit to take him off our hands before our alumni cease hanging him in effigy and get down to hanging him for real. Boy, do I recommend him!

> Sincerely,
> William E. Davis
> Executive Assistant for
> Student Affairs

To my dismay, Moe got the job. The Noon-Hour Basketball League was just not the same without him, and soon dissolved. Meanwhile, Red, Hardy and I took up noon-hour squash. We played a three-man version of the game by Jacoby's rules called "cut-throat." In characteristic fashion, the object of the game became that of Red and Hardy trying to hit the ball through the opponent rather than at the wall. And, if either lost, he threw his racket at you.

THE INTERVIEW

After almost two years at the University of Wyoming, in January, 1965, I received an inquiry pertaining to the presidency at a small college. With letter in hand I called on President Emeritus Duke Humphrey to seek his advice. (By that time Dr. Humphrey had retired as President but was serving as Administrator of American Studies.) He encouraged me to apply, but added that he knew of an opening that might interest me even more. He had just received a letter from the Board of Trustees of Idaho State University asking for recommendations for candidates for the presidency at that institution. He had visited the campus on a number of occasions and knew several members of the Board. Following our discussion, he submitted my name.

The months dragged by. Finally, in April, I received a letter from the chairman of the Board of Trustees inviting me to Salt Lake City, Utah for an interview.

I conveyed the good news to Dr. Humphrey. He eyed me carefully. "You got a suit?" he asked.

"No." I answered truthfully. "I'm not much for suits."

"Well," he grumbled, "that Board isn't going to be much impressed with your sport coat and slacks. Go buy a suit."

I bought a suit and departed for Salt Lake City.

On the big day, I entered the star chamber reserved by the Idaho Board for the inquisition. My throat was as dry as on that awesome moment before a kick-off. Straining to hear the first question, I sat on the edge of my seat.

"And what," asked the President of the Board of Trustees, peering at me through his horned-rimmed spectacles, "is your philosophy of education?"

"My God!" thought I, "What a question! This can't be for real."

But, sure enough, it was. I glanced around the room and five pairs of beady eyes stared back. There was the tanned, silver-haired, distinguished-looking head of a heavy equipment company

with his catbird grin; the gentleman farmer from Genesee who
kept glancing at his watch, no doubt bemoaning the fact that the
interview had infringed upon his dinner; the petite, dapper, feisty,
fast-shuffling lawyer from the mining territory who kept getting
up and walking around his chair as if looking for a bottle hidden
in the upholstery; the solemn Mormon transportation executive
from Pocatello with the baby blue eyes and a Boy Scout badge
sticking out of his lapel; and, of course, the smooth-talking banker
from Twin Falls who served as President of the Board. Yes, this
was for real. No quick wit with this crowd—no off-colored stories
—no careless language or split infinitives or dangling participles.
I reasoned I had better play this one straight—serious and straight.
I launched into my philosophy of education.

Somewhere, sometime, my discourse was interrupted by the
lawyer, who lifted an eyebrow and inquired, "You drink?"

Glancing cautiously at the Mormon out of the corner of
my eye, I replied, "Yes, I drink socially, discreetly, always. What
I mean is, I always drink discreetly, sometimes." That didn't
sound right either, so I tried to rephrase it, but the lawyer interrupted me again.

"By God, that's good!" he cried, slapping his leg and walking
around his chair. "I was on the Board once when we had a
president at one of the schools, and he wouldn't touch a drop.
Board meetings were drier than a Baptist picnic. Almost made
alcoholics of us all. We knew when we started the day there
wouldn't be a drop 'till sundown, so we had to fortify ourselves
before we assembled for the meeting."

He startled me by sitting on the arm of my chair. "Say," he
said in a confiding tone, "I ever tell you about the time I played
Shadow the Leaf in the play, "Robin Hood'?" I acknowledged as
to how this was a first revelation to me, at which point he embarked upon a most amazing story about this play given back at
the turn of the century in a small Idaho town called Weiner or
Weiser. The climax of his story was his (the lawyer, alias Shadow
the Leaf) leading a donkey onto the stage wherein he (the donkey) relieved himself. In my state of nervous tension, I admit the
whole thing just about broke me up. I glanced around to see how
the others were taking it. The banker was clipping his fingernails,
the heavy-equipment man was dusting his shoes with a doily, the
Pocatelloan was looking at the pictures of my family, and the
gentleman farmer was rubbing his growling stomach.

"My," I thought, "this *is* a casual group. These people certainly must have a lot of experience in interviewing." As it turned
out, I was quite right. I represented the fifth and last interviewee
in what must have been a long, dry day.

Self-consciously, I bowed my way out, backing over a cigarette stand, knocking over a floor lamp. I was proud that I didn't click my heels as I about-faced through the door.

And, I didn't really eavesdrop while waiting for the elevator. The talk in the room wafted through the transom and echoed down the hall as if through a giant megaphone.

"Open the cabinet; I need a drink," said the first voice. I smiled.

"Nice chap," boomed a deep bass. I glowed.

"Yeah, might have a fine career ahead of him" came another. I beamed.

"Would be a shame to throw him into that den of tigers," rumbled the bass. I frowned.

"Yeah," resounded the chorus. I climbed on the elevator.

In the privacy of my room, I shut the transom, locked the door, and called my anxious wife.

"How'd it go?" she asked.

"Great. I can't wait to tell you about Shadow the Leaf."

"Are you out of your mind?"

"Yes."

"What did you say to them?"

"I honestly can't remember."

"What did they say to you?"

"They'd let me know in a week or two if they were interested, and if so, would invite us to visit the campus."

"What are you going to do now?"

"Think about my philosophy of education."

WHY NOT ME?

During the next few weeks I spent a lot of time thinking about my philosophy of education—also about the job of a college president. The clearest, most lucid, and objective thoughts usually came as I shaved each morning. Then, at other odd times during the day and night, I carefully researched the subject on a more scientific basis.

During my close observations of the administrations of Quigg Newton at Colorado and Duke Humphrey at Wyoming, I had learned that an irreverent attitude toward presidents was not uncommon among the faculty. This was aptly illustrated in a penetrating article on "The Problems of a President" by Dr. J.D.A. Ogilvy of the University of Colorado, written at the time I was on my way out as football coach and Newton had just announced his resignation. Ogilvy had stated:

> To the faculty, criticism of administrators is less a privilege than a sacred duty. Any loyal member of the teaching faculty regards administrators as dictators activated by the basest motives, blinded to the best interests of the university by invincible ignorance, indifferent to the merits of the speaker and his department, but childishly gullible when it comes to resisting the preposterous claims of confidence men of other departments.

Ogilvy, graciously, did not confine his opinion of administrators to presidents alone, but went on to say:

> This description is . . . applicable to deans and vice presidents. The more charitable members of the faculty are inclined to regard the president as the innocent dupe of these monsters; but, of course, he must bear the blame for continuing them in office.

Ogilvy also modestly set forth some of the qualifications for a president:

The ideal college president (who has yet to be discovered) would be as wise as Solomon, as cunning as Ulysses and Machiavelli rolled into one, as patient as Job, and as honest as Simple Simon. He would be that rare combination, a master of diplomacy and a fearless fighter. He would also be quintuplets.

. . . The only respectable reason for becoming president of a state university is the willingness to forego nirvana for the common good. In the desperate search for college administrators, universities have turned to individuals who are rash enough for an undertaking which combines the attractions of a bath in a cement mixer with those of a trip through hell in a paper shirt . . . of a man who leaves a comfortable hotel for the cage of a family of hungry and irascible tigers.[1]

The cynics were not confined to the ranks of the faculty alone. Some came from the corps of college presidents. Dr. Robert Hutchins, formerly president of the University of Chicago, wrote: "If a man knows what it is like to be a college president and still wants to be one, he is not qualified for the job."

Clark Kerr, in a more satiric vein, while President of the University of California, delivered a series of Godkin lectures at Harvard in 1962. At that time he stated:

The university president in the United States is expected to be a friend of the students, a colleague of the faculty, a good fellow with the alumni, a sound administrator with the trustees, a good speaker with the public, an astute bargainer with the state legislature, a friend of industry, labor, and agriculture, a persuasive diplomat with donors, a champion of education generally, a supporter of the professions (particularly law and medicine), a spokesman to the press, a scholar in his own right, a public servant at the state and national levels, a devotee of opera and football equally, a decent human being, a good husband and father, an active member of a church. Above all, he must enjoy traveling in airplanes, eating his meals in public and attending public ceremonies . . .[2]

Kerr then suggested that to carry out these duties, the president must also possess such personal qualities as "judgment, cour-

[1]J.D.A. Ogilvy, "The Problems of a President," *Colorado Daily*, Oct. 9, 1962, pp. 1-5 of the "Gadfly" section.

[2]Clark Kerr, *The Uses of the University*, Harvard University Press, Cambridge, Massachusetts, 1963, pp. 29-30.

age, and fortitude—but the greatest of these is fortitude since others have so little charity."

If these personal characteristics were demanding, the professional criteria were equally as rigorous. Here, the academicians had to share both the credit and the blame, because most college presidents came stamped in the image of the very perfect model of a member of the faculty. When a vacancy is announced in a college presidency, the Trustees usually turn to the faculty for a screening committee to review the credentials of all candidates and recommend a number of nominees who meet the criteria (usually, also set by the faculty).

The basic qualifications frequently include a Ph.D. degree in a distinguished discipline (in academic circles, some are more distinguished than others); and, preferably, experience as a professor, department chairman, dean of the college (usually Arts and Sciences), graduate dean or dean of faculties or academic vice president. Publications, membership in learned societies, honorary degrees, and public service also add to the credentials. And, of course, a candidate should have all the personal qualifications set forth by Kerr.

Only a few names survived the cutting list, and few were the final candidates who lacked the above qualifications. Few, too, were the governing boards which dared to cross the faculty and break with the established traditions. Truthfully analyzing my own experience and qualifications against this background, I thought it would have to be a "rare" board that would pick me.

It was reasonable to suspect that in view of the much publicized hazards and rigors of the job, there also might be few candidates. But from personal experience, I had to laugh when I read about 300 vacancies a year in college presidencies and the accompanying alarm about filling the positions with qualified men. Like an opening for a college head football coach, no matter how bad the situation or under what miserable circumstances the last president departed from the campus, there were always five hundred willing souls standing in line to take his place. One only had to read any announcement of any appointment: "Dr. Eager has been selected for the presidency from an initial field of 500 well-qualified candidates."

I knew that when a presidency opened more than one of the number of hardy academic types on 2400 campuses throughout the country looked into the mirror as he shaved in the morning and wondered: "Why not me?"

At that moment I almost cut my throat with a dull razor.

124

FALLING INTO POCATELLO

The interview was in April. I alternated from high expectations to sullen resignation all through May. Meanwhile, Polly wanted a new piano; my eldest daughter, Debbie, wanted a horse. I kept them at arm's length. "No point in moving a piano and a horse to Pocatello, Idaho," I chided them.

"But who's going to Pocatello?" they chided back. May came and went, but not my optimism.

"Let's go camping and fishing in the mountains," chirped my youngest daughter and only son.

"I'm expecting a call from Pocatello," I said feebly.

"But who's calling from Pocatello?" they replied feebly. No one called from Pocatello. June came and went, and so did my last hopes.

On July first, I bought a horse and a piano and planned a fishing trip to the mountains. On July second, I received a phone call inviting my wife and me to Pocatello. "This is it!" I announced gleefully to my bride.

"I'll need a new dress," she replied, thoughtfully.

"They'll probably roll out the red carpet. They wouldn't have waited this long if they weren't sure," I said, kicking my heels in the air.

"Probably two new dresses," she mused, puckering her brow.

"Who knows what mysteries lie beyond yon mountains?" I added philosophically.

"And certainly some new white gloves," she added philosophically.

A boisterous group of friends accompanied us to the railroad station at ten o'clock that bright July morning to see us off. There were cheers, tears, moving farewells. Three hours later, we were still there waiting for the City of Portland to arrive. Our friends had gone home for lunch.

The train crept through Wyoming. I was sure the innumerable stops were to chase the buffalo off the track. The dinner in the diner stuck in my throat, and the reading in the Club Car was confined to the swashbuckling ISU Bulletin. My wife, meanwhile, was studiously memorizing the names and faces of the members of the Board of Trustees gleaned from an august portrait which had been carefully removed from the same dog-eared bulletin.

Thirty miles from our destination, we began preparing for our grand entrance into Pocatello. My wife donned her new white gloves, and we made our way to the vestibule. At last, the train slowed down, then stopped.

Polly led the way down the steps, I following after, lugging our two suitcases. At the bottom of the steps, she stopped, posed, pulled up her gloves, and surveyed the crowd, expecting to see the Trustees lined up in Napoleon-like, hand-in-the-coat manner, bearing us greetings. It was either plow right on over her with both suitcases, or step aside. I stepped to the side, missed the platform, and pirouetted into a free fall that ended only when I slammed onto the unyielding brick. Literally, I had fallen into Pocatello.

Fortunately, my fall had been partially broken by landing on the suitcases, which burst open at the impact. With pants torn and shins bleeding, I looked up to see my shorts and pajamas wafting in the balmy Pocatello breeze. Gritting my teeth, I crawled after them, ignoring the solicitous attention of the porter and the conductor.

"Are you hurt, suh?" one of them asked.

"I broke both legs," I groused stoically.

"Can I call a doctor?"

"Never mind. I'll set 'em myself," I growled, stuffing my shorts back into my suitaces and scanning the crowd to spot the Trustees.

At that point, I caught the eye of my ever-loving wife. Was she distressed and alarmed about my safety and welfare? Was she rushing to my side with sympathy and compassion? Not she. She was literally doubled over with laughter, the tears streaming down her face, her white-gloved hand over her mouth in a futile effort to control her uncontrolled mirth. Savagely, I slammed shut the suitcase and limped into the station.

Seeing that my humble, unpretentious entry into the city had gone virtually unnoticed and allowing as how I afterall had survived, I, too, permitted myself a wee chuckle. By the time we had climbed into a taxi, we were both laughing so hard that I am sure the driver thought we had been drinking in the Club Car all the way from Laramie, which certainly was not the case, considering the seriousness and dignity of the occasion.

It being past eleven o'clock, and there obviously being no more formalities to engage in that evening, we prepared for bed. The phone rang. Polly answered. "It's for you," she said.

"Hello," I said eagerly. "That was my wife."

There was a long pause at the other end, then, "My God, I hope so!"

The caller turned out to be Joe Hearst, Assistant Dean of the College of Liberal Arts, who had been assigned as our faculty host. He cheerfully informed me that he would meet us for breakfast at 7:30, and that the Faculty Screening Committee would interview us at 9:00 a.m., and the Board of Trustees at 11:00. I also learned that three other men and their wives were to be on campus the next day for similar interviews. The rest of the night we lay staring at the ceiling.

The meeting with the Faculty Screening Committee was most surprising. I had expected questions on philosophy, curriculum, faculty, books, articles, academic freedom, my background, experience—all sorts of things. Mostly, we talked about football. Polly got through the whole interview without more than a how-dee-do. Just when I thought things were warming up, the chairman gave me a crisp, "Thank you." I felt as lonesome and insignificant as a doughnut in a tire store. Hastily, we beat our retreat and escaped to the next interview.

Our enthusiasm somewhat subdued, we practically tiptoed into the Board room. Desperately, I looked for Shadow the Leaf. He wasn't there. I looked for the hungry gentleman farmer. He wasn't there. But, I soon learned, two new members had been added to the Board since the Salt Lake City meeting, and they were there—an attractive, cultured lady from Boise, and a smiling, red-faced potato tycoon from Rexburg. The latter got the session off on a cheerful note by leaning forward and asking, "What is your philosophy on education?"

After a pleasant hour or so on the griddle, the friendly banker adjourned the meeting, saying "Dr. Hearst plans to take you to lunch. During that time, we will come to a decision. Could we call you at the your hotel about 1:30?"

At that time, any type of call would have been welcome! At a Chinese restaurant, Mrs. Hearst joined us—a happy, jovial soul who strove mightily to relieve the tension. We ordered chop suey. Neither my spouse nor I could eat a bite. Joe, being an obliging host, ate our lunch.

We all then retired to the hotel to await *the* call. In a rare mood of bravado, I suggested we have a drink—just one. So we slipped into the hotel lounge. One-thirty came, and no call. Then two-thirty—three-thirty—four-thirty—five-thirty. By this time, I had finished my one drink, eaten the ice cubes, and was gnawing on the glass. Meanwhile, the Hearsts had kids to feed, horses to tend, and we had exhausted all intelligent conversation. Finally, Joe shrugged his shoulders and said, "Must be a hung jury."

"Yeah," I replied, affecting a nonchalance.

At this moment, the President of the Board walked in, shook my hand, and said, "Dr. Davis, it certainly has been a pleasure meeting you again. If you'll just send us a list of your expenses, we'll send you a check. We surely want to thank you for coming." With that, he excused himself and departed.

"School's out," I said to no one in particular. By this time, my emotions had had more ups and downs than a roller coaster.

Polly and I looked forward to dinner, thinking that in a lighthearted atmosphere of good food, a bottle of wine, and a chance to discuss the events of the day, we might find a moment of light humor. We were ushered into a long, red dining room and given a table in the rear. I was just about to make some clever remark about the meeting with the Trustees when I glanced at the next table. There was the gracious gent from Boise with his mother. We exchanged cordial greetings and introductions. Once more, we were seated. Then I looked the other direction. There was the distinguished lady Trustee from Boise. Again, we exchanged greetings. The dinner was eaten in absolute decorum— each bite filling the mouth like rising yeast.

The evening, however, was carefree and gay as we joined the Hearsts at their home for a gala party celebrating we knew not what.

Late the next afternoon we boarded the Portland Rose (I, most carefully) for the long ride home to Laramie. We could hardly wait for the train to leave the station before making our way to the Club Car for a quiet cocktail preceeding a greatly anticipated dinner on the diner. We walked through what I took to be the snack bar, but upon arriving at the end of the car, I found the door to be locked.

"Where you all going?" asked the surprised waiter.

"To the Club Car and diner," I replied simply.

"Ain't no Club Car and diner on this train," he smiled. "This is it."

Indeed it was, I thought, as I later munched on a ham sandwich washed down by cold, nourishing milk.

Our porter told us we would be in Laramie by 6:00 a.m. and promised to wake us up by 5:30. We slept the sleep of the exhausted. A lurch of the train and a sudden stop finally jarred me awake. Sleepily, I looked at my watch. It was six o'clock and light was streaming through the window. "Polly," I cried. "Look out the window and see where we are."

She looked. "We're in Laramie," she squealed. "There's the viaduct."

Leaping from the upper bunk, I urged her to dress quickly, fearing the train would pull out of town before we got off. In something like three minutes, we were fully dressed, and I was lugging our suitcases down the aisle. I bumped into the surprised porter.

"Where you all goin'?" he asked.

"Isn't this Laramie?" I inquired sheepishly.

"Heaven's no, suh. This is Rawlins. We won't be in Laramie for another hour and a half."

So, for the last lap of our trip, my long-suffering, patient wife and I sat in the Pullman staring at each other and dying for a cup of coffee.

The next day, I got the call inviting me to become President of Idaho State University.

WHY, OH, WHY DID I EVER LEAVE WYOMING?

After the packers had loaded our furniture on the van, all that remained to be transported to our new home in Pocatello was the family, one emotionally unstable cat, and our new horse, Comanche.

That horse was some prize, and well-named, for he was a hard-headed rebel if I ever saw one. Only a few days earlier, I had taken him off the hands of an Air Force Colonel in the ROTC program who had been reassigned to Rhode Island. What I had mistaken for generosity had really been desperation. But, at the time, I thought $150 for a horse with a saddle and bridle thrown in was a good buy.

It was only after we had consummated the deal that I learned Comanche's true pedigree. He really wasn't a thorough-bred, Arabian quarter horse with a dash of Appaloosa thrown in. What he was was a mustang from the Red Desert of Wyoming, half outlaw and half mad about having been gelded some two years before.

At first I thought about leaving him in Wyoming, but quickly realized that I would have to leave Debbie, too. Then I looked into the possibility of shipping him by rail. When I learned that it would cost three times what we paid for him, I dropped that idea. Finally, I borrowed a horse trailer from a law professor and thought our horse problems were settled.

The night before our great migration, we stayed with some neighbors—Joe and Betty Geraud. Leaping up with the dawn, we threw our bags in the station wagon while Doug fetched the cat. Traveling always upset her sense of security, and predictably she got sick.

I was wondering what else could happen when Debbie came riding up on Comanche. I had a hunch I was about to find out.

We opened the gate to the horse trailer and tried to coax Comanche in. He wouldn't budge. Neither oats nor oaths, pleas nor prods could get him into that trailer.

With a contemptuous leer, he bared his teeth, bolted, and galloped down the street. By taking a shortcut, I headed him off at the corner. He whirled around and raced for the back yard of our house, ripping off the gate as he passed through. Without breaking stride, he cleared the back fence and headed for the wide open spaces. It was apparent to all that that horse just didn't want to leave Wyoming.

Debbie finally found him back in his old pasture snorting at the prairie dogs. With a bucket of oats, she got him cornered, and, once again, rode him back to the trailer.

In the interim, I had acquired a long rope and considerable worthless advice from Joe Geraud, who, like me, had acquired most of his knowledge of horses from reading *Black Beauty*. With optimism, we wrapped the rope behind Comanche's rump and pulled. He sat down. We called for reinforcements. Half the faculty showed up, and we literally lifted the contrary animal into the trailer.

Meanwhile, all this excitement had upset our dumb cat even more. To the resounding cheers of our beloved neighbors and the indignant whinnying of Comanche, we were off. We made it just beyond the city limits before we had the flat tire.

At Rawlins, a distance of 120 miles from Laramie, we stopped for lunch. Upon returning from the cafe, I was horrified to find Debbie in the last stages of unbolting the door to the trailer. "What are you doing?" I roared.

"I was just going to get Comanche out and give him some exercise."

"Not on your life!" I threatened, slamming the bolt shut.

I had to put up with her sobbing the rest of the trip while Comanche tried to kick the tailgate down.

We arrived at Pocatello sometime after midnight and pulled into the old motel that was to be our new home for the next six weeks while the President's house received a face-lifting. The motel had been acquired by the University as supplemental housing for women, and while the three rooms reserved for the five Davises and the cat were adequate, it was obvious that there were no accommodations for Comanche.

Joe Hearst, the friendly assistant dean who had been our host when we had visited the campus, had volunteered his corral as a temporary haven for the lonely Mustang. So, after unloading Polly, Becky, Doug, and the cat, Debbie and I drove out of town to find the Hearst homestead on Johnny Creek Road.

We must have driven up every creek and road southwest of Pocatello before finally finding the Hearst's. Rousted out of bed at two a.m., he was delighted to see us and acted as if he enjoyed dragging an obstinate horse into his stable in the middle of the night.

As a full moon illuminated that quiet hillside overlooking the Portneuf Valley below, I could see that defiant glare in Comanche's eyes. If horses could sing, I would have expected that old refrain, "Why, oh, why did I ever leave Wyoming?"

134

HELLO, IDAHO

Despite the fact that I had put the horse and me to bed at a late hour, I awoke early that morning. It was August 28, 1965, and I was anxious to get to my new office for the first day on the job. That my arrival had been anticipated was apparent in the pile of mail stacked on my desk.

Since the announcement of my appointment, phone calls and letters had led to the suspicion that the news had not been greeted by dancing in the streets. Some reports indicated the reaction was more like climbing the ivy walls. I could well understand that my credentials might be suspect in academe.

Neither my degrees nor my experience fit the traditional route through the academic chairs to the position of president. Nor was I likely to impress anyone with my hoary years. At the age of thirty-six I still had most of my hair and only the sideburns were turning grey. To put it in another perspective, one of the senior deans had joined the faculty the same year I was born.

So, all in all, I could understand a certain sensitivity. This was easy because I was very sensitive about this sensitivity.

As I read through the newspaper clippings on my desk, I soon discovered that preceeding my arrival on campus, the discontent had flared into the open. I had a staunch defender in Perry Swisher, editor of a weekly publication, *The Intermountain,* who wrote:

> *Within the ivyless halls of Idaho State University, the appointment of Dr. William E. Davis of Wyoming as president is causing some anguish. There are faculty members who see themselves as great scholars and scientists who really should be in Harvard but are, instead, at great personal sacrifice, investing their unique talents in unappreciative Idaho. It is they precisely who are upset at the regents' choice: Imagine—this man was a coach!*

Swisher's baiting of the faculty had received a quick retort in a published letter from an irate member of the faculty, who had written:

> . . . *It is quite true that many of the faculty have criticized the Board's selection, but that criticism was far more broadly and sensibly based than Mr. Swisher would have his readers believe. The State Board, for instance, made their selection in opposition to the advice of a special faculty committee established for just that purpose by the Board itself. In addition, one need only compare the complete academic and administrative records of the University of Idaho's new president with that of Dr. Davis to understand why members of our faculty should quite sensibly be disturbed. A man is judged by his ability and by his credentials. In the academic world, one's professional audience is national or international rather than local, and consequently only his credentials are visible to most of that audience. A man's record will continually change, of course, according to his ability, but in the meantime it is easy to understand the academic world's sensitivity to professional credentials . . .*
>
> *Credentials that may be quite suitable for president of one kind of institution may not be so suitable for another. Idaho State University consists of three professional colleges, the excellence of which depends directly on the excellence of a fourth, the College of Liberal Arts. For better or for worse, many professors in liberal arts colleges and many in professional colleges as well, believe that university presidents should have reasonably extensive academic and administrative experience with the liberal disciplines. These people, not Mr. Swisher, are acquiring a new leader, and their wishes must be at least partly satisfied if Idaho State University is to remain an excellent university. In view of the qualifications and proven ability of the local candidate for the position, the need for an out-of-state candidate to be especially well qualified seems self evident . . .*

One of my first appointments that morning was with the chairman of the faculty's presidential screening committee. In a pleasant, straight-forward manner, he informed me that should he be called upon to submit a report for the presidential screening committee, he would have to state that I had not even been selected for an interview by the committee, but rather had been invited by the Board of Trustees.

He went on to add that of the five candidates interviewed, I had been rated as number five. Thus, the Board and the faculty screening committee had not reached any semblance of agreement, and I had been selected over the latter's objections. He concluded by saying that he thought I should know this before chairing the first meeting of the faculty.

At this point I made my first administrative decision. I decided that at the opening meeting of the faculty I would not call for any committee reports. And on this happy note I embarked upon the riotous road as president of Idaho State University.

BAGDAD ON THE PORTNEUF

As a newcomer to Idaho, I soon discovered that when one mentioned the name of Idaho State University outside the environs of the high Rockies, he often encountered a kind of vague, mystical stare. I also quickly learned that in such cases, one continued the attack and noted that it was located in Pocatello, Idaho. Not infrequently, the rejoinder was, "Where the heck is Pocatello?" Some even asked, "Where is Idaho?" (There are urban types who think it is somewhat north of Nebraska. As an initiate into the tribe of mountain men and fur trappers, I came to understand this kind of provincialism, however, because to us "back east" meant Jackson Hole, Wyoming.)

In no time at all, I, too, was singing the praises of ISU, Pocatello, and the state of Idaho.

For thousands of years primitive man camped along the banks of the Portneuf River where it left the mountains to empty into the great waters of the Snake. These nomadic tribesmen followed the natural highways in all directions, hunting and fishing along the routes of the streams. But winter often found them huddled in the Portneuf Valley, protected from the icy blasts by the brooding hills.

White men first passed through this area in 1811 when the Wilson Price Hunt party out of St. Louis, Missouri, floated the Snake on their way to Astoria. Later, the hardy trapper with an eye for the rich pelt of beaver worked the waters and lived and traded with the Indians. A roster of the early tourists included names like Donald McKenzie, Captain Bonneville, Jedidiah Smith, Osborne Russell, Francis Payette, the Sublette brothers, Peter Skene Ogden, Jim Bridger, Kit Carson—a veritable "Who's Who" of mountain men and adventurers who opened the West.

In 1834, at a site about nine mile north of where the Portneuf River flows into the Snake, Nathaniel Wyeth built a trading post and christened it "Fort Hall" in honor of the sponsor of the expedition, Henry Hall. This post in the heart of a lush meadowland soon became an important way-station for the thousands of emigrants heading west.

Known from the Mississippi to the Pacific as "the best beaver country, the best feeding country, and the warmest sheltered winter place for miles around," Fort Hall on the Oregon Trail joined those names destined to become legends in the romantic history of the West.

As the gold fever waned, the people stopped "passing through" and began "settlin' in." Pocatello, named after a Bannock chief, was founded in 1889. The first photographs of the area show teepees where University buildings now stand. At one time, the whole townsite was a part of the Fort Hall Reservation.

Among the inroads of civilization was the railroad, which had arrived in the 1870's. Eventually, it literally split the sprawling frontier town in two. This led critics to claim that Pocatello was the only place where both sections of town were on the "wrong" side of the tracks.

As a railroad stop, Pocatello developed a reputation for a "lively" night life, much to the consternation of the Mormon missionaries sent north from Utah to populate and farm the surrounding areas. More than one Mormon family on its way to colonize the Eagle Rock (now Idaho Falls) area reportedly made its kids lie on the floor of the buggy and cover their eyes as they drove through the sinful streets.

Along with the schools and churches and other trimmings and trappings of civilization, Pocatello, in 1901 became the home of the Academy of Idaho. Originally, it was intended as a prep school for would-be scholars on their way to the University of Idaho, some 600 horse-back miles north and west. An area of two square blocks was set aside for the new campus, and the pessimists of the day wondered what the governing board would do with *all* that excess land.

Sixty-five years later, the town had reached into the stream beds and along the mesas in all directions. The academy has become a college and then a University. Its 4,000 students occupied a campus that covered some 500 acres and included both the red brick of the first buildings and the beige and concrete of the new.

By 1965, the steam locomotives had been retired to the parks as relics of the past, objects of curiosity for jet-age youngsters who explored them from cow-catcher to stack. The lonesome wail of the whistle as a heavy-duty freight wound its way down from Inkom had given way to the blast of the diesel. Gone, too, were the volumes of black smoke belching from the stacks.

The old Oregon Trail had become Highway 30, which in turn had been replaced by modern freeways that literally passed over, rather than through, the modern community. Where, at dusk, the traveler once had stared at the winging glow of a campfire as a Bannock or Shoshone brave roasted hunks of buffalo meat for his evening meal, the tourist now gazes down upon the magic lights of Bagdad on the Portneuf.

But the natives proudly boast that some things never change —not the sunsets with the mountains silhouetted against the pink and purple hues that convey that vast sense of distance as vividly as a Russell painting from the past—nor the spirit of a people sprung from the stock of fur trappers, mountain men, missionaries, rail-roaders, merchants, ranchers, and farmers, augmented by occasional enlightened foreigners.

To them and me, Idaho remains a land where a man can flex his muscles and breathe deep and stretch to his full height— a land where, on a wintry morning, he can drive to work and see the hills overlooking the Portneuf valley bathed in snow and sunlight—or at nearby Skyline or Caribou, pause at the top of a ski run, cold wind in his face, and watch the clouds lift slowly over the Snake River Plain and reveal the sea of mountains rolling ever westward—or in the summer, where he can wander along the bank of a stream and catch grasshoppers to bait a hook for his son, and then witness sheer ecstacy as the boys lands a glistening trout.

One of the great American authors of this century, Ernest Hemingway, discovered Idaho for himself and shared it with all familiar with his work. In a tribute to a friend killed in a hunting accident near Sun Valley, Hemingway caught the splendor of this land, and wrote:

> *Gene loved this country . . . He saw it with the eyes of a painter, the mind of a trained writer, and the heart of a boy who had been brought up in the West. He loved the hills in the spring when the snows go off and the first flowers come. He loved the warm sun of summer and the high mountain meadows, the trails through the timber and the sudden clear blue of the lakes . . . Best of all he loved the fall . . . with the tawny, and grey, the leaves yellow on the cottonwoods . . . and above the hills the high blue windless skies . . . .[1]*

Best of all, I, too, came to love the falls, the tawny and the grey, the leaves yellow on the cottonwoods, and above the hills the high blue windless skies.

[1]Ernest Hemingway, *Idaho Statesman,* Nov. 2, 1939.

FACULTY HANDBOOKS

In getting acquainted with an institution, a new president must do a prodigious amount of heady reading—things like catalogues, bulletins, biennial reports, budget booklets, and, of course, The Faculty Handbook. The latter covers such rousing tid-bits as office hours for academicians, due process procedures, grading regulations, and vacation periods.

In scanning old faculty handbooks, I was almost lulled into complete lethargy when I came across some rare eloquence recorded in the words of Dr. Carl McIntosh, who from 1946 to 1959 had presided over the affairs of Idaho State.

On "Coffee Breaks," he took a hard but philosophic line, writing:

> Coffee Breaks: *From time to time different policies will be announced and followed in regard to 'coffee breaks.' Thus far no policy has been devised which has been satisfactory. No such policy is anticipated. The usual procedure is to announce a policy at the beginning of each academic year, then to observe the extent to which the policy is abused. When the policy has eroded away to the point that the practice is completely indefensible, reprimands are distributed or the more flagrant violators are fired, a new policy is announced and the procedure is repeated. Nothing that the college has tried works well, but the college does recognize the 'coffee break' as an inevitable, if not desirable, result of present society's attitude toward the working day, and all employees who exercise restraint, conservative judgment and a proper evaluation of whether the 'break' or the work is more important need not fear reprisals. Specifically, office telephones should not be left unattended, and offices should not be entirely vacant at any time. Checking into an office on time and leaving immediately to eat breakfast under the camouflage of taking an 'early coffee*

*break' is frowned upon. Those not taking coffee breaks
will not have their work week shortened or their vacation
lengthened in lieu thereof, as sometimes suggested. A
coffee break is defined as a 20-minute period taken at
a time most convenient to the office supervisor in charge.
During rush periods it may be necessary to forego coffee
breaks for several days. All are asked to face this un-
pleasant possibility courageously and stoically.*

A realist at heart, Dr. McIntosh was well aware that his
institution and state often offered salmon and scenery in lieu of
salary to its employees. Thus, his entry on the subject of "Hunting
and Fishing" reflected a rare insight:

Hunting and Fishing: *Hunting and fishing, like jury
duty and illness, pose certain special problems. It is not
unknown for an entire class to meet for an extended
evening session next week' in order to enjoy an opening
day 'tomorrow.' This cannot be authorized nor, for that
matter, can it be stopped. It is recognized that Idaho
offers unusual attractions and distractions to those who
enjoy these sports. Each faculty member is charged with
the responsibility of accomplishing the work he is assigned. In the event that any class is 'cancelled' or
'missed' it is his responsibility to report to his department
head and dean a satisfactory and acceptable program of
'make-up' work. Generally speaking, a professor in the
class is worth two in the bush. There are exceptions, but
the burden of proof rests with the individual. Specifically,
the president is not authorized to 'excuse' old friends,
newcomers, students, deans, directors, janitors or cooks
from observance of the regular schedule because of 'goat-
tags,' 'salmon runs,' 'tracking snow,' 'late northern flight'
or 'early steelhead runs.' This is strictly the individual's
problem and the dean's problem.*

An avid hunter and fisherman himself, the usually meticulous Dr. McIntosh neglected to mention whose problem the
president was. Anxious to find the solution to this mystery, with
renewed vigor I plowed into the stack of documents yet unread.

MEETING ELI

The old cliche about a man being a legend in his own time certainly applied to the University's librarian, Eli Oboler. Before we ever met personally, I was besieged with tales about the institution's learned keeper of the books. Students, particularly, could never be sure just when Eli had first arrived on campus. They just took it for granted that he had always been there. One legend purported that the library got its start when Eli showed up as a long-haired zealot fresh out of graduate school. Allegedly, he climbed to the top of the campus landmark, Red Hill, and after three days and nights descended with his head wreathed in light and carrying ten stone tablets.

As the years passed, he lost his hair, but never his passion. When the library was moved into a new building sometime in the Fifties, Eli adopted a defiant possessive air, almost as if he had laid each brick and placed each book upon the shelves. A fun-loving dean and an irreverent faculty member decided to put Eli's patriotic library fervor to the test.

They made a huge cardboard sign announcing a meeting of the A.A.U.P. They also cut the end off a large spike and glued it to the sign, with the effect that the spike appeared to have been driven through the sign. By using tape on the back, they fixed the sign so it would adhere to the brick wall.

They they carried the assembled masterpiece to the library, stuck the sign on the wall, and covered the floor in the area with crumbled plaster. By pounding on a two-by-four with a heavy hammer, they quickly attracted the attention of Eli, who, as usual, was prowling the premises hushing up students and rousing the lovers from behind the stacks. Reportedly, breathing fire from each nostril, Eli descended upon them like the Red Sea crashing down upon the armies of Pharoh.

With a buildup like this, it was understandable that as a newcomer to the Idaho State campus, I was anxious to meet Eli. Thus, I stalked him in his lair to have a dialogue.

I quickly learned that with Eli there is never really a dialogue—only an occasional leading question by oneself followed by much enthusiastic oratory by the ebuliant Librarian.

I tested him on his views of religious tolerance in southeastern Idaho and received this reply: "We had better be tolerant. Here the Protestants, Catholics, and Jews can band together and still be a minority." (He was, of course, referring to the heavy Mormon population.) Then he grinned and added, "In Idaho, you see, I'm referred to as a Gentile."

His mood became more somber as he surveyed me from head to foot. "I'm not sure you're qualified for the job of president," he quipped.

"I've heard that before," I replied. "But, what exactly are your reasons?"

"Well, to begin with, a college president should have grey hair and hemorrhoids."

I stared at him incredulously. "Why?"

"The grey hair to give him a look of distinction," Eli continued, "and the hemorrhoids to give him a look of concern."

"Eli," I said straight-forwardly, "do you like your job here?"

He traced a circle on the carpet with his toe, then looked up at me through his bushy brows, "Well, the pay isn't much, but I sure do meet a lot of new presidents."

I decided to take another tack. "Who," I asked, "is the big man on campus?"

Eli brightened up considerably. "I wouldn't want to come right out and say, but perhaps a little parable would serve as an illustration. Imagine, for example, that it is Homecoming at Idaho State, and I'm invited to drive an open car in the big parade. In the back seat there would be the Governor of Idaho, the President of the University, and a United States Senator. All of the people in Pocatello are lined up along both sides of Fifth Street, and as we pass, they nudge each other and ask, 'Who are all those characters riding with Eli Oboler?' " He bowed his head and blushed modestly.

I knew at this time that I had come to the right man for my political consultation. Anxious to get him on my side, I asked, "Eli, is there anything I might do for you?"

"Yes, there is one small matter," he cirped brightly. "The Library on our campus is known as the 'Idaho State University Library.' "

"Most appropriate," I volunteered.

He frowned. "You're missing the point. What I mean is that all other buildings have been named after persons who have made significant contributions to the University. I think we should choose an appropriate person to honor and name the library after him."

"Do you have anyone in mind?" I asked simply.

Again, he blushed modestly.

I got the message. "Eli," I exclaimed, "I have the answer. We can call your building '*Eli*brary Oboler' and inscribe on the plaque, 'In Memoriam—RIP.' "

That terminated the dialogue. The last I heard he was heading for Red Hill to pick up some more tablets.

HERE WE HAVE IDAHO

Dr Ernest Hartung assumed the presidency at the University of Idaho in July, 1965, just one month before I was installed in a similar capacity at Idaho State University. I am sure that neither of us was aware of the civil war that had long characterized the relationship between the two state supported institutions of higher learning. Mere logistics, terrain, and space seemed to preclude such a clash. After all, Moscow, the home of the University of Idaho, and Pocatello, the locale of Idaho State, were better than 600 driving miles apart. ISU was closer to Boulder, Colorado, and Laramie, Wyoming than it was to its sister state university. And the U. of I. was a bare nine miles from Washington State University and less than two hundred miles from the University of Montana. But—a civil war there had been.

Sam Day, the intrepid editor of the *Intermountain Observer,* once summed up the situation at that time by writing:

> Since the earliest days of statehood the waters (of higher education) have been churned by regional rivalries. Regional politics dictated the location at Moscow of the University of Idaho, which was a sop thrown to the territory's northern counties to keep them from drifting into Washington. As the state's population swelled south of the Salmon River, the steady growth of the university's southern branch at Pocatello became a continuing bone of contention between north and south.
>
> . . . The emergence of Idaho State College as a university in 1963 followed years of bitter rear-guard action by Moscow legislators.

If the feelings of the northerners were hostile toward the newly-minted ISU, the belligerency was returned in kind. From 1927 to 1947, twenty long years, the Pocatello-based institution was indeed an extension of the University of Idaho and referred to officially as "the Southern Branch"—a term still calculated to start a fight.

When Idaho State was finally emancipated by legislative action, the former parental relationship became more strained than ever. The mother institution was somewhat aghast at what it had spawned. The offspring reacted like a rebellious son who wondered who his father was.

But Hartung and I, having shed no blood in the ancient feud, mutually entered into a gentlemanly non-aggression pact between the two schools. We reasoned that together we packed more political muscle than either did alone, and the time might come when survival depended upon such an alliance. Thus, Hartung (described by Sam Day as an urbane, brahmin New England academic) and I (pictured as a pleasant, pipe-smoking chipmonk) marched into Idaho's political and academic arena, comrades in arms, holding high the torch of scholarship and stepping nimbly lest the hovering doves of peace got excited from all the heat.

Admittedly, in those early days, there were times I had reservations about all this fellowship with the University of Idaho. True, I was greeted cordially, even royally on my first visit to Moscow. A Chamber of Commerce group known as the Ambassadors ushered me into the Moscow Hotel beneath a canopy of raised canes. I ran the gauntlet quickly, expecting any moment to have one come crashing down about my neck and shoulders.

The occasion of my visit centered around the Idaho-ISU football game, the highlight of the Homecoming weekend in Moscow. My wife and I were wined, dined, and softened up with kindness by the time we finally arrived at the stadium. Then, the disillusionment began.

For several months I had been under the impression that "Here We Have Idaho" was the state song, and when the University of Idaho Vandal band burst forth with the tune, I dutifully placed hand over heart and sang along. Not until the closing bars did I realize that the words had been altered and I was singing the Idaho alma mater. It hardly did my morale any good to note that our esteemed Athletic Director and the head football coach were standing at attention on the bench and singing lustily. (I later learned they were both University of Idaho alums.)

The brisk and heated action of the game, however, soon compensated for my near treason. Unexpectedly, ISU took an early 7 to 0 lead and hung on through three bruising quarters. My wife and I, seated in Hartung's presidential box, cheered loudly and often. Midway through the fourth quarter, I realized we were cheering alone.

The terrible truth descended. There we were in the fourth quarter of the Homecoming game in Moscow, leading the vaunted

Vandals of the University of Idaho by seven points. Were that lead to hold up, it was clear that inter-institutional relations in higher education in Idaho could be set back for years. My wife was shouting, "Hit 'em again, harder!" oblivious to the icy stares and frozen silence. I dug an elbow into her ribs. "Give 'em the axe!" she cried. I cringed.

Fortune intervened as Idaho rallied in the final two minutes to score fifteen points and win the day.

As Polly and I sadly accompanied the hooting and hollering Vandal boosters and their jocular president across the Moscow campus, we could hear the nostalgic chimes pealing, "Here We Have Idaho."

VARYING DEGREES OF IGNORANCE

As a university president, one easily assumes a sense of expertise on all facets of education—higher and lower. And from my precarious perch on the ivory tower, I was generous in giving much unsolicited advice on the subject of raising and educating children. Then the grim realities of the unreasonable and non-negotiable demands of my first teen-ager, Debbie, began to take their toll on me.

I learned that when it comes to raising a teen-age daughter, there are no experts—just varying degrees of ignorance.

The turning point in all our lives came that night I heard Debbie and her mother arguing about the length of junior high skirts, with Debbie haughtily proclaiming, "But, Mother, this is *my* adolescence we are living through, not yours!" At that time I firmly resolved to be an understanding father, one who would see to it that his daughter got *through* her tens, not stuck *in* them.

So, I answered the telephone innumerable times an evening with fortitude and patience, steeling myself to the uncontrollable giggles emanating from the far end of the line. But I was hardly prepared for the night the phone rang and a husky voice asked, "Is Debbie there?"

"Who wants to know?" I growled.

There was a sudden click as the line went dead.

The next evening at dinner I carefully surveyed my brood. There was my wife, Polly, calmly trying to explain to my young son, Douglas, why he should eat his solod with a fork instead of both hands. There, too, was babbling Becky, my sixth-grader, globbling her dessert so she could get outside for a game of kick-the-can. And, finally, I looked at thirteen-year-old Dynamite Debbie, my first teen-ager, growing so fast that all her dresses were mini-skirts without raising the hem-lines.

It was an opportune time for a little father-to-daughter discussion. "Debbie," I said, "a boy called last night."

She looked up betwen helpings of mashed potatoes and gravy, eyes flashing, "Who?"

I shrugged.

"Who, Daddy? Was it Frank?"

"Frank who?" I grunted.

"Oh—just Frank."

"Who's Frank?" I insisted.

"The boy I go steady with."

I stopped my coffee in mid-swallow. "Go steady?" I said, trying to kep my cool. "Did you hear that, Polly? Debbie's going steady!"

My wife hardly looked up, being busily engaged in telling Doug he shouldn't eat his pudding with both hands. "I know," she replied in a tone of voice that was amazingly calm, considering the crisis.

"You know!" I exclaimed, walking around the table. "You know!"

"She's been going steady for a week," Becky volunteered helpfully, hoping that her sister, Debbie, was really going to get it.

"Don't you care?" I asked my wife, pleadingly.

"Would you like more coffee?" she replied.

"How can she go steady when she doesn't even date?" I shouted calmly. "What does going steady mean?"

My wife looked up patiently. "It means Debbie doesn't date any other boys either."

"Oh," I said understandingly, but not really. "Then *you* think it's all right?"

"All the other kids do it," Debbie chipped in.

"Do what?" I grumbled.

"Go steady."

"Why?"

"So they can dance."

I was thoroughly confused. "I don't see what going steady has to do with dancing."

Debbie patiently explained. "Well, Dad, it's like this. Every Friday afternoon at school, we have this dance and no one asks me."

"Asks what?"

"Asks me to dance. I just sit there."

"That's a heck of a note," I said indignantly. "Why don't those dumb boys ask Debbie to dance?" I glared at my wife. "Why don't you call the principal and ask him why they don't make those stupid boys ask the girls to dance?"

"Oh-h-h-h, Daddy!" Debbie cried in a note of total exasperation. (I was to hear this tone of voice often in the future.)

"That's just the point," my wife said, slapping Doug on the wrist. "Two weeks ago this boy named Frank did ask Debbie to dance. And now he dances with her steady every Friday."

"And *that's* going steady?" I inquired incredulously.

"Well, that's not all," Debbie demurred, dropping her eyes.

"What else?" I sighed, resigning myself to the gruesome details.

"Well, he walks to classes with me . . ."

"And . . ."

"I'm wearing his ring."

I glanced at her hand. Sure enough, right there, *right there* on the third finger, left hand *was* a ring. "Debbie," I roared, "that's where women wear a wedding ring. You can't wear a ring there!"

"But, Daddy," she pleaded, "everyone does!"

(I was to learn that this was the final rationalization for all her behavior—anytime—anyplace: "*Everyone* does")

"Take it off!" I demanded. Debbie didn't move. She just sat there and stared at me as large tears welled up in her eyes. "The ring," I said, insistently. "Give me the ring."

"Oh-h-h-h, Daddy!" She bolted from the table sobbing.

Later that evening, I got a long lecture from my wife on the manners and mores of the present junior high generation. En--lightened, but skeptical, I hid behind clouds of tobacco smoke, puffing furiously as the phone continued to ring.

As the days wore on, my curiosity began gnawing on me. "Just what kind of a boy," I wondered, "would be interested in my Debbie?" Chuckling to myself, I thought, "What happy-go-lucky, carefree, clean-cut young man willingly would subject himself to her moody, unreasonable disposition?" I could hardly wait to meet him and prepared myself for the big moment.

On the other hand, I felt some moral obligation to find out just what kind of a young man *she* might be interested in. Clearly, this was an overriding duty of a concerned father. So, I carefully drew up a questionnaire:

QUESTIONNAIRE FOR PROSPECTIVE BOY FRIENDS

Personal Data

Name: _____

Nicknames: (i.e., Stinky, Shorty, Fat-so, Butterball, etc.)
_____

Age: _____

Education: (Degrees) _____

Hair: Bleached _____
              Plastered _____
              Drunk _____

Haircut: Crew-cut _____
Sideburns _____
Flowing tresses _____
Beatle _____
Bangs _____
Shoes: Sneakers _____
Sandals _____
Shined _____
Scuffed _____
None _____
Eyes: One (in the middle of the forehead) _____
Two _____
Beady _____

Personal Habits

Smoking: Privately _____; publicly _____; never-ever _____
Cigarettes _____
Cigars _____
Pipe _____
Straw _____
Chewing: Gum _____
Tobacco _____
Sen-sen _____
Tongue _____
Drinking: Coke _____
Water _____
Milk _____
Coffee _____
Other _____
Language: English (sometimes) _____; (always) _____
Slang _____
Cussing (please list) _____
_____
_____

Bathing: Often _____
Sometimes _____
Right Guard _____
Driving: With parents _____
Like a little old lady _____
Drag racing _____
With aplomb _____
Recreation: Sports (please list) _____
Other _____
Girls: Others (please list) _____
_____
_____
_____
_____

Miscellaneous Manners

When your mother is shoveling the walks on a cold day, do you take her a cup of hot chocolate? Yes___ No___
When your mother is mowing the lawn, do you take her a glass of cold lemonade? Yes___ No___
On walking through a door, if a girl is following, do you open it for her? Yes___ No___
When playing ping-pong at our house, will you invite a little brother to join the game? Yes___ No___
On tying up the telephone for an hour, when you learn that there is an emergency, will you hang up within fifteen minutes? Yes___ No___
When other junior high boys give in to the mod craze, wear beads, and sport flowing locks, will you continue to dress sensibly in suit, white shirt, and tie? Yes___ No___

Likes and Dislikes

Do you like girls with clean, short hair that doesn't get tangled in the spaghetti when they eat spaghetti? Yes___ No___
Do you like girls who cheerfully clear the table, do the dishes, and empty the garbage without grumbling? Yes___ No___
Do you like girls who obey reasonable orders from their fathers, like, "Take off that ring!" Yes___ No___

All in all, I considered it to be a pretty keen survey. But, that had to be based on my own judgment, because, frankly, I was afraid to show it to my wife or Debbie before presenting it to Frank.

Finally, one Sunday afternoon, he came over to the house. Debbie brought him into the den where I was watching the pro football game. I looked him in the eyes. I don't know where he was looking because it was hard to tell, what with all that hair. I was pleased with one thing, however. It was obvious that in a fair fight, Debbie would be well-matched. She was an inch taller and a good ten pounds heavier.

Quick as lightening, I whipped out the questionnaire. *That* certainly was a surprise to everybody. In fact, it was such a surprise that nobody bothered to talk to me for the next week.

All on my own, I came to the conclusion that if a father is going to raise teen-age daughters, he might as well resign himself to the fact that for a few years, there probably will be some stray boys hanging around the house. And, most things considered, it is probably better to have a daughter attractive enough that boys will be at least mildly interested, rather than one they will ignore. A reasonable father should not presume that a daughter should go all through life sitting out junior high dances. I firmly resolved to do my best.

The next time Frank ventured into the house, I was ready. I had learned of his interest in tennis and carefully steered the conversation to what I knew would be familiar terrain for him. "Do you play often?" I inquired.

"Well," he said, studying a dirty tennis shoe studiously, "I've played in a lot of regional tournaments."

"Oh! Have you won any?"

"I have about fourteen trophies."

This whetted my competitive instincts. Priding myself somewhat on my own tennis prowess, I threw out the challenge. "I'd like to play you sometime," I ventured. "In fact," I continued, "I'll make you a litle wager. I'll play you double or nothing."

"Double or nothing what?" he inquired.

"Both daughters or none!" I cried jubilantly, slapping my thigh with great vigor. I thought it was a huge joke, but I was alone in my humor.

A week or so later, I overheard Debbie talking to her mother. Debbie was still in tears. In a plaintive tone, she pleaded, "Mother, I wish you could do something about Daddy. All the kids are laughing at him."

I smiled triumphantly as my wife lept to my defense. "Honey, that would please your Daddy so much. He thinks of himself as quite a comedian."

"But, Mother," she wailed, "you don't understand. They're not laughing *with* him; they're laughing *at* him. They think you married some sort of a kook! Can't you do *something*?"

I beat him to the punch. I decided to do something myself. I decided to go out in the back yard and play catch with my son. After all, there certainly was nothing complicated about his love life. He couldn't care less about girls as long as they weren't bossing him around. There are some advantages in being just six.

ON BEES AND BIRDS AND DIRTY WORDS

As things turned out, however, even with Doug, I had a few things to learn. For the first five years young Doug had been getting a lot of free advice and education around our house, mostly in the form of: "Brush your teeth. Blow your nose. Wipe your chin. Zip your pants. Tie your shoes." So, he shed no tears of remorse as he grabbed his lunch pail and at long last charged off for the first grade.

What tears we shed were mostly for his hapless teacher who had the unenviable task of telling him to be quiet and sit still while God was telling him to jump around. But first grade teachers and God *are* capable of miracles, and surely, that is what takes place as eager youngsters discover the ecstacy of reading.

It wasn't long before Dougie came home with the proud news that he was a "Bluebird." I would have much preferred that he be a hawk or an eagle or falcon—or perhaps even a mangy old crow. But he and the rest of the family seemed content with the Bluebird.

Soon, he was bringing his homework with him in the evenings, mostly in the form of books from the library to supplement his reading. But when he started writing, a whole new world opened up for him. He wrote with such intensity and bore down so hard on the pencils that he snapped off points with rapidity. The lead literally flew. It was on one such occasion that he inquired, "Hey, Dad. How do you spell 'loss'?"

"What do you mean, 'loss'?" I queried.

"You know. My middle name. Doug 'loss' Davis."

The first parent-teacher conference was a revelation. I was anxious to learn about his social adjustment—things like when he got hit on the playground, did he hit back? And more important, who won? Imagine my chagrin when his teacher reported that he didn't get involved in the playground brawls. In fact, she called him her little "peacemaker," commenting on how he couldn't stand to see other children quarrel or be unhappy. I was stunned. I had envisioned him as a fighting tiger. Instead, he seemed to be content to sit by the side of the road and be a friend of man.

That night I resolved to do my fatherly duty and asked him if he would like to put on the gloves and learn the thrill of a right cross finding its mark square on the choppers. He allowed as to how he would rather go out in his garden and check on the progress of his pumpkin crop. The only fight I got was a kick in the shins from Polly.

I was equally successful when I took him to his first college football game. The only orientation he profited by was the location of the refreshment stand. He devoured four boxes of popcorn, two hot dogs, and five cokes. By then it was half-time and he went home to tend his pumpkins.

One day, on the spur of the moment, I decided to visit his first grade class. I was greatly surprised to find him standing behind his desk at the rear of the room chewing up his pencils. Puzzled at this, I questioned his teacher, who replied, "Oh, Dougie always stands at his desk. I put him at the rear of the room so he doesn't bother the other children."

"But," I protested, "how does he write standing up!"

"Terribly," she acknowledged.

She was right. His papers were a study in chaos. Neatness was not one of his virtues.

Fearing some deep psychological block, I discussed this with his mother who made an appointment to discuss it with his teacher. Together, they decided that the reason the poor boy stood up was because he couldn't see. Whereupon the teacher moved him to the front of the room.

He sat down and his papers suddenly improved. Polly hustled him off to the doctor to get his eyes examined and have him fitted for glasses. The theory was shot when the doctor reported he had perfect eyesight. I guess he just liked sitting at the front of the room.

With spring he suddenly developed a great passion for bees. He rushed home one evening bubbling over with a thousand questions to which I had no answers. So, together, we dug up the *World Book*, turned to the section on bees, and began reading. He got the picture quickly. We learned about the queen who laid the eggs, and the workers who built the cells and gathered the honey and protected the hives. It was when we got to the drones that things got sticky.

"What do the drones do, huh, Dad?"

"Well, they fertilize the queen who lays the eggs."

That stopped him for a minute. I could see he was puzzled, and, not wishing to go into all the facts of life, took the easy way out. "That means," I explained, "that they are the daddies."

That satisfied him until a few paragraphs later we learned that at the end of the summer when the eggs had been fertilized and the drones had done their duty that the workers chased them out of the hives, refused to feed them, and let them die.

That was more than he could swallow. With tears streaming down his cheeks, he turned and said, "You mean they let the daddies starve?"

So much for the bees.

Not everything he brought home from school was so enlightening. Take the dirty word incident, for instance. One night after school he was playing in his room with a friend. They were building a covered football stadium out of Lego blocks, and the roof fell in. Just as Polly entered the room Dougie registered his displeasure by bursting forth with a certain barnyard expression. My wife was amazed, as was his friend, who looked on with great horror. Polly jerked Dougie up by the nape of the neck and the seat of the pants and rushed him to the bathroom to wash his mouth out with soap.

"What did I say?" he asked in blank amazement.

"You know what you said," she stated indignantly, washing with increasing vigor as he howled his protest.

At that moment I arrived on the scene, and Polly, after relating the gory details, suggested that I have a little man-to-man talk with my son. I took him into the den, sat him down, and with great dignity patiently explained that we were trying to raise him as a gentleman. I went on in some detail to say that with gentlemen, there were certain words that one did not use in the presence of ladies, and certainly not their mothers, and that he had just used one of them.

He looked up at me with his big brown eyes and asked, "What are the others?"

"You'll know," I said firmly.

"Hey, Dad. How am I going to know? You mean I have to get my mouth washed out every time I use one? Couldn't you just make me a list?"

Summer marked the end of that memorable first year of school, and he returned to his gardening, his tree house, and his hours of running in the sun. With less grace he also returned to the endless refrain of: "Brush your teeth. Blow your nose. Wipe your chin. Zip your pants. Tie your shoes."

The baby fat was hardening into bone and gristle, and those once chubby legs were getting lean and long. The bond with his loving sisters was less loving and more snarling as he began to demand *his* rights occasionally in the pecking order of the house-hold. And as a sign of his blossoming maturity, one night he crawled onto my lap with his latest book on bees, and asked in great seriousness, "Hey, Dad, can't we drop this 'Dougie' stuff. Can't you just call me 'Doug'?"

That seemed reasonable. After all, it was better than calling him by his middle name, "Loss."

STAMP OUT COMMENCEMENT SPEAKERS

Among the skills a president must carefully cultivate is delivering commencement speeches, because as a sometimes acknowledged leader in the field of education, he's going to be giving hundreds of them. Fortunately, I had a long acquaintance with commencement speaking before coming to ISU.

Perhaps the most effective commencement speech I ever heard was delivered by my Drill Instructor after I had survived ten weeks of Marine Corps Boot camp. Anxious to depart on our first liberty and eager for a glimpse of the outside world, my fellow PFC's and I, nonetheless, stood at ramrod attention drinking in his sage advice. We were afraid to do otherwise, ever mindful that a blink of an eyelid could invite swift and terrible retaliation.

"You are now United States Marines," he barked in a voice that bounced off the far corners of the parade field. "God help us all. You came to us as a group of miserable, flea-bitten, junk-eating, civilian coolies. But, today you are Marines, members of the finest fighting outfit on the face of the earth. As you go out that gate, just remember, *you* can lick any man in the world."

I believed him—every word. And that faith remained unchallenged for at least an hour until I tried to pass it off on some skeptical swabby in a San Diego bar. I told him I was a United States Marine, and that we could lick anyone in the world. He hit me right in the mouth. From that moment on, I have always been somewhat leary about commencement speeches and speakers.

In retrospect, as I look back on the epic moments of my life—my graduation exercises from high school and college, I can note little nor even remember what was said on these occasions or who said it. The speeches which allegedly highlighted these events were but lost murmurs on a crowd of nervous scholars perspiring beneath black robes while viewing the guest of honor over a sea of mortar boards. I do recall hoping that whatever earth-shaking advice the speaker had would be short so that the academic parade could pass in review.

But this intuitive and accumulated wisdom was obliterated in the ego-bursting flush of being invited for the first time to address a graduating class of high-school seniors. Filled with the completeness of knowledge that comes with a newly minted doctoral degree, I was eager to share. My problem was simple— namely, how to cram all the miscellaneous information acquired in preparation for my comprehensive examinations into a thirty-minute address for students and their parents. I literally labored for days, choosing each word with meticulous care, striving for just the right balance between scholarly dignity and pious platitudes.

To be sure, it was but a small high school that had issued the invitation, but I arrived armed with a message for multitudes. I seated myself on the stage and looked out at a gymnasium of smiling parents and screaming, wiggling kids.

The graduating seniors marched in with a hesitating two-step to the struggling strains of "Pomp and Circumstance." (Obviously, the key members of the band were graduating and their loss was being felt, or rather, heard.) At long last they arrived on the stage and seated themselves beneath a proud banner that in those stirring words of Tennyson's Ulysses proclaimed: "To strive, to seek, to find, and not to yield." This, I thought, was indeed an awesome challenge for the six, pimply-faced seniors whose ashen expressions suggested they would do a back flip out of their chairs at a loud clap of thunder.

During the invocation I could tell that the acoustics were great. The minister's prayer came back with a triple echo. Then came the parade of speakers. Everyone on the platform spoke at least once, some twice, as we heard the class history, the class prophecy, the class will, the class song, and the salutatorian and valedictorian addresses. Finally, after an hour and a half, I was offered up.

My opening remark was a real shocker. With a sweeping gesture toward the six graduates, I proclaimed, "Ladies and gentlemen, behold the leaders of tomorrow. The fate of our communities, our state, and our nation is in their hands." There was a moment of silence, then an audible gasp as the expressions of parental pride and satisfaction changed to cold, stark terror as my message struck home.

The rest of my speech was anticlimactic. At the conclusion of the ceremonies, I decided to mingle with the graduates and their parents and spread some good will. I was quite touched when an elderly gentleman shuffled up and offered me his congratulations. I beamed as I shook his hand, most appreciative that someone in the audience had responded to my eloquence. But my ego bounced off the floor when I discovered he thought I was one of the graduating seniors.

With each succeeding commencement speech, however, I learned. After a dozen or so, I had developed something of a reputation. This I discovered by overhearing a conversation between two superintendents. In answering an inquiry as to possible commencement speakers, one of them replied, "You might try Davis. He's not eloquent, but he's quick—and cheap."

Within a year or two I was accustomed to filling my May evenings and weekends with madcap dashes halfway across the state to inspire yet unenlightened seniors in their last hours as undergraduates. One such mission took me from my then native base in Laramie, Wyoming, some three hundred miles to a rural high school in the northern part of the state. It was a long, lonesome drive through country where there are more antelope than people. Turning off the main highway, I dead-ended into this small town some twenty miles into the mountains. I'm sure I was the first stranger to arrive since Jim Bridger showed up to trap beaver.

I drove to the only filling station in sight and proudly announced to the attendant, "I'm the commencement speaker for the high school graduation tonight. Do you know where I could get a good dinner?"

He studied me carefully before switching his plug of tobacco from his left cheek to the right. "Ain't but one place to eat, and that ain't very good." Then he jerked his head toward a building down at the end of the single block that comprised the town.

He was right. The food was lousy, but the action made up for what was lacking in the culinary arts. The senior class was celebrating the end of school, and two steely-eyed youths competing for the attention of a plump blonde stood toe-to-toe in the middle of the dining room and slugged it out for a good fifteen minutes. No one bothered to break it up, and it might still be going on had the blond not departed to go home and get her robe for the graduation exercises.

I skipped dessert and hustled out to the consolidated school for the eight o'clock ceremony. At a quarter till, I still was the only one who had arrived on the scene. Finally, a car drove up, and a man got out. He disappeared into the building, then came back out and began sweeping the steps in front of the gym. I walked over and announced that I was the speaker for the evening, acknowledged that he must be the custodian, and inquired as to where I might find the superintendent of schools.

He leveled me with a baleful glance and replied, "You're looking at 'im." The rest of the conversation was strained, and I was glad when the crowd arrived.

The gym was packed to the rafters with an attendance of well over five hundred. I remarked that this was quite remarkable considering the population of the town was only 250. "Not no other place to go," the superintendent grumbled. "Too late for huntin' and too early for smoochin'."

I chewed on his bit of homey philosophy through the march and benediction and preliminary speeches, then geared myself for my big moment as the superintendent rose to introduce me— or so I thought.

He began ominously. "Me and the Board of Education had a meeting this afternoon, and I want to tell you all right now, I wasn't fired. I quit." He went on to elaborate on the details for another thirty minutes before returning to the graduating class.

"This is just an average graduating class," he said. Then he paused. "Come to think of it, it isn't even average. One or two of 'em might be above average, but the rest are plumb below. For four years now I've been trying to teach them to say 'May I' instead of 'cain't I,' and 'isn't' instead of 'ain't.' But, as you can see, I didn't do very well. Our speaker for the evening is a professor from the University of Wyoming, Dr. Davis."

I should have learned from that episode that one should always test the political climate of a community before accepting a commencement engagement. But the strains of "Pomp and Circumstance" and a hundred invocations and valedictories lull you into a false sense of security. Some years later I was again to step into the cross-fire of an all-out war.

I first became suspicious when after a two-hundred mile drive to a mountain community, I stopped for dinner and picked up the latest edition of the weekly newspaper. The ink was not dry on the pages, it was so fresh from the press. In fact, it was so fresh that it reported in detail the commencement exercises of the night before and even referred to the inspiring speech by Dr. Davis. "That's what I call scooping the news," I thought to myself as I glanced at the dateline which was set for the following day.

What troubled me most, however, was a front page story with banner headlines indicating that the school district had finished the year $50,000 in debt, and that in a special election the entire board had been voted out of office and a new one selected. Further, the superintendent had just resigned to accept a new position in a neighboring state. So, it was with a sense of foreboding that I approached the high school.

My suspicions were confirmed. Nobody was speaking to anybody. I got my first hint when, after what I thought was the platform party was seated on the stage, an angry, beet-colored man stormed forward and demanded his chair. They got a chair.

We were introduced, and I learned that the late arrival was the ousted president of the school board. His mood matched his complexion.

The early part of the program was without incident, and I struggled through my remarks in an atmosphere that would have done justice to the Vietnam peace talks. But when it came time to pass out diplomas, the action began.

The high school principal suggested to the Board president that he would be happy to read the names of the graduating seniors while the president handed out the diplomas. To which the president replied, "I'll do it myself."

At that, he stood up, grabbed the microphone, and planted it vigorously on the front of the stage. Now, it really wasn't a stage, but rather a large piece of plywood balanced on a series of tables. Hence, there was considerable bounce anytime a person crossed the platform. The president had placed the mike in the bounciest part, and even dainty footsteps sounded like the charge of the Light Brigade. The solicitous principal tried to explain all this to the obstinate president, but he was beyond taking any advice. The mike stayed put, and the principle returned to his seat muttering under his breath, "Let the dumb bastard put it where he pleases."

He did, and picked up the first diploma, squinted, pulled it close to his face, then held it at arm's length. The principal nudged me in the ribs and chuckled, "They're printed in Old English. He can't even read new English."

After a long pause, the president began. "Connie Anderson," he announced proudly. The audience tittered. Connie was really Lonnie, and he stood fidgeting at the edge of the stage, all six-feet four of him.

With agonizing slowness, the procession passed by. I timed the ceremony, and for the first twenty-five graduates, it took exactly twenty-five minutes. Noting that we were only half through, I studied the stack of diplomas. I was puzzled by the strange table upon which they were sitting. I had a nagging hunch that something about that table didn't fit into the program. I was right. As the president ran out of diplomas near at hand, he proceeded to pick up the table and move it closer to him. The principal was half out of his seat when the president froze him with a whithering eye. With a sigh, the principal sat back down, and the president grabbed the table and plopped it down near the front of the stage.

It sounded like a cannon shot over the speaker system. But what really surprised me was the unfolding of a portable sewing machine, which it was, scattering diplomas hither and yon, while the inside of the apparatus dropped out on the stage like an umbilical cord.

I was speechless. So was the president as he stomped off the stage and into oblivion.

In the aftermath, I was confronted by a nervous individual who introduced himself as the treasurer for the School Board. Having just read of their financial situation, I couldn't blame him for being nervous. "Mighty fine speech, Dr. Davis."

I thanked him.

He coughed. "I don't know whether they mentioned any financial arrangements when they contacted you?" It was in the form of a question.

"No, they didn't," I said modestly.

"Expenses?"

"No."

He looked relived. "Well, should we pay you something?"

"Oh," I replied self-consciously. "Whatever you like. But I love to make commencement speeches. I really do it for the fun of it."

He smiled. He believed me. I was left with a sweaty handshake and a thousand priceless memories.

I now proudly take my stand with those who would do away with commencement speakers altogether.

COMMAS, NOT PERIODS

But in doing away with commencement speakers, I certainly wouldn't do away with commencements. These ceremonious occasions do serve as punctuation marks to the academic parade—hopefully as commas rather than periods. One needs such reminders that time, indeed, marches on. Caught up in the milieu of events that demands more hours than there are in any day, a president's existence seems to be characterized by leaping from crisis to crisis. Happenings that at the moment are sharply defined blend into a hazy series of days, then months, then years on the job. Classes graduate, and within four or five years, hardly a student remains on campus who can remember a time when I *wasn't* President of ISU.

Thus, as the stormy Sixties neared their end, I found myself no longer the anxious newcomer, but a rapidly-greying veteran held accountable for the record.

Sitting on the commencement platform watching the academic procession file by provided ample pause for reflection. With relief, even gratitude, I appreciated the outward symbols of traditional dignity and joy that marked such occasions—no bare feet, no clenched fists, no shouts of defiance.

I was reminded of the theoretical commencement address which had appeared in a June issue of *Life* magazine, wherein the alleged speaker lamented the fact that the esteemed university president could not be present, having been locked in his office for three weeks by the ad hoc Committee to Define Radical Alternatives. He had been unable to meet all 31 demands of the Students Alienated from a Sick Society (SASS) "for a searching new look at the university's decision making process."

Watching the faculty and students take their places before the panorama of parents and friends seated in the stadium, I often thought that behind each diploma lay a story. I reflected upon all the individual struggles within the classrooms and laboratories as each student tried to predict what devious formula the professor would apply in computing a grade, the cumulative impact of grades and credits and averages, and the haggling and bargaining with the registrar. I well knew of the many trials and tribulations, including the bare logistics of eating and sleeping and keeping alive while climbing the academic slopes, organizing one's love life so that it would conform to the University's unreasonable rules on women's hours in the dorms, or standing spread-eagled with hands to the wall as the Librarian searched for missing books. I also was aware of the bitterness and disillusionment when a student discovered that a professor's evaluation of his work sometimes fell short of his own objective views on the subject.

Collectively, there were few affluent students in the crowd, no big spenders. Most were first-generation students, in that their parents had not attended college. They came from small towns in Idaho, and if one would draw a circle that would encompass a 175 mile radius from Pocatello, he would encircle 75% of the student body. Many came from farming communities, bringing with them a side of beef or home-canned products, renting a room, and participating in a type of communal living in the best sense of the word.

Hard cash was scarce. Over half the students were virtually self-sustaining, paying all or most of their way through college. To them, education represented a solid investment in the future, an attitude reflected in their seriousness of purpose. So commencement was an occasion of triumph and fulfillment.

But it did not belong to the young alone. Grey hair beneath many of the mortar boards revealed that. Among the graduates were those who had renewed their formal education, a luxury denied in their own youth.

In one graduating class, a father, his son, and his daughter-in-law received diplomas. The father, after raising his family, had decided to go back to school and do what he always wanted to do, become a pharmacist. The family sold its home, moved to Pocatello, and his wife went to work while he entered the University as a freshman. The story behind his diploma would be well worth telling.

So would that of his son. I knew him best his senior year, when, in addition to a full academic load, he worked forty hours a week at a near-by fertilizer plant as a book-keeper. He also managed to participate actively as a student leader and attend meetings of the National Guard. I slept well at night just knowing that he was awake. In fact, I never figured out just when he slept. Because of the great demands on his time, I doubt if his grade point average fully reflected his capabilities, but I never had any doubts as to his potential for success in his chosen field of business administration.

His lovely wife was a language major. In addition to a senior year that included student teaching and a husband in orbit, she also found time to direct the choreography for the campus musical, "Kiss Me Kate." Upon graduation she planned to become a junior high teacher.

This was but one family, and yet, in a way, it symbolized all of the pooling of effort and resources and energies leading up to the triumphant moment of conferring degrees. In a sense, it also symbolized the high regard for education that people would so sacrifice and persevere and strive to achieve these goals—a fulfillment of the dedication to the continuity of learning and the habit of acquiring new knowledge, then putting it to work.

I was proud to be a part of this academic parade. And the years passed in accelerating swiftness.

THE RESTLESS CAMPUS

Considering the nature of our campus and student body, I was surprised when in the spring of 1969 I received a letter from a congressman in which he stated that Idaho State University had been listed as one of the college campuses characterized by student uprisings and disruptive protest. He invited me to list the details and comment on legislation which would deny further funds to student insurgents.

In an era tormented by repeated headlines announcing riots and turmoil on college campuses from Columbia to San Francisco State, perhaps it sounds like a cry from the Idaho wilderness to call attention to the fact that throughout this country on the majority of campuses, the majority of students are not engaged in bloody rebellion. And I was complacent enough to think that Idaho State University and its students fell into the latter category. But, somehow, *we* had made the congressman's *list*.

There are places, I told myself, where such an inquiry might have all the innocence of a valentine. But in Idaho, experience with lesser catastrophes has taught me to regard such a missal as a potential state scandal. Under the circumstances, one is tempted to take his phone off the hook, burn his correspondence, send his family to the in-laws, get his credentials up to date, and hightail it for the hills. But, I chose the bolder route. I decided to pick my way back through the four years I had been at Idaho State University and analyze the student disorders—their causes and their effects.

Having arrived at Idaho State University in the fall of 1965, I recall that I did not have to wait long before encountering my first student demonstration. T'was on a grey December day. The campus was lulled into a sense of false serenity by Christmas carols and glowing anticipation of the coming holiday. But, underneath the surface, the natives were restless.

One enterprising student who had read about the turmoil besetting various colleges in the country wondered what would happen if we had a demonstration at Idaho State. He had nothing in particular to protest about, so contented himself with painting a sign that read, "Peace on earth." Nailing it to a long pole, he proceeded to march up and down in front of the Student Union.

Shortly thereafter, another student happened by. Thinking the one-man parade was a peace demonstration, he decided to join the march. He, too, soon had a sign—this one reading, "To hell with McNamara."

A Vietnam veteran who had just returned to school that fall took exception to both signs and soon was following them with a placard which proclaimed, "To hell with you."

About this time, the eleven o'clock classes let out, and a crowd of some hundred students formed in front of the Student Union. Glancing out of my window, I wondered what the excitement was all about, put on my overcoat, and wandered over to take a look. By the time I arrived, eight sign carriers were tromping back and forth through the snow, cheered on by the hecklers in the crowd.

Suddenly, however, the atmosphere changed as photographers and cameramen from the local newspapers and television stations arrived.

That night and the following day, I was amazed to see my picture on television and in the newspapers accompanied by the caption, "Peace Riot on ISU Campus as President Looks On."

Somehow, lost in the shuffle was the fact that while the alleged "peace" demonstration was taking place outside the Student Union, some five hundred students were inside that same building donating blood for the southeastern Idaho Red Cross blood bank. I philosophized that emphasis makes the news.

That spring we did have a bona fide peace demonstration in our community. It had been well advertised and coincided with a nationwide peace march scheduled for that day. I had forgotten the date, however, and might have missed the whole show had I not dropped by the campus post office that Saturday to pick up my mail.

Noting a cluster of newspaper and television reporters around the Student Union, I asked what was going on. When reminded that this was the beginning of a peace march, I went into the building to listen to the speeches.

About thirty to forty students had gathered with various members of the clergy and townspeople. The program began with a prayer, followed by a pledge of allegiance to the flag. Various persons spoke about the blessings of peace and the immorality of war. Then, in a very orderly manner, they left the building, marched through the business district, and proceeded to a bridge above the Portneuf River where they concluded their demonstration by throwing a wreath into the river.

That night on television, I heard about the peace marches in New York City, San Francisco, California, and *Pocatello, Idaho*. The following week, an ROTC review which involved some 200 Idaho State University students in uniform went virtually unnoticed.

There was a moratorium for several months, during which time the Trustees formalized a speaker's policy for the state's institutions of higher learning which permitted students to invite speakers of their choice to the campuses. Our students, eager to test the Trustees, the policy, and, undoubtedly, me, scheduled Dr. Timothy Leary, the alleged psychedelic drug advocate, to appear at Idaho State University.

He showed up in velvet pajamas and dispensed his philosophy to an overflowing crowd that included students, some faculty, townspeople, and representatives of the State Drug Control Board. For the most part, student reaction was extremely negative. In the open discussion period, their questions were penetrating and devastating while, in my opinion, his answers were qualified and evasive.

But the appearance was news-worthy. A neighboring newspaper published an editorial entitled, "Is ISU Becoming Another Berkeley?" and went on to say:

> *What in the world is the administration of Idaho State University trying to do? Follow in the footsteps of University of California and pave the way for more moral breakdown? . . .*
> *ISU's permitting the speaking appearance in the Student Union Ballroom of such a person as former Harvard professor, Dr. Timothy Leary, billed as the 'self-styled prophet of the Turned-On Generation,' is nothing more than condoning and encouraging drug usage and idleness among students at the college . . .*

Leary's appearance was followed by the usual aftermath of threatening anonymous telephone calls, abusive letters from throughout the state, and accusations regarding my dereliction of duty, subversive tendencies, moral laxity, and probable communist affiliations.

On the campus, the incident was quickly forgotten as students continued plodding their weary way through the groves of academe—content in the knowledge that yesterday's crisis is today's yawn, but satisfied that they had tested the administration with a real hullabaloo.

The issue was not to be resurrected until two years later when a state official, in justifying his proposed two million dollar slash in the university's budget request, referred to the Leary speech and stated:

> *He [Leary] was selling dope . . . If any of you doubt that, come to my office, and I will show you a text of his speech which one of our narcotics officers got for me.*
>
> *This is what is going on in our universities and Dr. Bud Davis let it happen when all he had to do was open his eyes and read a few books and he would have known it was going to happen.*
>
> *I'm getting sick and tired of this kind of thing. I don't like my money, and I'm sure you taxpayers don't either, spent on this sort of thing.*

Meanwhile, there was no outward violations of public opinion on the part of the university from February, 1967 (the Leary speech), to April, 1968. Then, in his waning weeks as editor of the student newspaper, a bearded graduate student chose to use certain barnyard expressions in an editorial. The University Communications Committee (composed of students and faculty) advised him that the policy of the paper was to adhere to acceptable, professional journalistic practices and proceeded to set down certain guidelines.

The student elected to stay on as editor subject to the restrictions, but protested against what he labeled censorship. To aid his cause, he enlisted the help of the National Student Press Association, which was quick to condemn the university and its administration for its alleged high-handed abridgement of freedom of the press.

The student editor issued numerous statements to local and state news agencies and was interviewed on television. His bushy appearance made for great picture coverage, and the university was the subject of numerous editorials, both pro and con. On the campus itself, he received little support.

As a token of the editor's righteous indignation, the next issue of the student paper appeared with the entire editorial page blanked out. (Some considered it an improvement.) When that failed to get the desired response, the editor announced to his staff that he was going to refuse to publish the year's final edition of the paper. His staff replied that with or without him, they were going to publish the paper and then proceeded to do so.

When the papers arrived on campus, the irate editor quickly confiscated them and locked himself in his office. The local reporters and television stations rushed to the scene and photographed and interviewed the embattled editor.

A television reporter, however, had the presence of mind to interview one of our co-eds to determine student reaction. Her remarks were devastating to the editor's cause as she stated:

> *Oh, Frank! Everyone's laughing about this. Let him sit in his office with those papers. Maybe they'll hatch. At any rate, when he gets tired, he'll come out, the papers will be distributed, and life will go on.*

She was right.

The following year, we had a new editor, a former tackle on the football team. In line with the expectations for the job, he, too, grew a magnificent beard and roamed around the campus looking like an intellectual Paul Bunyan. Admittedly, however, there were those among the faculty and student body who regarded him as a subversive; he occasionally had a kind word for the administration—a type of academic heresy.

The 1968-69 academic year was disarmingly quiet. We just about had a disruption, however, after the joint student-faculty production of the musical comedy—"A Funny Thing Happened on the Way to the Forum." The show was such a hit that tickets were at a premium, and some students were rumored to be scalping their activity cards. The chief crisis revolved around a member of the math department who played the role of the lecherous old senator. Surrounded by a harem of lovely coeds, he so relished the part that he was reluctant to give it up when the show closed. His wife quickly squared him away, however.

International Student Night was also something of a sensation. By tradition, this annual performance by the foreign students featured their native folksongs and dances. All went well until an Egyptian faculty member took his daughter out of a convent and enrolled her as a freshman at ISU. Her native folk dance was a show stopper all the way—the greatest maneuver since Little Egypt did her own thing at the World's Fair half a century ago. The proud father accepted the plaudits of the crowd with a modest shrug of his shoulders, commenting, "It's in zee blood." But the rest of the men went home and threw rocks at their wives.

A later protest (from the public) occurred after the appearance of our student body vice president on television in regard to his testimony before a legislative committee on human rights. I received several indignant telephone calls to the effect that this articulate, well-groomed black student had had the audacity to wear a mustache and goatee, a turtleneck sweater under his sport coat, and, of all things, love beads. The love beads, for whatever it is worth, turned out to be the microphone hanging about his neck.

This about sums up the students disorders over a four-year period. For the most part, the major disruptions had come from without, not within.

That same spring, for example, an elected state official called on the American Legion to help restore law and order to our Idaho campuses. Addressing the Legion's fiftieth anniversary banquet, he said, "It's going to take some guts to fight some of these knotheads who don't have any respect for our country. I'm sick and tired of hippies, yippies, peaceniks and beatniks." He then went on to say he also was concerned about rioters, looters, arsonists, draft card burners, insults to the American flag, deserters from the armed forces, campus demonstrations, and the rapid incease in the use of dangerous drugs, pornography and obscenity.

I wondered at the time what adult over thirty wasn't concerned, but I could hardly believe he was relating these general statements to the local scene. I was wrong. With an air of mysticism he continued, hinting that he was dissatisfied with some of the "goings on" at the Idaho institutions of higher learning. He did not list the details or the specifics, nor did he divulge his sources of information, but in an ominous tone, he added, "If you knew what was going on . . . I don't know what you would do."

All of which brings me back to the letter from the congressman. I wonder who told on ISU?

THE HAIR REBELLION

Idaho prides itself on its remote and rugged setting. For example, our Idaho State University campus is located so close to the primitive area that when a long-haired, bearded student shows up from Pierre's Hole or Mud Lake, we don't know whether he represents the "now" generation or one of Jedidiah Smith's fur trappers. And from good accounts, the missionaries Brigham Young sent north to settle and populate this region arrived with luxurious facial adornment. Yet, its remoteness and isolation do not guarantee any immunity from the attitudes and fads that sweep the country. There may be a time-gap or "cultural lag" between what is happening on the East Coast and its impact on Idaho, but, eventually, it gets to us—including the hair rebellion.

So here, too, on the last frontier where manes and whiskers have long been symbols of hardy individualism and rugged manhood, there is something about seeing long hair or beards on a university campus that sends otherwise rational men into orbit. The irrational tend to form vigilante committees armed with razors and shears.

The father of one of our students formed his own one-man posse to track down his long-haired son. He stalked him through the Student Union, across the campus, and in the dorms, finally locating him on the golf course (putting for an eagle three). There he tackled the surprised youngster, pinned him to the green, yanked out his scissors, and whacked away. No doubt 6,000 fathers in absentia would have cheered this audacious act, had they not been tracking down their own sons.

For the historian, the modern reaction of decently barbered citizens of the Sixties and Seventies to the hair explosion should come as no surprise. More than one father in greeting his son after the latter's prolonged absence in college would empathize with Saint Wulstan, who, a thousand years ago, whenever a long-haired communicant knelt before him, would whip out a knife, cut a good handful of hair, and then would throw it into the startled offender's face, threatening him with the fires of hell unless he chopped off the rest.

The fact that beards had graced the countenances of such red-blooded patriots as Abe Lincoln, Robert E. Lee, and Ulysses S. Grant, is little consolation to the well-clipped distressed father who first sees ringlets curling down the back of his prodigal son's neck.

As a Dean of Men at the University of Colorado in 1962, I grew up with the first roots of the hair rebellion. In part I attribute it to the influence of the Beatles. When they introduced the "beat" of the Sixties, their flowing ringlets bobbed in rhythm. At first it was such a novelty that a favorite show-stopper in campus musical productions featured pseudo musicians with mops on their heads, faking at the instruments, while a Beatle record blared over the P.A. system. I remember my being amused at their absurd appearance.

As a college president, however, it became a horse of a different color—or hair of a different length. As the crew-cut became a relic of by-gone days, dangling locks, drooping sideburns, flopping mustaches, and flowing beards began to thrive. And as the hair grew and gained stature on campus, the reaction from the hinterlands became gnarled with hostility and suspicion.

A picture of a bearded group of students listening to a guest speaker on campus was sufficient to rate a front-page editorial in a neighboring newspaper, entitled: "Is ISU Promoting Hippies?"

One father took this instance to make a thirty-minute, long distance phone call to me protesting about the bad influence the University was having upon his son—a freshman of about some six months standing. I took the trouble to procure a photograph of the young man in question taken on the day of his matriculation. It revealed long, yellow hair hanging down to his shoulders. He was, in fact, a striking version of a six-foot three-inch Goldilocks. His father was irate because in six months the University wouldn't do what the old man had failed to do in eighteen years—namely, tell his son to get a haircut.

In times of crises such as this, I often flip back to a treatise on the "Problems of a President" written by one of Colorado U.'s distinguished profs, Dr. Jack Ogilvy, who has become an expert in advising college presidents. Predictably, Ogilvy, writing in 1962, had forseen the hair problem and philosophized:

> *If a certain number of faculty and students elect to grow beards, and to appear in rather informal attire, the university stands convicted of moral turpitude in the eyes of certain well-meaning citizens, and the ad-*

ministration is accused of moral laxity, dereliction of duty, and probably subversive tendencies.

Ogilvy went on to conclude:

It is hard to point to any law of God or man which forbids the wearing of beards. In fact, for long periods in history beards were regarded as one of man's principal adornments, and they have been worn by innumerable highly respected citizens from Sampson to the Smith brothers.

A university administration which forbade faculty or students to wear beards . . . would be attacked as hopelessly fuddy-duddy, Victorian, outmodedly puritanical, and probably fascist.

Heeding his sage advice, I kept my cool and sat tight while the hair flourished unabated.

Turning philosopher myself, I soon rationalized that beauty is in the eye of the beholder. This was passionately illustrated when ISU's bald-headed Athletic Director, Dubby Holt, took exception to the shoulder-length ringlets of our star hurdler. (Some attributed Holt's attitude to tonsorial jealousy.) I was sitting beside Dubby watching our local hero warm up for the Big Sky Conference track meet. Holt growled, "Damned kid. I told him to get a haircut before the meet. But he thinks he's Sampson. I just hope he doesn't get his curls caught in his spikes while going over the hurdles."

After our star had won the 440 yard dash, the 400 meter hurdles, and anchored two winning relay teams, I remarked, "That long hair didn't seem to bother him tonight."

Holt widened his baby blue eyes and replied, "What hair?"

Outwardly, I adopted an attitude of strict neutrality. But inwardly, I was a hairy traditionalist. Within my own family, I never had any trouble with my son, Doug. I would set the stage by telling him of the Spartans in ancient Greece who shaved their heads and beards so that in combat their opponents could never grab a hunk of hair as they whacked away at their heads. While Doug pondered over this bit of history, I would plop him on a chair in the kitchen, whip out the clippers, and peel him like a Marine Corps boot. Hairwise, he was neat, sanitary, and happy— and never uttered a word of protest. But, then, at age eight, he had never learned that his hair could grow more than three-quarters of an inch long.

My teenage daughters witnessed all this with weeping and wailing as they pleaded, "Daddy, please don't cut his bangs."

Despairing with this futile approach, they turned their attack on me. The big blast came the night of a Rotary family picnic, when fifteen-year-old Becky protested, "Daddy, you embarrass us. Look at all those other Rotarians with long hair and bushy sideburns. Everyone thinks you're some kind of square."

As I sulked under her cutting remark, I also saw a cheerful side. "As soon as those college kids see these long-haired Rotarians," I chuckled, "we'll be back in the era of crew-cuts."

WHAT DID HE MEAN BY THAT?

After several years in office, I found that it was easy for a president to become afflicted with academic paranoia—almost to the point that he might well catch himself tip-toeing around corners, confining his press releases to his wife, censoring all publications for pictures of nudes, or flinching at each fresh edition of the student newspaper. At times it got so bad that when our football team went into its huddle, I thought they were talking about me.

These attacks of paranoia became particularly acute when I was scheduled to speak to a faculty meeting—for I knew that gathered before me were representatives of the world's most critical experts on every field known to God and man—and a few that aren't.

On such occasions, I always tried to speak from a carefully edited and prepared text, because I knew that in the sanctity of the faculty lounge it would be pulled apart in detail. No punctuation mark would go unchallenged, no split infinitive or dangling participle or agreement of tense. Terminology, phraseology (probably even cosmotology) would be scrutinized with meticulous care as the wily scholars sought to learn: "Just what did he mean by that?"

A suspicious lot, these professors. I've never quite figured them out. Thus, I leave the definition of the breed to the academic types themselves—men such as Marten Ten Hoor, who, in his articles, "The Species Professor Americanus and Some Natural Enemies," described a professor as "a prophet without authority, a preacher without unction, an orator without sex appeal, a martyr without a crown."

Ten Hoor went on to ask these thoughtful questions:

Why is it . . . that in Europe an ordinary mortal when he sees a professor, tips his hat, whereas, in these United States he taps his forehead? Why is it that in Europe the professor is the jewel of the salon while in the United States he is the skeleton at the feast? Why is it that in Europe a professor is a lion who is diligently hunted by the arbiters of society, while in the United States he is a lone ass braying in the wilderness?

I don't know. I don't even pretend to know. I just know I'm not foolhardy enough to go around making jokes about them.

Actually, to use an old cliche, "Some of my best friends were professors." Occasionally, some even dropped into the office without a request for more funds. I became leary, however, about dropping into their offices or the faculty lounge. When I did, all conversations stopped.

I also was cautious about curbstone opinions. These get you in trouble. Once on a casual stroll across the campus to view a new display in the museum, I was intercepted by our bright-eyed librarian (who doubles as a professor). He commented, "The stacks are getting full, and we sure could use some more room for books."

I nodded appreciatively and hurried on. Three days later, I found I had committed myself to a new four million dollar library building.

Once I heard that a man might be a successful college president if he could solve three problems: football for the alumni, sex for the students, and parking for the faculty. But that was before the tyranny of alphabetical organizational initials. In these perilous times he is confronted by such combinations as SDS, NSA, NSPA, BSU, LSD, and AAUP—but the greatest of these is the AAUP. I got so that when I heard the name of this omnipotent organization, I crossed myself (which is something for a Methodist), and muttered a silent "Amen." I shared the superstition of the Indians that even to mention the name of an auspicious landmark (such as a mountain or the AAUP) was to invite certain disaster.

There were times I suspected that the fire-breathing members of the AAUP in their missionary zeal would do away with administrators altogether and totally restructure the institution. I wondered if the result would be: sex for the alumni, parking for the students, and football for the faculty (using an administrative head for the pigskin).

I even got suspicious of the modern Ph.D. programs, and wondered if alongside such basics as language requirements there did not also exist a course in revolutionary expertise. Time and again, a newly hatched Ph.D. arrived for his first teaching assignment, and within three months became an authority on budgets, sabbatical leaves, academic freedom, student rights, and due process procedures.

His type fits the axiom set forth by a former Idaho State University president, Dr. Carl McIntosh, who wrote: "In the academic world everyone's expertise in administration increases as the square of the distance from his own responsibilities."

Yet, with all the talk of reform, I have to chuckle when anyone refers to the faculty as liberal. This has to be one of the most conservative bodies in American society. There are those who are for change all right, but not now, and especially not if it affects them or their respective departments. This is sometimes called the "snout in the trough" theory. The academic trough is regarded as full, and any new program represents another snout with which to share the already meager fare (or funds).

I also learned, however, that faculty firebrands and gadflies on the campus are a minority—that the most productive scholars and dedicated teachers shun petty intramural quarrels like they would the Chinese rot. They are too engrossed in their profession to engage in excessive campus or departmental politics. While they pull their tour of duty on faculty government and committees, they are well aware of that admonition of Professor Carlos Baker, who in *A FRIEND IN POWER*, stated:

> *No more committees, please. I'm on enough committees, as it is . . . They say it's the price you pay for democratic government in a university . . . But who pays the price of scholarship? Who writes the books on Shakespeare, Sophocles, Voltaire? No books were ever written while a man sat at a committee table.*[1]

As a president, I stand in awe of the true scholars and their talent and knowledge in their respective disciplines. I am well aware that in comparison the science of administration is inprecise and the art inconstant. In the classroom, by far the majority are enthusiastic and dedicated teachers. Out of the classroom or lab, for the most part, these men are good companions—the kind you would like to go fishing with or light up a pipe with or spend an evening with just talking.

Such men form the hard core of academic excellence on any campus and probably do more in terms of personalizing the instructional programs and making the curriculum relevant that the instant reformers who lead the charges and also the retreats.

Still, I hate to face their collective wisdom in a faculty meeting.

[1]Carlos Baker, *A Friend in Power*, Charles Scribner's Sons, New York, New York, 1958, pp. 23-24.

But, no matter how firm my resolve not to let academic paranoia get me down, I still have lapses. Just the other day as I was crossing the campus, I ran into a new member of the faculty. He nodded and said, "Good morning."

I watched him walk away and wondered, "Now, what did he mean by that?"

THE NUDE

From the first moment I saw her picture I knew I was in trouble. To be sure, she was a lithesome beauty with more curves than a mountain road. Her back was turned discreetly to the camera, and the art students in the picture industriously absorbed in their painting, but I was confident my ever-ready critics would not be confused by the setting or the facts. For, there she was, in all her unclad splendor, smack on the front page of the 1969 Special Idaho State University edition published by the usually discreet local newspaper, *The Idaho State Journal*. And she was being mailed to every high school senior in Idaho under the alluring caption: "The Academic Life at Idaho State University."

I anticipated the letters, and the first was not long in arriving. It read:

Dear President Davis:

Please cancel my daughter's name from your mailing list. She is a senior in high school this year. We are very ashamed of your college paper that had the picture of the nude woman in it. Do not send this pornography to my daughter. You are lowering your moral standards at that university to accommodate a few students with low ideals and standards. Why push the entire University into the mire because of a small minority?

We were always so proud of our Idaho State University. We used to have a university that all citizens of Idaho could be proud of, but so many young people with long shaggy hair and long bearded men that look so unkept have been admitted to our fine university that it is lowering the standards for all students. The Idaho State University is not the University it use to be because the minority are allowed to rule.

There is quite a Communist movement in our colleges, let us be aware of what is really taking place to undermine the morals of our youth.

Sincerely,
(signed) Mrs. Patience Little

Truthfully, I was at a complete loss as to how to answer that one. Far from being prudish, I rationalized that one could scan the covers at any neighborhood drugstore news stand or read the advertisements in almost any household magazine and see far more suggestive pictures. A picture of a life-drawing class seemed innocent enough in comparison. But, knowing ultimately what the reaction from some quarters would be, I braced myself for the onslaught.

But, if I was prepared for the letters, I hardly expected the matter to be brought before the Legislative Council and Fiscal-Budget Committee. Thus, I was shocked when I read the following news release:

LEGISLATOR IS UPTIGHT ABOUT ISU NUDITY

A Lewiston legislator criticized Idaho State University for sending out promotional material showing a nude model posed before an art class.

Rep. Joe Wagner, D-Lewiston, caused a brief flurry during a meeting of the Legislative Fiscal-Budget Committee when he questioned the taste shown by the institution in sending out such materials to high school seniors.

He passed around to sometimes laughing committee members a supplement to the *Idaho State Journal* of Pocatello, which he said was mailed to his son in an effort apparently to induce the youngster to ISU.

Sen. J. Marsden Williams, R-Idaho Falls, said the supplements to the Pocatello newspaper were mailed out by the university to high school seniors throughout the state, adding his own child received one.

"I'm no prude, but I don't think this is a policy of good taste on the part of the school or the paper," the red-faced Wagner told the committee. He said he felt that perhaps nude models might be needed by art students in their classroom work but he strongly objected to mailing out pictures of them to prospective university students.

The picture in question was on the front page of a supplement slugged *"Academics."* It showed a female model lying nude on her side with her back to the camera.

"The nude may be necessary, but I don't think it should be publicized," Wagner said, emphasizing his displeasure with the publication.

At this point Rep. Helen McKinney, R-Salmon, questioned whether this committee was the proper sounding board for such objections.

"We are not here to judge what is pornographic or not," Mrs. McKinney told the committee. *"We are here as a fiscal-budget committee."*

Rep. Jenkin Palmer, R-Malad, committee chairman, pointed out to Wagner that the paper in question was a professional publication and not a publication of ISU.

"Joking aside," Palmer said, *"I don't think it is the prerogative of this committee to judge lest ye be judged."*

Sen. Walter Yarbrough, R-Grand View, said he disagreed with Mrs. McKinney and that he felt as a taxpayer and as a legislator he had the right to dissent if he felt something was wrong or in poor taste.

I replied as best I could:

November 6, 1969

The Honorable Jenkin L. Palmer
Representative
Route #1
Malad, Idaho 83252
Dear Mr. Palmer:
   I read the enclosed clipping entitled, "Legislator Is Uptight About ISU Nudity." Allegedly the quotes refer to a meeting of the Legislative Fiscal-Budget Committee. I must admit, I didn't even know we were on the agenda. I certainly had no intention of pleading our case for supplementary appropriations on the basis that our academic programs were so naked we could not afford to clothe our models in a life drawing class.
   I confess, however, that when I first scanned the special ISU edition of the Idaho State Journal *and saw the section on Academic Programs, my reaction was similar to that of the sailor in the opening lines of the play, "Mr. Roberts" when he exclaimed, "My God! She's bare-assed!" No doubt, Representative Joe Wagner had much the same response.*
   Please believe, however, that we are not promoting pornography, promiscuity, free love, or dirty pictures. Drawing classes are conducted in an atmosphere of appropriate academic decorum; and, to the artist, the bare lass probably had no more appeal than a brass vase.
   I hope this explanation covers the subject thoroughly. I am always appreciative of your concern, your understanding and your support.
                         Sincerely,
                         (signed) William E. Davis
                         President

I was glad when the legislative and public interest turned from nudes to football.

CHEERS FOR DEAR OLD MOM AND DAD

To the avid football fan seated high in the safety of the stands watching Saturday's heroes, the action and mayhem on the field are an awesome sight. When a mammoth defensive tackle rips the opposing lineman with a vicious forearm, whomps the fullback on the helmet with a blow that resounds like a busted melon, and scratches and claws his way to crunch the unwary passer beneath 240 pounds of bone and muscle, the crowd cheers. But, most likely, some mother gulps and holds her breath until the pile untangles and the object of the assault rushes back to the huddle. Then she breathes again, for she, above all, knows that the unlucky quarterback is not some stalwart invincible gladiator, but *her own baby boy*. And, no doubt, somewhere else in the stands, another mother is thinking the same thoughts about that big, ugly, brute of a tackle.

The mother's anguish was vividly brought home to me in a 1969 Idaho State University football game. For us, it was the game of the century inasmuch as ISU had never defeated its sister institution, the Vandals from the University of Idaho. Our hopes rested on the strong arm and power running of our talented quarterback, Jerry Dunne. I sat behind his parents at the game.

ISU jumped off to a quick 21 to 0 lead, then we jointly suffered as it withered under a furious Idaho passing game. In the final half, our foe would strike swiftly and pull within a touchdown margin, then Jerry Dunne would move his team the length of the field to again widen our lead.

By the latter stages of the third quarter, Dunne's mother had had all she could take—she bugged out—thus missing a thrilling finish where her son led his team to a 47 to 42 victory. The boy had displayed all the poise and confidence of a young Napoleon while his mother personified the Wreck of the Hesperus.

Meanwhile, the father stayed and survived every play. His post-game comments were classical as he overlooked his son's four touchdowns by rushing and one by passing and wryly stated,

"Jerry would never have had those two interceptions if he had gotten the nose of the ball higher . . ."

As one who has experienced almost a lifetime of football both as a player and an observer, I have come to appreciate the personal involvement of parents in the throes of a game—or even a scrimmage.

To me, my dad was always exhibit "A". My first contact with varsity football came as an undistinguished sophomore quarterback at Loveland High School back in 1944. Much to my embarrassment, my dad just couldn't stay away from the practice field and each night stopped by on his way home from work. I begrudgingly accepted this, but only on the condition that he stay behind the fence and out of sight.

One night as we prepared for our game against Longmont High (from a neighboring Colorado community), our fullback stepped from the huddle and informed the coach that some mysterious stranger was hiding behind the fence and scouting our plays. I knew who the mysterious stranger was, all right, but I wasn't talking.

The coach called us together and said, *"We've got a Longmont scout hiding behind the bushes there. Now on the next play, run the ball over to the sideline, then take off and catch him."*

I participated with mixed emotions. Fortunately, for me, and, for him, my dad saw the mob race through the gate. He managed to keep a few strides ahead, reach the safety of the car, and roar off. His anonymity, and mine, was preserved.

Later, when I was playing football at the University of Colorado, it was still preserved—that is, up until my senior year when we met the University of Oregon. It was Dad's Day, and the fathers of the players were invited to sit on the bench. I think my Dad was proudest of all. My college career had been fraught with much frustration and little glory, but this obviously was to be a high point.

In the fourth quarter, we were sitting on a comfortable lead when Coach Dal Ward called me off the bench. *"Davis,"* he said, *"for three long years your dad has been coming to these games, and he hasn't seen much. Now get in there at blocking back, and for heaven's sake, don't embarrass him."*

The only embarrassment my dad suffered was the fluttering of 30,000 programs as spectators flipped through the pages to find out who number 25 was rushing onto the field.

But my father was nothing compared to Harry Narcissian's mother. Harry, the mad Armenian, was a splendid athlete—a 9.8 sprinter in track and the star tailback on Colorado U.'s football team. On one notable occasion, in the Kansas State game, Harry broke loose on an end run and headed for a long touchdown.

His mother promptly jumped over the retaining wall and raced down the field with him, matching him stride for stride and yelling, *"Go, Haree-ee-ee!"* She beat him to the end zone by a full five yards.

She wasn't the only mother I have seen on the field. Years later, when I was coaching football at the University of Colorado, we were in the waning seconds of what had been a long afternoon. We ran what we thought was the final play, and the gun sounded. Amidst much confusion, the crowd rushed on the field as the players started off. But, there had been a penalty on the play, and the officials called the teams back on the field for another down.

A mother of one of our players had been caught in the chaos and she, too, remained on the field. With great dignity, she walked over to our huddle, accosted her son, and said, *"Well, I'll bet you're surprised to see* me *here."*

To which he replied, *"I certainly am, Mother. I certainly am."*

More recently, I have discovered that the problems of football parents even carry over into college administration. One fall afternoon, I called Chuck Kegel, our Academic Vice President, about a minor crisis. His secretary registered some surprise and blurted out, "He left a half hour ago for your office for your Administrative Council Meeting." Later, on my way home, I stopped off to take in a Little League football game. There, with a sheepish expression on his face, was the truant Academic Vice President, watching his son play center for the Franklin Flyspecks. Earnestly, he pleaded with me never to divulge his secret, lest it impair his reputation with the more academic types of the faculty. And earnestly, I promised him I never would.

That same fall I received a phone call from an anxious mother in a neighboring farming community renowned for its big, strapping football players. Her son was coming to Idaho State on a football scholarship, and she wanted to know if I would mind meeting him at the train station. I replied that we usually tried to provide transportation for students from the station to the campus.

"Well, that really wasn't all I was asking," she continued. "What I really meant was would you keep an eye on him personally? You know, little things like seeing that he changes his socks and underwear regularly, eats three square meals a day, and gets to bed early. Furthermore, I don't want him smoking or drinking or chasing around with those wild university coeds."

"That's a pretty tall order," I pointed out.

"I know it is," she replied, "but, you see, this is the first time he has been away from home—except for the four years he was in the Marine Corps."

I muffed my first two chances at being the parent of a football player, and cheerfully settled for two daughters. But on the third try, we had a boy.

At age eight, he showed great promise—little things like sleeping with his football or stopping off on the way home from school to watch the ISU Bengals practice. I know that these symptoms are but fore-runners of my test as a football parent. But when my time comes, I firmly resolve not to be one of those fathers who scrutinizes every move his son makes on the field, charts his findings in a notebook, then reviews each play with him at home. I, if anyone, should know that this makes the boy self-conscious, nervous, and apprehensive. For the record, however, my son runs the Z-out, the fly, the post, and the hook patterns with great enthusiasm. Now, if he would just set his feet further apart on his stance, get his tail up, relax his hands when he catches the ball, and . . .

Football parents are an incorrigible lot, especially when they learn that the slowest kid in town emptying the garbage is the fastest back on the field carrying a football under his arm.

DEBBIE AND THE DRILL TEAM

What with all the nostagia aroused by the reflections on parents and their sons and football, I began to be troubled by a guilty awareness that with the exception of Doug (who shared breakfast with me), I hadn't seen my others kids for some time, namely Becky and Debbie. The more I thought about it the more it appeared that something mysterious was going on the way they were gone before daylight every morning and didn't return until after dark.

Finally, my curiousity got the better of me, and one morning over my shredded wheat, I asked Polly, *"Where are Debbie and Becky these days?"*

"I'll bet if you had two boys on the football team you'd know where they were," she snapped.

Slightly chaagrined, I meekly added, *"So, where are they?"*

"Well," she replied with an irritating smugness, *"Becky's practicing her cheerleading, and Debbie's at drill team. You remember drill team?"*

"Oh, boy," I thought, *"did I remember drill team!"*

When Debbie first started to Poky High, I didn't even know what drill team was. As an ex-coach, I had been vaguely aware of the presence of cheer leaders and pom-pom girls during the course of ball games. Also, I had some hazy notion that during half-times, the band did its thing while husbands, fathers, and boy friends stood in long lines for hot dogs and cokes. But, drill team, that was something else.

It all started innocently enough. First Debbie had to be selected for the Pep Club. She passed that muster in good style. We purchased her three costumes, and her career was launched. Little did I know at the time that it would soon develop into an academic major.

In the spring of her sophomore year, however, I began to suspect that something was cooking. There was a certain tension in the air as communications broke down and the panic level went up. I thought for awhile that Debbie had acquired some physical affliction or nervous tic. She marched around the house snapping her head at odd angles, turning square corners, making violent gestures with her hands and arms, and counting—always counting.

My patient wife explained that this was Debbie's way of rehearsing for drill team tryouts. I was further informed that on a crucial day in May, some one hundred and fifty aspiring females would be competing for twenty highly coveted positions on the drill team. I volunteered as to how if I were Debbie, I'd much rather sit in the stands and watch the ball games. I was ignored.

As the fateful day approached, however, I sensed that this was no trifling matter of merely being selected for a team, but rather something that could profoundly affect her whole life. At least, that was the incredulous pitch that was made to me.

The day of the big try-out, I rushed home from the office to learn the results. Anxiously, we waited dinner, while Debbie stopped off on the way from school to bury her anxiety in three milk shakes. At last she arrived, heart-sick. She had been out of step twice, and on her splits her bottom had been a foot from the floor.

"Enough of the details," I snapped. *"Did you make the team?"*

"I won't know until tomorrow morning," she sighed, rushing off to call her friends and commiserate on how poorly they all did. From the sound of things, I anticipated that no one had made it.

As she left for school the next morning, her mother instructed her to call as soon as she saw the list posted on the bulletin board. As I left for work, I instructed my wife to call as soon as Debbie called.

Not much business was transacted that day as I nervously eyed the phone. When five o'clock came and there was still no word, I resigned myself to entering into a long period of mourning and joylessly headed home. Debbie and I arrived at the same time, and I could tell by the fact that she was doing handsprings up the front walk that something good had happened. Little did I know.

The first rehearsal for the new members was scheduled for 6:00 a.m. the following morning. That meant getting up at 5:30 to take Debbie to school. I accepted this begrudgingly as the least I could do to assure my daughter's successful career as a high school student without realizing that it was to be a daily event.

Thus, the first jolt was to hit our sleeping habits. The second, however, hit my pocketbook. I was to discover that the drill team needed more changes of costume than the chorus line in the

Ziegfeld Follies. The family sewing machine was soon humming like a garment factory.

As an old, retired coach, I could appreciate the importance of regimentation and discipline, but the seniors in charge of shaping up and training the neophytes made Marine Corps Drill Instructors look like Sunday school teachers. They were tough. I got the idea from Debbie that if one missed a practice, they probably chopped your head off, or at least a leg. Snow, rain, fog, or illness were no excuse. On at least a couple of occasions, when she had the flu, she would get up for drill team practice and then come home to go to bed.

I foolishly reckoned that this silliness at least would end when school let out in June. But, I was wrong again. Morning and evening practices were scheduled all through the summer months. Plans for a family vacation were set aside so that Debbie could march in every county fair within hauling distance.

I groused about the fact that if the football coach were to make the same demands on his players throughout the summer, he would be strung up by the thumbs for over-emphasis. At one point, I even threatened to call the principal to protest. But not wishing to spend the rest of my life alone, I demurred and kept my silence.

The first home football game of the season also marked the inaugural half-time performance of the drill team. It was a miserable day with a chilling wind whipping across the field at about thirty knots. Before the game I had pleaded with Debbie to wear some warm underclothes under her scanty costume, or at least take a heavy coat. But she paid no heed. I could picture her sitting in the stands—just one big purple goosebump.

For the first time in my life, the outcome of the game was of secondary importance. My great concern was how Debbie would do with the drill team. Again, I had been led to believe that if a girl got out of line, the only way she could atone for her sin was to commit hari-kari on the high school steps the following Monday morning. I had real butterflies in my stomach as half-time approached.

Finally, the gun ended the half. The teams rushed off the field; the drill team marched on. Doug got up to go get a bag of popcorn. "Sit down," I growled, "and watch your sister."

"Which one is she?" he asked.

"Darned if I know," I replied as sixty girls strutted between the goal posts, arms swinging, heads snapping, eyes popping, teeth shining. (I could not help but reflect that there must be a lot of happy, wealthy orthodontists in the crowd.)

The drill went off without a hitch right up to the finale. The grand climax consisted of each girl leaping eight feet in the air and coming down in the splits. I cringed at the very thought.

All performed the ritual, however. But when they got up to march off the field, it was obvious that one girl had become locked in the splits. It took four football players to carry her off in that position. All through the second half I kept watching her, which was easy enough. With one leg going each direction, she took up eight seats in the cheering section. I kept hoping it wasn't Debbie.

So it went, all through the football and basketball season. Pre-dawn practices, long bus rides, strained muscles, more costumes. With the conclusion of the state basketball tournament, I thought the worst was over. But, again I was wrong. I didn't know of the state-wide drill team competition in Boise. If anything, the pace became more hectic and frantic.

There was an outside chance that Debbie might not get to go. Only the best were to be selected for the big meet, and she was an alternate. But her luck (and mine) held. One of the first-stringers pulled a ham-string (probably the same one who got hung up at the football game), and Debbie leaped into the fray.

The morning of the great adventure, she got up at 4:00 a.m. to pack her lunch—three twinkie cup-cakes and a box of cheese crackers. With great expectations, she took off, literally.

They left on a Friday and planned to return after the final event on Saturday night. That meant an all-night bus ride, so Saturday night we left the door unlocked and went to bed.

At 5:30, my wife and I were still awake. She noted with some alarm that Debbie was not home. I calmed her apprehensions by noting that it was at least a five-hour drive from Boise, and allowing three more hours for them to eat, they should arrive by six.

For once, I was right. Debbie came dragging in just as the sun came up. I could tell by the look on her face that something terrible had happened.

She gave us a blow-by-blow description, beginning: "Daddy, there were over 1300 girls in that meet, and, Daddy, you just couldn't believe the squealing and confusion."

I acknowledged as to how I really could believe it.

"Well," she continued, "we all had to dress in the locker rooms of the gym at one of the high schools. And we got the boys' locker room. You know boys' locker rooms?"

I nodded. I knew about boys' locker rooms.

"They have only one mirror—one little tiny mirror. We couldn't get our make-up on or our hair combed, or anything."

I chuckled. My wife gouged me in the ribs as Debbie went on with her tale.

"Well, they gave us these directions for the parade. We were supposed to march up to this block where the judges were, and when a man signaled with his arm, go into our drill routine. Well, we marched beautifully, right up to the judges' stand. The man signaled and signaled, but Bubbles, that's our head drill leader, didn't see him. She just kept smiling and smiling and strutting and strutting, and we never *did our routine. We marched right by the judges and into oblivion."* At that, Debbie broke up completely.

"Poor Debbie," I thought. "Poor drill team. And, above all, poor Bubbles. Probably no one will ever speak to her again. All that work and no routine."

I was tender; I was understanding; I was compassionate as I kissed Debbie good-night (or good-morning). After all, I could afford to be. There were no more drill team events that year. And, glory be, the next year Debbie would be a senior, and the following year she would be out of drill team and into college.

But, as I trundled off to bed, I was hit by the cold, stark realization that my second daughter, Becky, would be a high school sophomore the coming year and a candidate for the team. As I lay in bed staring at the ceiling, I wondered if I were up to it.

Boy, did I remember drill team!

BECKY DAVIS' RESIDENCE

Becky is the kind of girl, who, when her dad is watching a pro football game on television in the den, brings him a bowl of hot buttered popcorn. She aims to please. Unlike her big sister, Debbie, who thinks that getting ahead in life means to run faster, jump higher, and hit harder, Becky is an advocate of smiles and loving diplomacy.

This contrast in sisterly character affected the discipline pattern in our household. By laying it on Debbie, one seldom had to raise his voice with Becky. She was so impressed with the chaos and turmoil in Debbie's life that she studiously avoided the conflicts and confrontations that plagued her elder sister.

When Debbie first got interested in boys and singled one out—ZAP! The poor fellow never had a chance. Napoleon never calculated a campaign with a cooler eye for detail. With Becky, it was the other way around. She just smiled and waited for the phone to ring.

Fortunately, I had anticipated that with two teen-age daughters the President's house should have an alternate line in case someone had to reach me in an emergency. But Becky foiled the plan. She talked on both lines—at the same time. (Statistically, I have observed that one out of twenty phone calls is for me.) The traffic became so heavy that I began answering, "Becky Davis' residence."

But while I became embroiled handling the problems of the University, Polly handled the problems of Becky Davis' Taxi Service. It usually began in the pre-dawn (7:00 a.m.) hauls for drill team (in junior high!) practice and the countless rounds of after-school junior high athletic events, social functions, and activities. But, on occasion, I got the duty.

For example, there was the night Polly asked me if I would take Becky and her friends to the picture show and pick them up afterwards. I grumpily laid down the evening paper and complied.

Little did I realize that it would take a good hour just for the collection. She had a friend in every corner of town.

Popularity, however, had its rewards, because the fall Becky was a ninth-grader, she was nominated to try out as a cheerleader. She worked hard in preparation for the big event and pacticed her gyrations in the living room—until the evening one mighty leap ripped off the light fixture. That night I was sound asleep when I heard this steady thumping in the house. I crawled out of bed to see if the wind was banging an open window. It was only Becky giving three rahs and a tiger in her bedroom—at 1:00 a.m.! By the time the big day arrived, she was so stiff and sore from all her contortions that she could hardly hobble to school.

She was elected, thank God! And I was glad. Otherwise, I would have been wearing a black armband in mourning for the rest of the year.

Later that fall, (by this time I was playing the role of the interested, dutiful father) I attended a junior high football game to watch my daughter perform. There were more cheerleaders than spectators on this raw, miserable day. A biting wind had turned the cheerleaders' legs bluer than the royal blue of the Franklin Junior High Flyspeck uniforms. But the girls were oblivious to the goose bumps and chill-blains as they loyally leaped and cheered from the opening kick-off in what they regarded as Pocatello's version of the Super Bowl.

Shivering and shaking before the blasts of the biting winds, I could stand it no longer. Finally, I went down to Becky and offered her my coat. The silly goose refused and even seemed embarrassed. "Daddy," she protested, "Get back in the stands."

Feeling a little foolish, I then volunteered to teach her and her friends some new yells. That met with an equally chilly reception as she gave me that "Daddy, how could you?" look.

Greatly chagrined, I slunk back to the stands.

After the game, I delivered her friends to their respective homes (in every corner of town) in my most amiable fashion. But I was shocked to learn that not only had they never seen a single play in the game, they did not even know the final score! It was enough that they had cheered fiercely.

As my bright-eyed Becky raced from the car to the house to answer the ringing phone, I began to worry. With her philosophy of never wanting to hurt anyone's feelings, I wondered how she would ever measure up to her mother's ability to say, "No."

A SMALL BOY IN A BIG HOUSE

What Doug liked most about his dad being president was the big University-owned house we got to live in.

The President's home at Idaho State University has a charm and mystique all its own. Built by a Basque sheep tycoon in 1918, it was purchased by the college in 1949, and since that date has served as the residence for the respective presidents and their families.

It is a spacious dwelling rising three stories above ground. In all, it contains some sixteen rooms; but its chief excitement lies in the hidden nooks and crannies that delight a small boy. For example, a long bannister running down the stairway to the front hall provides an exhilarating slide for one desiring a quick descent. Hideouts for times of crises plague an exasperated mother searching for a wayward offspring. And an eight-year-old can throw a fair-to-middling forward pass the length of the upstairs hallway.

On sunny days a thousand footsteps echo on the stairs as hordes of neighborhood youngsters race up to the balcony overlooking the front lawn—the scene of the launching of many a paper airplane or the dropping of a ball to a friend below. On the dreary days, there is the laughter around a game of Monopoly or Stratego in front of the living room fireplace.

The house is so ample that one is prompted to share—an urge amply reflected in our son, Doug, the year he was eight. With no reservations, I approved, for example, the setting up of a lemonade stand in the front yard. I had no notion, however, of the instincts of the entrepreneur that led to his other enterprises until one August day I was in my den typing a speech. With some surprise, I greeted Doug, accompanied by a delegation of five or six youngsters who were strangers to me. He obviously was giving them a guided tour of the house, which included my own hideout. His narrative was a little startling as he carefully explained, ". . . and the University pays for all the heat and lights and telephone bills and when something gets broken Mom just calls up and . . ."

"How nice," I thought, "but I'll have to have a talk with him later and explain that we don't advertise all these details to the general public."

My alarm increased several fold, however, when I walked out the front door. The lemonade stand, obviously, had been doing poorly, and his business venture had taken on a new twist as the sign now read:

"TURE THE MANSHUN—10c"

The house also lends itself to a lot of entertaining—another family activity Doug enters into with great exuberance. He greets guests, carries coats, and picks up empty plates. Occasionally, he adds a touch all of his own.

That summer, following the Commencement exercises, we invited a large group of parents and students over for dinner in the back yard. Now Doug took great pride in the back yard, especially in the fountain which featured the head of a lion spewing water into a small pond. With his own artistic flair, he poured a box of Ivory Flakes into the pool. When we arrived with our guests, the suds were a good five feet high and Doug was frantically throwing them over the back wall with a snow shovel. The lion spat beautiful suds most of the summer.

His gardening added another dimension. The pumpkin and squash growing up the Greek columns on the side of the house were one thing, but when the corn stalks began to poke their way through the roses on the patio, we all were amazed.

His big moment for front-stage, center, was yet to come. In retrospect, I am sure that the October 15, 1969, Moratorium protesting the war in Vietnam was observed in a variety of ways on the campuses throughout the country. At our house, however, it took a most unusual twist, thanks to Doug.

He was still in the throes of a thrilling football victory over Montana State University and a gala homecoming celebration the previous weekend. Reading that a group of students were planning a parade through Pocatello to be capped off by a rally on our front lawn, he naturally interpreted this as an extension of the Homecoming festivities. He aimed to give them an appropriate welcome.

Mustering a group of neighborhood chums, he called on a near-by fraternity house and talked the willing students out of the remnants of their Homecoming float. The loot included signs that read:—"We want blood!"—"Scalp the Bobcats!"—and a large crepe paper display that proclaimed—"ISU—We're Number One!"

Arriving home from the office on the eventful evening, and barely a half hour before the scheduled demonstration was to appear, I found Doug and his buddies industriously winding orange and black paper around the pillars in front of the house. The rest of the display had already been erected.

We were still tearing down the display when the peace marchers (some three hundred) assembled in our front yard. While I held forth on the fundamental right to peaceable assembly and protest, Doug and his friends were marching around in a fair imitation of the Idaho State cheering section chanting, "We're Number One! We're Number One!" When the peace marchers gave him the two-fingered symbol for peace, he happily flashed it back, thinking it was the Cub Scout sign.

Someday, hopefully many years from now, another president and his family will look at the name scratched in what was once fresh cement, or find a forgotten baseball bat in a hidden corner, and know that once a small boy lived in and loved this home.

GROWL, BENGALS, GROWL

There was a time when I thought that three children was a nice-sized family, and that anyone with four or more kids was either under-educated or over-sexed. But I had to revise my philosophy in the fall of 1969 when it became apparent to even the most casual observer that Polly was pregnant *again*!

The Idaho State University fight song is, "Growl, Bengals, Growl." It could well have been the theme song of our household during the Christmas holidays of 1969. In Polly's pregnant condition, nothing very funny happened.

For example, take the day when Doug came home from school with his shoe laces untied. Polly burst into tears. I was amazed. For eight years Doug has been running around with his shoe strings untied. Meekly, I inquired as to why that should upset her at this time. Sobbing, she replied that he *could* tie his shoes and *wouldn't* and she *would* tie her shoes, but *couldn't*.

Later, deciding that too many holidays banquets were taking their toll on my waistline, I engaged upon a crash program to lose ten pounds. When I succeeded, she pouted because I had slimmed down just to embarrass her by contrast.

Everybody worked hard to boost her morale. Doug washed his face. Becky quit shaking the foundations of the house with her cheer-leading gyrations. Debbie turned her radio down to a low roar. Even the cat tip-toed around the house.

The University alumni director also got into the act. For the Christmas edition of the alumni news, he featured a picture from the previous year's holiday ball, showing my wife, trim and svelte, in front of the punch bowl holding a glass of cranberry juice and sherbet. Alongside was her chubby friend, puffed up like he had just eaten the Christmas goose.

Even this, however, backfired, as the nurse in the doctor's office inquired at the bi-weekly check-up: "Who is that woman standing with your husband?"

The following week, I opened the office mail to find an anonymous letter from Logan, Utah, (the home of Utah State University). It was addressed to my wife:

> *Mrs. Davis:*
> *Couldn't you pose without a glass in your hands? It surely gives a questionable impression on the kind of people who are the "first family." I'm sure you'd never find any of our "first families" posing this way. We have too much of this in this world without those who are supposed to be leaders to set this kind of image.*

I never delivered the letter. I did, however, instruct the University photographer that at that year's Christmas ball to refrain from taking pictures of my pregnant wife, lest some blue-nose suspect we had been doing worse things than drinking cranberry punch.

The unkindest blow of all came at the pre-holiday basketball game between ISU and Boise State College. Everyone jumped up when our band played, "Growl, Bengals, Growl!" By the time Polly got to her feet, the fight song was over—and so was the game!

AN ANXIOUS CHRISTMAS

In the waning days of 1969, as we were sitting around the breakfast table one morning picking out possible names for the anticipated newest arrival in the Davis family, eight-year-old Doug piped up, "I don't care whether it's a boy or a girl," he said with a sigh, "I just hope it is a *nice* baby."

"Me, too," his sister, Becky, chimed in.

This provided their mother with the entré for an illustrative discussion on how whether or not it was a nice baby would depend on how it was treated by the rest of the family—whether we loved it, played with it, taught it to do things. Doug chewed on this weighty philosophy for awhile, then noted, "Poor Debbie. She had no big brothers or sisters to play with her. She never had a chance!"

Poor Debbie, indeed, sitting there with her hair piled high in curlers, grease all over her face, eating her toast while filing her nails. Thank heaven, she didn't always look like that—not by a long shot.

A short time before as a high school sophomore, she had discovered boys. About a year later they discovered her. The latter was no accident, but rather the culmination of a cold, calculated, and expensive campaign. It had involved $600 worth of braces to straighten one slightly crooked front tooth, contact lenses so prospective admirers could appreciate the blue makeup on her eyes, and a wardrobe that would bring out the best in her. Wistfully, I sometimes wondered if life were not simpler when she had crooked teeth, wore horn-rimmed glasses, and was flat-chested.

As she rushed from the table to answer the phone, I reflected on how Debbie *had* been the trail-blazer in the family—a kind of pioneer in all the love and affection and high expectations parents traditionally heap upon their first-born. Nostalgically, I thought back on our first meeting. She was a year old when I returned

210

from Korea, and as the carols on the radio wafted about the kitchen, I remembered that first Christmas with her.

From an old baby album not opened in years, I dug out a letter I had written to her on that occasion when she was a bouncing, babbling, fifteen-month-old baby girl.

It is almost Christmas Eve, my Debbie. And yet you sleep in the same soft, fuzzy way, bottoms up, in your crib. No "visions of sugar plums dance in your head," and St. Nickolas is only the funny man in the red suit and white beard who gave you your first sucker some days ago; probably already forgotten. You have accepted the wonders of Christmas in much the same manner you have crowded turning over, walking, and your first baby words into your fifteen months of wisdom. You have been delighted at the tree, the tinsel, the music, and the packages; and still, I wonder if you will ever know how much more special and wonderful you have made this Christmas for all of us?

Can I ever forget how you helped us trim the tree? How you helped me fix the base by crawling beneath the branches and grabbing the screw driver and hammer and running away in high glee. It was while we were stringing the lights that you pulled the tree over on you, and peered out in amazed surprise between the branches.

You especially loved to pat and stroke the branches and yell, "Purdy! Purdy!" at the top of your lusty voice. The ornaments were fascinating. You would pat them with increasing firmness until you had them swinging like punching bags. And the icicles! Well, you delighted in taking them one by one and draping them in your own delicate way on the tree, knocking a dozen off for every one you added. But it was good sport and worth it all to see your face light up when the lights went on that night.

As for the Christmas music, you don't distinguish "Oh Come All Ye Faithful from "Semper Fidelis," but you dance well to either in your up and down bouncing style.

And the presents! You grab them one by one and march from room to room, clutching them with the same tenacity you hug your teddy bear or drag your doll around by the hair. And your mother is thankful you haven't discovered that if you tear off the paper you will find something even more delightful and interesting inside. Christmas morning should add that bit of useful information to your mounting store of knowledge.

I have tried to explain to you about Santa Claus. But it is difficult to put that wonderful legend into terms that you can understand with your vocabulary of, "Doll, ball, purdy, peese, dog, buoy, and hot." But I have a hunch you have the general idea.

For weeks, your grandparents and your mother and I have been happily anticipating this Christmas morning when you will look beneath your tree and find the rocking horse and dolls and train and clothes and all the bright, colorful things calculated to please the heart of a fifteen-month-old baby girl. And while you sleep peacefully in the other room, we can hardly wait!

Yes, my Debbie, no cherub's cheeks are as fat and rosy as yours. No ornament on the tree can match the sparkle of your bright eyes. No song brings the pleasure of your delighted laughter. And no candle matches the glow of your smile. So, a very merry Christmas to you, Debbie, for the merry Christmas you bring to all of us!

I agreed with Doug. I, too, hoped it would be a *nice* baby, just like the other three we have loved and enjoyed so much.

WOULD YOU BELIEVE TWIN GIRLS?

"Would you believe twin girls?" I was stunned. The doctor looked at me sheepishly. "But," I stammered, "you promised me one nice big baby?"

He shrugged and smiled, "Win a few, lose a few." Then he walked back into the delivery room while I nibbled the stem off my pipe.

"Would you believe twin girls?" I passed the word on to Becky via the telephone. That was like flashing is on the ten o'clock newscast. Her communications network crackled and sparked and took off in all directions. I could relax. I knew in thirty seconds the message would be all over town.

Meanwhile, back at the hospital, I rationalized that this time I was very much on the scene. As I watched the nurses clean and polish the new products, I speculated on what I knew about twins, and came up with nothing.

They were beautiful—faces like two pink rose petals—curly black hair—tiny features complete down to the last dimples on their dainty, clawing hands. They greeted me with a yawn, then a whimper. But my first look at them was a moment of sheer ecstacy.

"Would you believe twin girls?" Everywhere I went the news was accompanied by a laughting—"You've got to be kidding!" To which I replied, "Yeah—twice!"

Doug accepted the big event with stoicism. Now he was surrounded by girls—two above and two below—a hundred per cent increase in sisters in five minutes, and all he had wanted was someone to play catch with. Parodying that Doublemint advertisement, he went around singing, "Double your *trouble,* double your fun . . ." But at least he had a tidy bit of gossip for show and tell. He threw the third grade at the Campus Laboratory School into an uproar by announcing that we were going to name them Avis and Mavis Davis. I had twenty protesting phone calls from irate mothers.

The family council, however, vetoed that inspiration and settled on Bonnie and Brooke.

Messages came pouring in. One legislator wired: "We're impressed by your handling of the problem of overpopulation. Now what are you doing about air pollution?"

Anxiously we looked forward to getting the mother and the twins home. I raced around buying two of everything. Doug raced around taping all the drawers and cupboards shut so the twins wouldn't get into everything. (It was hard to explain to him that it would be some time before they could play catch with him.) Becky and Debbie and my mother-in-law just raced around.

Brooke, who was four minutes younger but one pound heavier than Bonnie, came home with Polly. Doug could hardly wait to get his hands on her, having never seen anything that tiny. But he was in his usual after-school state of muddy disrepair. His mother promised he could hold the baby if he would take a bath. I never saw such immediate action on his part. We started calling him "Mister Clean."

In retrospect, aside from my own pride in my contribution to the great adventure, I acknowledged that Polly also had done well. She had managed to sandwich the event between an Idaho-ISU basketball game and a legislative hearing. But while I appreciated her efforts to make me the Father of the Year for 1970 among college presidents, I wondered if she were not showing off just a bit.

Reflecting on the traumas of steering two daughters through their turbulent teens, I firmly resolved that the twins certainly would never be spoiled in the manner of their elder sisters. In the meantime, I allowed as how I might as well go out and shoot baskets with Doug.

For some time after the birth of the twins, we received congratulations, condolences, admonitions, and advice—often all in the same message. Most apropos was a greeting from my friendly banker who welcomed Polly and me to the "3+2=5 Club." (He and his wife also had a nice family of three children before adding twins.) His warm remarks concluded on this chilling note:

Raising twin daughters certainly does complicate the college problem. But if you immediately start saving and living frugally for the next 18 years, you will be able to send them both to some fine girls' school. Then, for the next four years, you and Polly can be extremely proud while you are living in abject poverty.

A quick mathematical calculation also reminded me that by about the time Bonnie and Brooke were graduating from college, their parents would be going on Social Security.

Meanwhile, our household adjusted to a routine wherein someone was eating or crying around the clock. The regular schedule called for feedings at two, six, and ten—p.m. and a.m. The irregular schedule asserted itself when Bonnie was on the two, six, and ten schedule and Brooke was on the four, eight, and twelve. Polly finally got them synchronized, which meant that they were both hungry and howling at the same time.

For me, there was no way out. At first I tried burrowing my head under the pillow while Polly attended to the chores. But when my ribs turned black and blue from the sharp jabs of irate elbows, I cheerfully got out of my warm bed to feed whichever twin was handed me.

As the weeks passed, I did get to see a lot of my wife, however, as we visited during the nocturnal feedings. In the daytime, it was hard to see her at all behind that pile of five dozen diapers. There were moments I thought it would have been more appropriate to have named the twins Donnie and Brooke.

But the joys of "fatherhood rediscovered" did provide the entré for a light touch as I was introduced at various events on the winter banquet circuit. In fact, I began to view my prowess and virility with considerable pride until I read of a couple in Provo, Utah, who had had *two* sets of twins in *one* year. That whetted my competitive instinct. With grim determination, I announced, "A challenge is a challenge." To which Polly replied, "Why don't you go skiing?"

It remained for fifteen-year-old Becky to have the last word. I asked her how her friends had received the good news of the twins. She replied, "Well, Daddy. Twins are very embarrassing. It's bad enough that my friends know that mother and you do *it* at all. But, Daddy! Twice in one night!"

216

A CONVENTION OF PRESIDENTS

While steering and herding my family through this series of exciting events in the fall and winter of 1969-70, from time to time I *was* involved in presidenting.

As a general rule, I hold to the theory that a president on campus is generally worth two in the air, and try to limit my out-of-state travel accordingly. But occasionally I succumb to the urge to find out what is going on outside these "everlasting" hills and join my presidential colleagues in some kind of national meeting.

Outwardly, a gathering of college presidents may resemble a convention of morticians. The traditional uniform consists of conservative gray suits and dark ties, while the atmosphere reeks of an air of mourning. But far from being a pious, stuffy lot of faceless conformists (attributed by their respective faculties with a collective low animal cunning sharpened by an uncanny instinct for survival), inwardly, there beats many a stout heart of defiant individualism. One such convention of presidents rekindled my conviction that the flames of passion and potential militancy were rampant, indeed.

During a discussion of unrest on the campus, one courageous soul (camouflaged in a gray suit) orated on the evils of tenure and the need for change. Audaciously, he proclaimed that he had never known a genuine student movement that was not faculty inspired. "If presidents are to survive," he warned, "they had best band together in an organization of their own—such as the President's Protective Association, or, perhaps, The Society for the Preservation of College Presidents."

There was a stir amongst the crowd, and even a feeble, "Hear! Hear!" Encouraged, he ventured to propose that one way to re-establish the administration would be to "do in" those who were seeking to "do in" administrators.

An audible gasp shook the ranks. There was no lack of awesome respect for his Nathan Hale approach of having but one life to give for higher education. In fact, there was a kind of touching nobility about his desperate plea. But his torch of enlightenment was snuffed out in a hurry by his more rational colleagues. They were of the same breed who, had they been present when Washington shoved off to cross the Delaware would have cautioned, "Sit down, George, old boy, you're rocking the boat."

In short, they belonged to the Silas Marner group—squint and grope. But if the brave proposal had been shouted down, at least the sparks were there.

I was among those timid souls who sat on their hands and glanced about suspiciously. And as the talk turned to the safer and more dramatic topic of modern campus architecture and its relationship to the poverty program, I mused about presidents I had known who had reacted to crisis in an individualistic manner.

I chuckled quietly as I recalled the president who administered his campus in the grand style of a Teddy Roosevelt—the Rough Rider all the way. After years of procrastinating on whether or not to tear down the old stadium in the heart of the campus in favor of constructing a new one on the fringe area, his cautious Regents finally acted. When the news was released, however, sentimental alumni and the anti-athletic element of the faculty put the heat on the Regents to reconsider their decision. Whereupon, the chairman of the Board called the president and instructed him to defer any further developments until the next meeting.

The president answered (allegedly with straight face): "I'm sorry, sir, but the demolition process is already underway." Upon hanging up, he quickly called the head of Buildings and Grounds to instruct him to get out there with a bulldozer and knock the stadium down. That night, they put the torch to the remnants of the structure in what must have been the grandest bonfire in the history of the school.

Then there was the prototype of Renfrew of the Mounties— he always got his man. From the day he arrived on campus as president, his chief antagonist and chief critic had been the well-entrenched registrar—a man who had never been away from the institution since arriving as a smooth-faced freshman at the turn of the century. For several decades, the pair fought and scrapped, giving and taking no quarter. Finally, the registrar was scheduled to retire. The president, by virtue of a one-year extension of his own retirement, at last had the upper hand.

The morning following the registrar's last official day in office, he had the audacity to pay a final visit to the administrative building and park in his old parking place. With great glee, the president called the campus police and ordered the registrar's car towed away.

Not all presidents dress or act in quiet, somber tones. There are a few dandies. One such president had all the flair and flash of a Gaylord Ravanal, the riverboat gambler. He was resplendent in sartorial garb that included pink shirts and a Pepsodent smile. Forbearing the customary hearse-like Cadillac, he roared around the campus in a Stingray, much to the delight of students and consternation of the liberal members of the faculty.

He also was a physical-culture fiend, and created quite a stir when he dug up the rose garden in back of the president's house and installed a heated swimming pool. Soon, his daily routine included an early morning jog of some three miles around the campus, followed by a brisk dip in the pool. The sub-zero weather was not deterrent, and his contempt for the elements was much admired.

All went well until the night the heating unit in the pool failed and the water turned into a solid sheet of ice. In the pre-dawn darkness, the intrepid president ran his three miles, shed his sweat clothes, and executed a brilliant jack-knife off the board.

He later moved to a more hospitable clime.

Turning closer to home, I proudly recalled a sterling individualistic performance by the President of the University of Idaho, Dr. Ernest Hartung. When the debonair Hartung arrived in the state in 1965, he was regarded in some quarters as an Ivy Leaguer all the way, what with his degrees at Dartmouth and Harvard and professional career in New England institutions. But as testimony that a man can overcome his environment, his performance at a legislative hearing endeared him to the hearts of all true Westerners.

In essence, he overwhelmed the senators and representatives from Sirloin Row with logic and rhetoric and emerged as the man in the white hat on the white horse. It all came about when the chairman of a budget and finance hearing asked the president if the University of Idaho budget request could be chopped with the understanding that if the cuts worked a hardship, the legislature might appropriate more money the following year. Hartung's reply was classic. "You are a rancher," he answered the senator, "and you know that once you castrate a critter, you can't do anything about it a year later if it proves to be a mistake."

That carried the day. On the evening news telecast, the reporter referred to the urbane university president as a "poet of persuasion."

Such men stand out like windmills in a wheatfield.

Meanwhile, back at the convention, as the session droned on, I turned from notalgia to philosophy and mentally dwelled upon the dilemmas of a modern college administrator.

If the college president purports to know the answers and shows confidence in his decisions, there are those who will call him arrogant.

If he "runs a tight ship" (regardless of how hard he tries to govern by democratic processes), there are those who will call him dictatorial.

If the university goes to seed under his leadership, many will call him inept.

A president I knew well once called a subordinate into the office and instructed him to find out just what the faculty thought of their president. The unlucky messenger returned and with considerable embarrassment stated, "Mr. President, I am sorry to report this, but the faculty regard you as arrogant, dictatorial, and inept."

The president chewed on this awhile, then with a wry smile, replied: "Arrogant, perhaps. Dictatorial, maybe. Inept—*never!*"

The banging of the gavel signalled the adjournment of the session. I wearily gathered my notes and agendas while my less conservative colleagues raced for the bar. Casting aside my innate shyness, I firmly resolved that at the next convention I would assert my individualism by doing something truly innovative and daring—like wearing my plaid slacks and my orange blazer.

WHEN YOU'RE NOT LISTENING

At this convention of presidents I was scheduled to have my moment on the podium. When asked to present a paper on some aspect of campus goverance, I readily accepted and chose to bore in on the topic of student participation in University affairs. Ignoring my usual trepidation that pious preaching invites ready disaster, I plunged into my subject with the same boldness that characterized General George Armstrong Custer when at the battle of the Little Big Horn, he admonished his troops, "Remember, men, take no prisoners."

I confess to a certain air of smugness. The indices of disruption at ISU had been low at a time all hell was breaking loose on campuses across the country. Further, I had been paid the supreme accolade when in the late fall of '69 the student newspaper had stated that I was responsive to the opinions of students, that the doors to my office were open, and that I was a president who "cared." (I admired the editor's insight and perspicacity.) It was one of the high-water marks of my term as president, and, as Shakespeare would have put it, at that moment I would have scorned to change my state with kings.

Buoyed up by this heady experience, I was in a perfect mood to share my wisdom and insights with my colleagues.

I pointed out that there should be a continuous and overall effort to involve students in affairs and decision-making within the university and to allow them to come to grips with significant issues on the campus, particularly those which affected them. What students lacked in continuity and background, I felt they could more than make up in terms of creativity and freshness of ideas. Their impatience with red tape and maintenance of the status quo also was stimulating.

I emphasized my theory that the real power students possessed was the power of their ideas and their persuasiveness. I also advocated inculcating a sense of fiscal responsibility by acquainting them with the budget requests and fiscal management of the institution, including the relationship of their own budget and the student fee structure.

I stressed the importance of effective student participation on all of the standing committees of the university where hopefully they would learn that there were no secrets, and, often, no simple answers to complicated problems.

Finally, I added that in working with student government, the administration should be supportive to the extent that if the students could not handle a student situation themselves, the administration would—but, in most cases, after giving the students the first shot. I strongly felt that a president through his administration and actions must demonstrate a confidence in the leadership and mature judgment of students. I noted that to be sure, there would be disappointments, but that an institution could absorb and tolerate a lot of errors—something that does not hold true for the individual student to whom *his* education is a very personal thing.

Later, in reviewing this speech, I am grateful that I concluded my remarks with at least a modicum of humility, stating:

> *And now, after all these pompous pronouncements, my next phone call will probably be from our Dean of Students informing me that the Administration Building has just been occupied—serving as a reminder that in working with students, victory is never final and defeat is always close at hand. But what great consolation it is to know that within each entering freshman class lies either the seeds of democratic leadership or bloody rebellion, and that the role of the president is to approach that uncertain future with the calm confidence of a poker-playing Christian holding a pair of deuces and betting into a pat hand.*

The words were prophetic. Within a short time I did indeed receive a phone call informing me that my office had been selected as a target for a student "sit-in." Thus, one April morning (1970) when my office opened at 8:00 a.m., I was greeted by a delegation of about forty students who were protesting the non-reappointment of a non-tenured member of the faculty.

I invited the students into a large conference room and listened to their grievances, explained the processes involved in non-reappointment procedures, and informed them that in this case the matter had been carefully reviewed and that I chose to accept the recommendations of the department chairman and the dean.

When I did not accede to a prepared list of what the students termed were "non-negotiable" demands, they broke off the discussion and informed me that they were going to sit in my offices until the demands were met and the professor reinstated. With that, they left the conference room and moved into the outer presidential offices.

At that point, I noted that the dialogue had terminated and a confrontation had begun. Subsequently, I informed the students that their actions at that time constituted disruption of the affairs of the institution and directed that the building be vacated within fifteen minutes. Further, that those remaining in the building after that time would be summarily suspended from the institution.

Three left. Thirty-eight stayed. After the expiration of the fifteen minute period, I announced that those in the room were suspended. This had a sobering effect, and after a short period of discussion, the dissident students decided to leave peacefully prior to the issuing of court injunctions.

Because of their quick termination of the disruptive action, I later determined that the suspensions would be held in abeyance pending individual hearings before the university discipline committee. This committee, after the hearings, recommended that the suspension be reduced to "conduct probation", which meant that the students could continue in school providing there were no further repetitions of such behavior.

Feeling that the chief purpose of university discipline is to maintain and preserve order on the campus, and, if possible, rehabilitate the offending student, I considered that the first goal had been achieved and the second was possible, so I approved the recommendation. (This, predictably, was criticized by those extremists who would not have been satisfied by anything less than erecting a gallows in front of the Administration Building.)

Within a month, the movement of troops into Cambodia and the Kent State and Jackson State tragedies precipitated what might be termed as a national crisis on college campuses throughout the country. Many shut down.

On our own campus there were those who advocated a general strike and a cessation of the educational activities. I could not agree that the shutting down of the institution would be justified and notified the Administrative Council that in the event there was a general strike which closed the university, no credit would be given for academic work that semester and all salaries would cease that same day except for the custodians needed to maintain the plant and provide security.

Actually, this probably wasn't needed. Throughout the campus there was overwhelming support to keep the university open.

In the light of these two events, however, my campus image (at least in the eyes of the students involved and the student press —by then under a new editorial staff) had radically changed. Instead of being a president who "cared," I was charged with ignoring the views and petitions of students, denying due process, wielding the power of my office to shut off dissent and protest, purging faculty members who defended student rights and opposed the administration, selling out the students to appease the Governor and legislature and people of the State, and, in general, stifling academic freedom on the campus.

Perhaps politics by demonstration and confrontation were but a sign of the times in higher education in the first year of the Seventies. Obviously, success on some campuses had given an air of legitimacy and some acceptance to the practice. There is no escaping a certain sadness when this is the *modus operandi* and persons on both sides are locked into rigid situations where hard-line decisions must be made.

Likewise, there is no joy in a campus confrontation, no sense of elation regardless of your own justification of your decisions. Even rationalization is difficult, and the fact that the uproar involved less than .5 of one percent of the total student population is of little consolation. But appeasement is no answer, and non-negotiable demands are just that—non-negotiable.

I had discovered the hard way that with this sample of dissident students, when you weren't agreeing with them, you weren't listening.

UNRAVELING THE GREAT PAY-RAISE MYSTERY

In 1970, what started out as a bad spring for college presidents began to deteriorate rapidly during the month of May. Thus, when a starry-eyed reporter asked me, "Dr. Davis, has there been any unrest on your campus as a result of President Nixon's global strategy and Vice President Agnew's colorful rhetoric?"—I was reminded of that line: "Other than that, Mrs. Lincoln, how did you like the play?"

But with commencement over and the students more interested in pulling out of town than pulling down the establishment, I was relieved I had survived the rigors of sit-ins, peace marches, and protests; albeit, to a segment of students, my image was somewhere to the right of Ghengis Khan or Atilla the Hun.

In this cheerful, carefree mood, I planned a weekend of complete relaxation, highlighted by the annual Administrator's Challenger Cup Golf Match with Chuck Kegel (the Academic Vice President who moonlights in the summer as ISU's touring one-man golf team on the Idaho circuit), and Bill Bartz (the Financial Vice President who makes Shylock seem like a spendthrift). After an hour's futile rummaging through basement and attic, I learned my seventeen-year-old daughter had loaned my golf clubs to her boy friend. I stomped into the kitchen to complain to my wife, and the phone rang.

It was a newspaper reporter asking whether I would confirm the report that 37 faculty members at Idaho State were getting 33% pay increases. I replied, "Don't be ridiculous!"—and he quoted me.

During the next half hour, I was deluged with similar calls based on a story from the State Capitol that the Legislative Council had received a complaint from the Governor and the Director of the Budget about the exhorbitant salary increases granted ISU personnel. Quotes attributed to various Senators and Representatives ranged from protests about my blatant disregard for the taxpayers and an obvious recession to suggestions that we should be cutting salaries as a token of patriotism.

I frantically tried to contact my golf-playing associates, but they had already teed off.

Knowing that this type of rumor would hit the campus with the same stupefying impact of a gold strike on Red Hill, I could envision how the professors were taking the news. I could picture my staunchest critics in the Faculty Lounge doing a dance around the May pole, each with the expectation that he was one of the mysterious and lucky 37. In the eyes of some of them, it would mark the first time I had done anything right since I had arrived on the campus. I could have cried. This might have been my finest hour.

Chuck Kegel and Bill Bartz spoiled the occasion by arriving from the golf course resplendent in their knickers and spiked shoes. Kegel was angry—he had been putting for a birdie. Bartz was merely sullen. "Obviously," Bartz groused as he heard the news, "there's been a mistake. Some of *these* guys didn't get *any* raise."

Retiring to the Gold Room in the administrative towers, we began to trace the story to its origin. It wasn't easy. In inverse order, the trail led to the State Director of Higher Education, the President of the Board of Trustees, the *Idaho Statesman,* United Press International, the Legislative Council, the office of the Governor, the Director of the Budget, and back to us.

Meanwhile, the headlines announced:

DAVIS CHALLENGES BUDGET DIRECTOR

TO RELEASE THE 37 NAMES!

I wasn't challenging anyone. I was desperately looking for some small clue in what must have been the best-kept secret since Boise stole the state capitol from Lewiston.

Thanks to Dr. Donald Kline, the State Director for Higher Education, who threatened to set fire to himself on the Capitol Building steps if he didn't get the list of names, four days later we got the lead that broke the case.

A typist had transposed the monthly salary rates for seven departments and had erroneously listed the monthly rate of pay for nine months of teaching as the monthly rate for twelve months. It was only a small error. To give some idea of how small it was, a professor scheduled for an annual salary of $14,000 suddenly would be making over $20,000. The predictable end result would have been 37 deliriously happy and surprised faculty members gratified that their services had at last been properly acknow-

ledged, 317 disgruntled faculty members in bloody revolt, a legislature meaner than a swamp full of alligators with the swamp
gone dry, and a Governor in orbit.

That night we had a summary court martial in the administration building for the guilty secretary. I had envisioned ripping
the buttons off her blouse and drumming her out of the campus
quadrangle.

She showed up looking as dewey-eyed and innocent as last
fall's homecoming queen. She would have looked even more like
the homecoming queen had she not been eight months pregnant.
And when she cried, I cried.

I couldn't fire her. She had already quit. Her husband, whom
she had been putting through school, had graduated the previous
Friday after an undistinguished undergraduate career that covered six years and three and 8/9 children. In fact, her children
and husband were home cooking the last supper for the family
before they all departed for *his* first job.

What could I do? I told her it was too bad she was leaving
because I would put her in for a 33% pay increase if it weren't
for the restrictions imposed by that tight-fisted legislature.

The next morning as I was departing from my office to go
to Boise and explain all this to the Board of Trustees and the
Legislative Council, I noted the flag was flying at half mast, no
doubt as a symbol of mourning for that insensitive and incom-
petent president who had fouled up again.

Graciously, I agreed to accept all the blame. Kegel and
Bartz, before taking off for the golf course, acknowledged that
this was as it should be.

As the plane flew over the now-quiet campus, I refletced on
that old educational aphorism (I'm not sure whether it came from
John Dewey or Kingman Brewster):

> *When you are up to your ass in alligators——it is
> difficult to remind yourself that your initial objective was
> to drain the swamp.*

And when I closed my eyes, all I could see was alligators.

228

TEEN-AGE DAUGHTERS AND
GOD'S INFINITE WISDOM

My good friend, Larry Rice, not only is a Professor of English, he also is a philosopher, which seems only right because that is what he is a doctor of. As a philosopher-scholar, I'm not in his league. What we both have in common, though, are seventeen-year-old daughters, and that would make a philosopher out of almost anyone.

Believe me, I tried to be sympathetic while giggling myself silly one night in early June, 1970, as he reflected on his theory of God's divine plan for teen-agers and their relations with parents. His carefully modulated tones oozed with self-pity as he reported the events of the day—namely how he had given his daughter, Carlyn, permission to drive his coveted Scout on a picnic for some junior class girls. It had been begrudging permission, to be sure, because Larry is chary about loaning his hunting rifle, his hunting dog, or his hunting station wagon to anyone. He more cheerfully would share his pipe. But family pressure wore him down, and he foolishly gave in.

His afternoon meanderings over the tales of Chaucer were interrupted by a telephone call. The plaintive, humble tones on the other end of the line were in such contrast with the accustomed authoritative, self-righteous outbursts from his daughter that he immediately began to suspect that something was wrong. There was that sinking feeling in his stomach as his thoughts raced to the welfare of his beloved Scout.

His worst premonitions were confirmed. She had driven it off a small cliff. The girls were all right, the sandwiches were soggy but edible, and, while the canned pop had later exploded upon opening, the picnic, by and large, was still a success. The Scout, however, was totaled.

Like I said, though, he was philosophic about the whole thing and attributed it to a part of God's divine plan. According to Larry, it goes something like this.

If all children were as lovely and delightful as they are at age four or five, parents could never bear to kick them out of the nest. So God invented the teen-ager, and made her behavior so obstreperous and rebellious, and, at times, so downright outrageous, that frustrated fathers can hardly wait to send them away to college or give them away in marriage.

I verbally agreed that this indeed reflected infinite wisdom. But to myself I quietly chuckled and thought that poor old Larry had been carried away by a most emotional and traumatic experience.

I wasn't chuckling or giggling, however, later that night as at 2:00 a.m. I was sitting on the front stairs waiting up for *my* seventeen-year-old daughter, Debbie, who had not yet arrived home from a drive-in movie that had let out at 1:30. When her boy friend's car pulled up, I flashed on the front lights, the hall lights, and greeted them at the door. The balmy May night suddenly took on the chill of a February blizzard.

Debbie's attitude was downright belligerent, as she showed no concern for the fact that we were all up past our bedtimes. She stormed by me with a look that would wither Frankenstein's monster, leaving me holding the door open for her startled boy friend. (I think his name was Elmer.) I said the first thing that came to my mind: "Good night."

Had this been but an isolated incident, I might have forgotten the whole thing. But as I lay awake, I recalled other grievances that had accumulated—such affairs as driving the car without permission, fighting with her sister over the hair dryer, grumbling about taking her little brother to Little League practice, arguing about whose turn it was to set and clear the table, refusing to wear her warm coat on cold nights, and now, forgetting what time she should be home. It was a long and formidable list. In short, it clearly was high time that she either "shape up" or "ship out." And considering how understanding I was, I had no doubt that when confronted with my reasonable approach, she would choose to "shape up."

On this happy thought, I closed my eyes, resolving to have a little reckoning in the morning.

Debbie, of course, slept through breakfast, but this just gave me additional time to finalize my plan. A direct confrontation with Debbie, I reasoned, was enough to ruin the day for the whole family. Thus, I chose the less noble route of writing her a letter— one wherein I tempered laying down the law with making little jokes—a refined blend of justice and humor. When she marched into the kitchen, eyes flashing, fire rolling from her nostrils and smoke from her ears, I quickly handed her this missal.

June 10, 1970

Miss Debbie Davis
Pocatello, Idaho
Dear Debbie:

Your mother and I love you very much and want you to grow up and be a bright, strong, happy, healthy girl. We applaud your fine marks in school, your horsemanship, your snappy drill team routine, your shiny straight teeth, your shiny straight hair, and your eye makeup. We appreciate your being willing to get a job, your making your own clothes, and your getting yourself up in the morning on school days. We also know we should be thankful for those things you are not, such as—a hippie, a drop-out, a pot-head, a boy-chaser, a sitter-inner.

There are, however, one or two things which could be improved. One can, for example, hardly walk through your room without tripping over a bra or yesterday's underwear. We don't care whether you change diapers on you new baby sisters, just as long as you aren't howling louder or more often than they. Affection or a kind word to your brother or sisters understandably can be reserved for Christmas or birthdays, but a friendly smile occasionally would go a long way.

There also seems to be some confusion about who is running this household in terms of what time we get home, whom we ask for the car, when we get permission to stay all night with a girl friend. No doubt I am responsible for this communications gap and have failed to make myself clear. As the chief money-changer and provider in this household, I, or my designated authority, am the boss. From time to time I delegate this authority to your mother—on rare occasions to you, infrequently to Becky, seldom to Doug, and almost never to the twins, Bonnie and Brooke.

In the past few days I particularly feel I have been had. I interceded to relieve you of baby-sitting (while your mother and I attended Commencement) by bribing Becky and a friend. Instead of gratitude (which one comes less and less to expect), I am greeted by a sullen hostility and bloody rebellion. You take the car without permission, write a note stating you are spending the night at Cindy's, stay up until two a.m. this morning, and arrive home as irascible as a hungry barracuda.

Your mother attributes this to your overall exhausted condition and the hectic pace you have been following during senior week at Poky High. In this condition you have been ornery, irritable, unreasonable, and sometimes obnoxious. Your words come out not in gracious *pear-shaped tones, but more like a snarl of an angry woverine who has just had the trap snap shut on his tail. Much as I would like to overlook these small deviations from your normal, sweet, loving behavior, I feel that it is my duty as a father to register our protest and dissent —also to invoke a little discipline, painful as it may be for us all.*

Thus, you are to be home by 10:30 each evening (providing we let you out in the first place), are to drive the car only by specific permission in each instance, are to spend the night with girl friends only with prior approval, and are to love your brother and sisters and mother and father. Relief from these arbitrary and capricious rules may be granted only by formal petition and unanimous vote of your supervisors.

Your loving father,
William E. Davis

From the expression on her face I learned a startling fact about my eldest daughter—she had no sense of humor.

"Ten-thirty?" she asked, increduously.

I nodded firmly.

"Ten-thirty?" she asked her mother. My wife just turned her palms upward and shrugged her shoulders. I suppose I can be thankful that she didn't also tap her forehead and point at me.

"I'm leaving home," Debbie announced.

"Good," I said jovially. "I'll help you pack."

"I *mean* it. I *really* mean it."

I decided to play along. "Where do you think you'll live?"

"I'll go live with Cindy."

"Oh, no," I protested. "Cindy's mother works. Her dad works. They have enough family to support without you—what with your appetite for clothes and food."

That stopped her for a minute. "Then I'll rent an apartment and live alone."

I guffawed at that. "You can't. You're under-age. It's against the law." I was only guessing, but my tone implied that I was sure of my ground—I thought.

Debbie was getting desperate. "I'll go away to school."

"Great!" I shouted. "Let's pick out a nice nunnery."

Her tone dripped with sarcasm. "*That* wasn't what I had in mind."

"I know, I know," I replied with real compassion. "But I'd settle for any good school that required reasonable hours—like 10:30—and no dates except on weekends."

"Daddy," she pleaded, tears welling to her eyes. "I'm not a child. I don't need hours."

"Neither are the Marines," I argued. "And someone tells them what time they have to be in."

"Daddy, this is not the Marine Corps!"

"Sometimes I wish it were," I sighed. "It certainly would be simpler to command a regiment than to raise a teen-age daughter."

"I know . . ." she said, changing the subject.

"Know what?"

"I'll get married?"

"To whom?"

"Elmer."

"I'll bet *that* news would gladden his day," I chortled. "Tell me, has he seen you with your hair up in curlers?"

She glared. "He'd marry me. I know he would."

"Oh, yeah," I bluffed. "Well, let's get this settled right now. You just call him up and tell him to come over here. In fact, I'll do it for you." I walked toward the telephone.

"I'll do it myself," she said, snatching the phone from my hand.

"She's bluffing," I told my wife as Debbie dialed the number.

"Hello, Elmer," Debbie cooed. I could hardly believe the change in her voice. "Can you come over for a few minutes?" Debbie continued. "I just told my father we want to get married."

There was a long silence on the other end of the line. Debbie clicked the phone, "Elmer, Elmer, are you there?" Evidently he said something, because she hung up and announced, "He'll be here in a few minutes." As that thought sank in, she sprinted up the stairs and into the bathroom.

By the time the doorbell rang, she emerged as her most glamorous going-out-in-the-evening self. I could hardly believe the transition. Elmer was ushered in in an atmosphere of strict formality. We seated ourselves around the family hearth. He practically sat at attention as he blurted, "Mr. Davis, I think Debbie is a nice girl, but we're too young to get married. I'm only nineteen!"

I had to give Debbie credit. She survived this blow without blinking an eye. "But, Elmer . . ." she purred.

"How come she talks to him like a contented kitten and to me like an unhappy bobcat?" I thought to myself as she continued.

"But, Elmer, you don't understand how miserable things are around here. You've got to take me out of all this."

Good old Elmer—he looked very skeptical.

Debbie was losing her patience—also her composure. Suddenly, the tears popped out, slopping up her mascara. "Here," she said, throwing me a defiant glance as she handed Elmer my letter, "read this!"

Elmer read the letter, then laid it on the coffee table. Without giving him a chance to comment, Debbie launched into a tirade about how tyrannical and intolerable life in our household had become, concluding with the proclamation that she had no choice but to leave home.

At this point Elmer looked me in the eye and shrugged, "Mr. Davis, I know just how you must feel. We had to go through this at my house a couple of years ago with my older sister."

Debbie looked as if she'd been whacked by a two-by-four. But I had to give her credit—she was resilient and rolled with the punch. Within the flash of a second she was smiling sweetly and fluttering her eyelashes demurely as Elmer continued, "I don't think these rules are unreasonable. I'll get Debbie home whenever you say."

At this tender moment, I could not help but think about Larry Rice and his theory on God's divine plan. I put my hand on Elmer's shoulder and said, "*Son,* I'm going to barbecue some steaks tonight. How'd you like to stay for dinner?"

THE HALF-ASTRODOME

One of the big events on the docket for September, 1970, was the official dedication of Idaho State University's unique minidome, the first covered football stadium and sports arena on a college campus. And while I shared the enthusiasm of the completion of the final stages (and the anxiety as to whether or not the facility would meet all our high expectations), I well-recalled its humble origins.

When Idaho State's Athletic Director, Dubby Holt, first started talking about building a covered football stadium, I wondered if he hadn't been sitting at too many track meets with his glistening dome exposed to the sun. But, Dubby can be very persuasive. After all, a man who can coach a championship swimming team when he can't dog-paddle across the pool, or who can be an Olympic Boxing coach when he can't even whip his wife in Indian leg wrestling, has to have something going for him.

Dubby pointed out that the old stadium (nostalgically called the Spud Bowl) couldn't hold the assembled student body and faculty in an all-school "sit-in." On the opening day of pheasant season, he sighed, one could fire a shot-gun in the stands without hitting a spectator. (I thought these two arguments contradictory, but hesitated to interrupt.)

He alleged that in basketball, trying to pack the fans into our gym was like stuffing a shot-putter into a mini-skirt. As for track, one had to have the constitution of a polar bear to participate in or watch a meet. Dubby claimed to have almost lost a star sprinter when the latter broke the tape on a hundred yard dash. The string had frozen and nearly beheaded the unlucky athlete.

Then Dubby played his trump card—money. He moaned that gate receipts were so poor that we had to pass the hat to pay officials, and that if we lost even one athletic supporter, we faced a financial crisis.

His face lit up and his mood changed as in glowing terms he proposed a covered sports arena that would house our varsity football, basketball, and track events; expand our capabilities for physical education and intramurals; attract cultural and other musical events; and provide sufficient seating to help balance the budget—all in a controlled climate.

I yawned, told him I had some payroll vouchers to sign, and sent him to see Bill Bartz, the Financial Vice President. We don't call him Cassandra Bill for nothing. Bartz can find a dark cloud behind every silver lining, and I was confiident his firm "no" would chase Holt out of his office at a faster clip than a 9.4 hundred Dubby claims to have run in his salad days.

In retrospect, all I can figure is Holt hit Bartz on the same day Bill's son got a haircut and joined the Marine Corps. Contrary to his reputation as "the Friendly Undertaker," old reliable Bill was in a happy, charitable mood. He reacted just like he was hoping someone would walk in and suggest building a covered football stadium. Taking out his sharp pencil, he calculated the project could be completed for less than three million dollars, including 12,000 seats, offices, concession stands, artificial turf, a portable track and a portable basketball court, and parking. Then he called up a local architect, Cedric Allen, and asked him if he could design such a facility for that price.

Cedric got out *his* sharp pencil and replied that we were over-estimtaing the cost. He thought the project could come in at around $2.8 million.

When I made a preliminary report on all this to the Trustees, they suggested I take a couple of days off and go fishing.

Construction of any non-academic building on a college campus can be fraught with brinkmanship in diplomacy—but to propose an *athletic* facility virtually guarantees a conflagration. Probably overly sensitive to anti-establishment and anti-athletic sentiment because of my own personal background and identification with these worthy targets of criticism, I reasoned that it was high time we pool the silent majority of students on these issues. I presented the matter to the Student Senate, which in turn decided to conduct a student referendum to determine not only whether or not we should build a covered sports arena to be financed by student fees, but, in addition, whether we should continue a varsity inter-collegiate athletic program—also chiefly financed by student fees.

Predictably, the scheduled student referendum brought out the anti-athletic and anti-president factions in full force. Headed by a music major and coached from behind-the-scenes faculty, a "Ban the Dome" committee was formed to head off the alleged transition of the school to Jock Strap U.

Some faculty members were alarmed at their role of non-combatants in a campus furor, and requested a meeting of the faculty. After a presidential report, one noted campus liberal proclaimed, "This is too important an issue to be left to the students." Subsequently, it was decided to have a faculty vote by secret mail ballot to be tallied and announced on the same day as the student referendum.

Meanwhile, our audacious venture was attracting attention beyond the confines of the campus. A sportswriter on the Twin Falls *Times-News*, in a somewhat emotional vein, took exception to the election and nominated me for the "Idiot of the Year" award. Giving full vent to his skepticism, he wrote:

> *Our first reaction was, if you can imagine, one of speechlessness. But we quickly regained our composure at the latest news from the "educational leaders" of our schools of higher learning and are now prepared to discuss what we consider to be the silliest situation that has hit the area in a long time.*
>
> *We're not talking about things that fate might eventually force upon one. We are appalled that someone went out and really asked for a decking.*
>
> *This refers to the proposed referendum at the Idaho universities to see if the students want a football program. Whoever came up with the idea can claim the idiot of the year award. Let's look at the record.*
>
> *In the first place, the students of the universities are in no position to make such answers as such a policy would have to emanate from the board of trustees. If $20,000 a year college presidents need advice from students on this type of situation, they certainly aren't worth their pay.*
>
> *Doing a little speculation, we think that someone overthought on a bubbling idea at Idaho State. In the first place, that school has come up with the figure of two and one-half million dollars for a bubble-topped stadium that will seat 15,000 persons. We frankly doubt that a brand-new open-air stadium seating 15,000 to 20,000 in the site proposed could be built for much less than that figure and forget the bubble top—cheap plastic or expensive concrete.*

The unhappy editor went on for several paragraphs stating all the reasons a majority of students would vote against athletics and the proposed covered stadium, then concluded

> *Student leaders assure us that there is ample majority support for the program. If so, we are whistling by the graveyard. If not, it'll be humble pie time.*

The debate continued right up to the day of the election. Winston Churchill probably survived the parliamentary crisis at the time of Dunkirk with greater confidence and aplomb than I did that election day. But the project substantially carried with both the student body and the faculty, the dome was underway.

Thinking that the community would be overjoyed at having a major athletic and cultural center located in its midst, we selected a campus site on 40 undeveloped acres of sagebrush and ragweed. No sooner was the locale announced than we were deluged by protests from neighbors who had envisioned that area as a national park or at least a golf course.

Leading sorties against the poor, defenseless, mute, unborn building were legions of physicians who protested about the proximity of the proposed site to the Bannock County Community Hospital. Among the criticisms were the potential noise factor and the traffic snarls during our football games. We promised to cheer quietly. Our solemn assurances did little to pacify them. It was like fighting motherhood.

Bartz took another tack and began dropping the hint that we were thinking of converting that 40 acres back to an airport (which it had been twenty years earlier when the University obtained the land), or perhaps a shopping center. The criticism and protests ebbed, but the wounds were still raw.

Plans were completed, bonds were sold, ground was broken, and construction began. By June, 1969, six massive steels spans loomed above the 4½ acre hole that defined the limitations of the arena. Then the steel workers went on strike and walked off the job, leaving not the Seven Pillars of Hercules as a monument, but rather six naked arches howling in the wind.

But that didn't stop the dirt movers, who attacked the prairie with a vengeance, uncovering levels of dust that hadn't been touched since primitive man first camped along the banks of the Portneuf River. Their vigor was matched by hearty winds. Soon the area was covered by yellow clouds of powder, and hostile natives began sending me the cleaning bills for drapes and carpets. I sent them to Bill Bartz.

Bartz sent for John Korbis, the campus plant engineer, and told him to plant grass. John planted grass and covered it with healthy Idaho fertilizer. Bartz then commented, "The only thing worse than 40 acres of blowing dust is 40 acres of blowing fertilizer."

The greeting on the heights of Pocatello that summer soon became: "Where were you when the campus hit the fan?"

By the spring of 1970, the arena was almost completed. The roof had shed the snow and the artificial turf was blooming. We had calculated the drainage system carefully after studying all the rainfall records in Pocatello since the pioneers first wandered through on their way to Fort Hall. We figured we were in good shape as long as we didn't have more than two inches of rain in a single hour—something that had never happened.

Then it happened! A slick, slimy layer of mud oozed onto the street at the lower part of the arena site and covered the intersection next to the home of the local member of the Board of Trustees. At two a.m., a carefree, light-hearted, empty-headed student drove through the intersection, hit the mud, ripped out twenty feet of the Trustee's concrete fence, and slid to a stop inches from his front door. For the next two weeks it pained me deeply to drive by and watch Bill Bartz and Dubby Holt out there mixing concrete and mending fence.

The Trustee was a good sport about it all, and feebly joked, "I didn't say anything when the girders on the dome first shut out the sunrise, or when the roof finally blacked out the sky. But when the student body comes driving into my living room . . ." I called Bill Bartz in, and he called John Korbis in, and we re-routed the traffic and the mud along Bartz Boulevard and Korbis Creek.

The spring inter-squad football game was the first official function for the new dome. It was a gala night, and we were proud of the dome and the students. Some 8,000 people attended, more than had ever been at an athletic event in the area. The beautiful, artificial Polyturf sparkled, the acoustics were perfect, the climate was delightful—in fact *everything* worked, and the crowd left in a jubilant mood. After all the anguish, there seemed to be a genuine pride in a structure that was the first of its kind in the world.

Then came the June flood. Now one wouldn't ordinarily expect a flood on a high plateau—but then one wouldn't ordinarily expect a water main to break just outside the arena.

Bartz broke the news to me. (He later reported that they had drawn straws and he had lost. The reluctance was based on historical data that Ghengis Khan always beheaded the bearer of bad tidings on the outcome of a battle, and they all knew how much I admired Ghengis Khan.) "Merry Christmas," he said. "The dome now has a foot of mud and water."

Our University relations man, always alert to put the best possible construction on any catastrophe, prepared the following press release:

Pocatello: June 30, 1970—Idaho State University, home of the world's largest swimming pool, said today it will bid for the 1972 Olympic swim trials.

*New water polo coach Ed Cavanaugh (formerly var-
sity football coach) meanwhile, said he has skin divers
working to plug up a few leaks that sometimes result in
losing water at the 50-yard line. He also said he plans
to put up "No Fishing" signs at the west end of the Mini-
lake.*

*University President William E. Davis said he intends
to spend the remainder of the summer on the new presidential yacht, relaxing in the shadow of the goal posts
and planning a mode of plank-walking to be used this
fall by the disciplinary committee.*

*Student radical leader, Shoal Warning, said if Davis
refuses to come ashore this fall, his flaming liberals will
sit-in in wet suits.*

*Meanwhile Biological Sciences Professor Allan Linder
says he is applying for a grant to see if the artificial Polyturf, when well-irrigated, will grow.*

Bartz took command and soon had John Korbis bailing water,
digging canals, and manning the pumps. By fall, 1970, the arena
was ready for its inaugural season. Neither wind nor rain, nor
dust nor floods had stayed the steady flow of progress.

Thinking the last catastrophe had been weathered, I relaxed.
Then came the name crisis. Dubby Holt waltzed into my offices
with the *ad hoc* committee on naming the sports arena. Much as
I appreciated his inspirational leadership on this way-out project,
I had to reject the committee's unanimous recommendation to call
it the "Dubby Holt Half-Astrodome." After considerable man-
euvering, we resolved to let it stand as the Mini-Dome until we
could schedule another student and faculty referendum.

As the committee departed mumbling about the President
having put them off again, John Korbis, that crazy Greek of a
plant engineer, came rushing in to inform me that a local mortician
had just given the University four Greek columns which John
had erected on Red Hill. Korbis then launched into this great
proposal on how we could cover them with a dome and produce
the first Greek Parthenon in Pocatello. I yawned, told him I had
some payroll vouchers to sign, and sent him to see Bill Bartz.

FROM THE WRONG END OF THE CATHETER

Broad and comprehensive as my duties as a college president were, I never bargained for a bout with kidney stones as part of the agenda. It seems that there should be some kind of presidential immunity from such things. (There should also be some kind of immunity from that tired old gag pulled on me by the President of the Board of Trustees when he wired me in the hospital: "Sorry to hear about your surgery. The Board voted four to three to wish you a speedy recovery." Big joke!)

But as I lay in bed convalescing, I could rationalize that when it came to kidney stones, I, at last, had had the full course— not from a scientific medical standpoint, but from the patient's. My urologist (who has never had a kidney stone) says he hears that the pain is excruciating and that it is worse than having a baby (he's never had one of those either).

Whatever the standards of comparison, however, there is no mistaking the symptoms. If you have ever had a severe leg cramp (or any kind of cramp), you begin to get the picture, only this cramp is happening deep inside you where you can't rub, scratch, or grab. In another sense, it feels as if your insides are locked into two vices which are then rotated in opposite directions.

Personal reaction to this pain probably varies. For me, my toenails curl up, my knees draw up to my chest, my eyeballs bulge, and that white stuff under my fingernails is the wallpaper where I have climbed the wall in the above position. I've also discovered that the most immediate relief is to gnaw on a bed post if one is handy. Obviously, it is a little awkward to get to the hospital under these conditions, but in such an emergency, I just rip off the bed post and take it along.

At the hospital, you don't have to tell anyone what your problem is. They take one look at you and know. They slap you on a cart (still in the fetal position), and rush you into X-ray. There, they try to unwind you for your photographs. With me, this is always quite an undertaking. If they stretch out my legs,

242

the upper part of my body follows so my chest and knees still meet. If they lay me on my back, here come the knees again. They finally solved this problem my having someone sit on my feet and head.

Somewhere in the red, foggy distance, the X-ray technician says, "Take a deep breath. Let it out. Hold it." Then, "z-z-z-z-z." "Now breathe," she adds pleasantly. Once, on about the third picture, the doctor walked in just as she said, "Hold it." They oh'd and ah'd over their handiwork like Rembrandt admiring a finished potrait while I turned purple waiting to be told to breathe.

If you are lucky, the stone begins to move. This might be compared with having a knife imbedded deeply in your lower back, drawn slowly across the crest of the hip bone, then pulled diagonally across the groin. About two days later, in the final act, the stone reaches the penis. The latter reacts by puffing up and coiling like a striking cobra, hiccupping, and in a flash of blinding pain, spitting out the stone. Then it gasps and goes limp for the next six years.

The Spanish would refer to this as *la hora de verdad*, the moment of truth. The appropriate medical term, however, is *meteoritus a-go-go*, which is some kind of Latin.

I went through all this (which might be called Phase I) with stoic good humor, and six years later had, indeed, just about recovered when I awoke one Thanksgiving morning with this old familiar pain and my leg drawn up to my chest. As I hobbled off to the hospital, my spirits were buoyed up by the optimistic notion that in two or three days I could breathe again. Little did I know that I was heading for Phases II and III.

The doctor and X-ray technician expressed their customary exuberance at finding the stone. Then, the doctor, with a long face and a clucking noise, carefully explained that it appeared the stone was too large to pass through the *easy* and customary process and would require some *minor* surgery. I was flattered with all the attention as they wheeled me off to the operating room.

There, they gave me a spinal block—probably for two good reasons: one, so I couldn't feel anything—the other, so I wouldn't get up off the table and walk away in righteous indignation. As yet, I was not used to my private parts getting such public exposure. First, they tilted me down so I couldn't see, then they heisted my legs over these stirrups to get the proper angle. (I was probably lucky that this all took place over the Thanksgiving break at Idaho State University. Otherwise, I might well have had the entire ISU nursing class sitting in the gallery.)

The doctor patiently explained what was going on, or in. He inserted a catheter into my penis, ran it into the bladder, detoured it to the right and into the urinary tract, and finally plunged it into the kidney. Judging by the comments of the assembled assistants, he must have been doing a masterful job. I could hear them mutter in awed tones: "Nice shot, doctor! Beautiful touch! Oh-h-h, you hit it *right on!*" To which he nonchalantly replied, "Reel out more line."

From my biased and limited point of view, I knew it must take a lot of skill and finesse to run a radiator hose up an Eversharp pencil. (The medical term for this little operation is *penis delicti. Penis*, of course, refers to a portion of the anatomy; *delicti* is a Latin word inferring a punitive civil wrong or misdemeanor.)

When they wheeled me out of surgery, I had more tubes sticking from me than a space-walking astronaut attached to the mother ship by his lifelines.

What shreds of modesty remained quickly disintegrated as for the next day and a half, every nurse in the hospital checked my plumbing every hour on the hour. But I could have cared less. What with being torn between a constant urge to urinate and the sensation of being a wiener roasted over hot coals, it was difficult to concentrate on any rational thoughts. The inspecting doctors took it casually enough, however, and even made little jokes, like: "Did you hear about the college president who was so dumb he had to unzip his fly to count to eleven?" I wasn't laughing.

Finally, it was back to the X-ray table, where I was greeted with the good news that the doctor couldn't find the stone. Apparently, the catheter had broken it up and it had either dissolved or passed.

In the relative privacy of my room, the doctor proceeded to remove the catheter. My elation turned to stark terror, however, as he pulled out a long needle and inserted it into a bottle, drawing forth a full measure of clear liquid. Somehow, the prospect of his inserting that needle into my poor, defenseless, abused organ was more than I could bear. "What's that?" I gasped feebly.

"Oh," he chuckled, "that's just mineral oil to lubricate the catheter." Sweat popped out on my forehead and I ground my teeth as he approached wielding that dripping needle. Then I almost collapsed with relief as he inserted it not into me, but into the catheter tube.

The actual removal of the catheter was like pulling up the anchor on a small boat. He would haul in about three feet of line, throw it over his shoulder, haul in three more feet of line, throw it over his shoulder. Finally, after pulling out more line than it would take to go up an elephant's trunk, the deed was done. I looked at it lying in coils on the floor and was mightily impressed.

As I checked out of the hospital, however, I admit to some disappointment. I had no visible scars for my ordeal. I wasn't even wearing a sling. And the whole affair was certainly nothing

I could discuss in mixed company. Nonetheless, I practically danced all the way home full of relief and well-being.

All that lasted about two days. Then, in the small, dark hours of the morning, the demon hit me again. I called the doctor, who, by this time, was getting accustomed to beginning his days with my urgent cries for help. Back to the hospital and the X-ray room. By photographing me from all angles, they finally located the elusive missile. It was hiding in the tissues of the kidney behind the lower rib. The doctor gravely announced I was ready for Phase III. He would have to go into the kidney and dig out the stone. But, disconcerting as this news was, I was so ready I was willing to wheel the cart into the operating room myself.

This time, there were no graphic descriptions or friendly conversation. When I awoke, there was a hole in my side comparable to the opening of Carlsbad Caverns and on the table beside my bed was a bottle containing the stone. It was about the size of the nail on my little finger—a pathetic token of so much trouble.

My wife was disappointed. She had envisioned something the size of a football at least. She hurried home and soon returned with a lava rock the size of a half dollar floating in a pickle jar. We labeled it with an appropriate Latin inscription, *"In sic transit gloria,"* (which roughly translated means, "This, too, shall pass"), and glued it to the jar. My visitors the next few days were properly astonished.

I had one more crisis to endure. Twenty-four hours after the operation, a male orderly appeared and gleefully announced, "The doctor says you haven't passed any water and your bladder must be emptied." I couldn't have been more in agreement. With that, he handed me a cold, steel pitcher. I tried as best I could, but it defied the laws of gravity and nature to urinate straight upward while lying flat on my back.

"Too bad," he sighed. "The doctor said if you couldn't urinate, I'd have to drain the bladder with this catheter."

As he pulled out the hose, I jumped out of bed and snatched the pitcher from his hand. In this more familiar, upright position, I filled the damned thing right up to the brim. It was easily one of the most satisfying moments of my life.

In retrospect, my jaundiced eye might have exaggerated some of the details, but from my end of the catheter, these were the highlights I best remember.

Sometime during the period of convalescence, my mood changed from resentment, hostility, and aggression to acceptance, charity, and forgiveness. Philosophically, I rationalized that the whole ordeal was like going through Marine Corps boot camp: I was proud to have survived; I wouldn't look forward to doing it again.

And, for a college president, it *is* pleasing to be an expert on something besides faculty tenure and student revolts. As I said in the beginning, I've had the full course on kidney stones. And much as I would like to add, "Every urologist should have one," I won't. I wouldn't wish that on my worst enemy, let alone my friendly physician. Besides, there's no way of knowing when I might have to call him again in the middle of the night.

HOW ROOM VISITATION CAME TO IDAHO STATE

The academic year 1970 proved to be one of many transitions. Perhaps most difficult for me was the advent of room visitations. From the beginning, I made no apologies. There was no doubt that the adventures of a misspent youth had hardened my prejudices against open room visitation in college dorms. For example, if I were to write a prescription for trouble with a capital "T" for an innocent, guileless maiden, it would be to lock her into a room with one of my amorous college fraternity brothers for ten hours on a rainy Sunday afternoon listening to soul music (which in our day was Glenn Miller and Guy Lombardo). What instinct or cunning did not suggest, boredom eventually would.

I was constantly reminded (with some urgency) by the 1970's crop of collegians that "life styles" had changed. Indeed they had. The span of twenty-five years that separated their generation from mine puts me and mine back into an era as remote as the middle ages. They charged I was suffering from "future shock", while I maintained that what I was suffering from was a lucid memory and a certain nostalgia for that day when men were men and women were women and you could at least tell the difference by the way they cut their hair.

Admittedly, my classmates at the University of Colorado had been subject to some human frailties and red-blooded urges (even in the 1940's) as we waged frustrating and often losing warfare against such Victorian customs as getting our girl friends back to the women's dorm before midnight on Saturday night.

I well recalled the misfortune of my roommate (a male), who after a steak-fry and beer-bust in Bluebell Canyon roared up to the girls' dorm with his date five minutes past the bewitching hour. Faced with the alternative of ruining her social life for the year with a list of demerits that would "campus" her for an apparent eternity or the chance that by keeping her out all night and returning her safely in the morning her absence might go unobserved, he (naturally) chose the latter route. But a conscientious housemother foiled the plot, and, accompanied by the Dean of Women, greeted him and his date as they arrived with the sunrise.

His protests that a night in a sleeping bag had really been in the young lady's best interests (after all, he had kept her from the foggy-foggy dew) were to no avail. She got demerits. He got busted out of school. By the prevailing standards of the time, he was not so much a knight errant, but rather an erring knight.

Amazingly, nobody considered this a miscarriage of justice—simply bad luck.

That there was a certain acceptance of the University's infringement upon individual rights of courtship and fraternization between the sexes was apparent in at least another well-known episode at the University of Colorado during my undergraduate days. It occurred at the time I was hashing at the Gamma house, so I was familiar with the details.

Final exam week for the spring semester coincided with the balmy nights of late May, and the temptations to break the tedium of cramming got the better of three passionate Delts. Noting that the lights were burning brightly at the Gamma house, they wandered over for a visit. They beckoned through an open window to three glamorous Gammas industriously burning the midnight oil. The conversation must have gone something like this:

Delts: "It's too lovely a night for studying. Look at that moon!"

Gammas: "Sigh."

Delts: "Why don't you jump out this window and join us for a beer at Timber Tavern?"

Gammas: "We can't. It's past midnight. We're locked in and you're locked out."

Delts: "Sigh."

The boldest of the Gammas: "But if you came through this window and kidnapped us and carried us away squealing and kicking, *we* couldn't be blamed for that!"

That terminated the conversation. The fun-loving Delts climbed in the window, threw the Gammas over their shoulders, and marched out the front door with the girls obligingly squealing and kicking.

A bleary-eyed sister of the bond on the way to the john heard all the commotion and dutifully reported to the housemother, who dutifully reported to the police, who dutifully reported to the newspapers.

By three a.m., the whole state was alerted as the morning newspapers carried the headline:

THREE COEDS KIDNAPPED FROM COLORADO U. SORORITY HOUSE.

By four a.m., when the Delts returned the Gammas (a little beery but otherwise none-the-worse for wear) to their multi-pillared abode, unbeknownst to them the house was surrounded by a cordon of police. As the Delts boosted the girls up the fire-escaps for their re-entry, the place lit up like the granddaddy of all Fourth of Julys. Pinned in the glare of spotlights, the much-sobered Delts were soon spread-eagled against the wall. (Mean-while, the Gammas had scurried up the fire escape to the waiting arms of their sisters.)

No one was shot, but three promising academic careers were held in abeyance for a year. As usual the girls went free.

All of this justice had a lot to do with *en loco parentis,* which the University thought it was. No doubt such traditions dated back to pioneer days when a common reception for a young swain's returning his loved one from a midnight rendezvous included an irate father and blood-thirsty brothers with shotguns held at the ready.

Like I said earlier, all of this was readily accepted twenty-five years earlier. But *en loco parentis* had a different connotation on the collegiate scene in 1970. In this latter era kids arrived on campus, looked at the faculty and administrators, and said: "You remind us of our parents and we don't like you either." Parents, on the other hand, sent their kids off to college and when they returned said: "We don't like what we see and it's all the fault of you permissive educators."

With such scenes indelibly imprinted upon my mind, as a college administrator I acknowledged a certain respect for the grand old traditions. They seemed safer.

In such a mood I was approached by a delegation from the Men's Residence Hall Council with a petition bearing the signatures of ninety-nine percent of the campus requesting that Idaho State University adopt a policy of "open visitation" for the dorms. It was obvious that as the figurehead of "the estab-lishment," I represented a less than one percent minority. None-theless, I said, "No."

"What's the matter?" they wailed. "Don't you trust us?"

"No."

"Why? *You* make us go half-way around the world to wage war against innocent peasants, *you* allow industry to pollute the air, and now *you* won't even permit us to invite a girl to our room *to study.*"

"Study?" I said, trying to raise an eyebrow.

"What else would we do?" They asked the question with such innocent candor that for a moment I felt like a dirty old man. But they frittered away their tactical advantage by adding that grossest of insults: "The trouble with you is that you're too old to remember what it is like to be young."

"Oh, ho," I said, coming out of my swivel chair with a vengeance. "The trouble with me and your proposition is that I remember only too well what it is like to be young. You think I don't remember running around the campus after a long, cold winter shouting:

> *Hoo-ray, hoo-ray!*
> *It's the first of May.*
> *Outdoor lovin'*
> *Starts today!*

They looked shocked, so I pressed on. "You think you guys invented sex. Let me tell you, we also prowled the campus like predatory goats trying to lure unsuspecting coeds into our rooms."

One unabashed delegate harrumphed: "Did you ever succeed?"

"Not often, but just like you, we were always trying." By this time I was really carried away. "Once in awhile a guy would get a girl in the dorm or frat house. We even had a little signal rigged up. If a man had a girl in his room, he would hang a tie on the door."

"Amazing," someone clucked.

Another delegate queried, "Yeah, but President Davis, *even* in your day places like Yale had open visitation."

"I've heard that," I acknowledged. "They also had a rule that the door had to be open the width of a book. They got around this by inserting a match-book."

There was a token chuckle.

I decided to take another tack. "I was in the Marine Corps," I reminded them.

"Yeah, we know," someone mumbled.

"Well, the Marines didn't allow girls in the barracks. In fact, our sergeant used to say, 'If the Marine Corps wanted you to have a girl in the barracks, they would have issued you one.' "

No one laughed. I sat down, and the chairman of the delegation stood up. "President Davis, what you are saying is, 'No.' "

I nodded. Then I played what I thought to be my trump card. "Besides, even if *I* were to agree, I am confident the Board of Trustees would say no. Our sister institution, the University of Idaho, has requested open visitation on seven occasions, and each time it has been turned down."

Quietly, the delegation began to file from the room, but the chairman threw out a parting shot, "Gawd, you sound just like my dad."

I went home that night feeling pretty low. My decision *had been* a "no confidence" veto. The generation gap was opening like the Snake River Canyon. At forty-two I was becoming a dinosaur on my own campus, suspicious, doubting, untrusting. After all, I rationalized, a room in the dorm *was* a home away from home. Maybe today's generation of collegians *was* different, what with its creed of peace and love. Perhaps the motives of today's youth were more noble, more lofty, more pure. Human nature, like "life styles" (their words), can change. Maybe they did want to take girls to their rooms *just to study.* Perhaps we were forcing upon them an unnatural and oppresive value system and tradition that no longer fit the times—one more attempt to press upon them a standard of morals that often as adults we did not impose upon ourselves. And, as young adults, in a matter of weeks or months or years, they would be experiencing that freedom where a guy with impunity could indeed bring a girl to his room *just to study.*

At dinner, I was in a blue funk which my wife sought to relieve by saying, "Let's go to the movies. *Love Story* is on and *that* should get your mind off your problems.

As we stood in the line two blocks long that represented a good portion of the faculty and student body, I watched most of the delegation from the Residence Hall Council file by with their girls friends—good-looking, clean-cut kids, all of them. Probably, after the movie, they would go back to their dorms and study, in the lounge, of course. I hoped my sense of guilt didn't show.

In the dark of the theater, I scootched low in my chair. The film turned out to have a college setting. I was shocked at some of the language used at Radcliffe and Harvard. It wasn't falling on tender ears. I had heard it all before in construction work, the barnyards, the locker rooms, and Marine Corps—but Radcliffe and Harvard! I shuddered at the Puritan I had become. But I bit the bullet and munched on my popcorn.

Then *it* happened, right before my eyes, *room visitation!* This Harvard "preppie", Ryan O'Neal, got this innocent coed, Ali McGraw, into his dorm and seduced her *while studying.* And when I saw that old signal of the necktie on the door, I stood up and started shouting, "See! See! They haven't changed at all!"

As my wife dragged me out of the theater, the hero and heroine were romping in the snow and I was raving, "He'll never make the All Ivy-League hockey team that way!"

In the ensuing weeks as the pressure kept mounting and I was visited by further delegations and the Dean of Men and Dean of Women, all advocating *some* visitation policy, I realized I was fighting a lonely battle. Only the firm resolve of the Board of Trustees seemed to reinforce my precarious stand. But I had not reckoned on Women's Lib.

Our aforementioned sister institution to the north, the University of Idaho, elected its first lady student body president. In her initial meeting with the Board, she fluttered her baby blues at the august Trustees and the open visitation policy was adopted. The dam had burst, and I knew that it was but a matter of time before we had a similar policy at ISU.

As we walked out of the meeting, something in my demeanor must have said to the President of the Board, "How could you do this to me?"

The Trustee put a fatherly arm around my shoulders and remarked, "Being President of the Board means never having to say you are sorry." (Obviously, he had just seen *Love Story*.) "Besides," he continued, "I have a son who has been going to Harvard the last four years. His mother hopes he'll come home looking like Ryan O'Neal, and I keep hoping he'll bring home some Radcliffe girl like Ali McGraw."

In the final confrontation, I was able to effect some compromises, like entitling the new policies as "visitation privileges" so they wouldn't be confused with inalienable student rights—registering guests in and out so the dorm councils could keep track of who was studying in whose room—limiting the hours and specifying certain days so that those coeds without boy friends could run up and down their own halls in curlers and grease paint—and keeping the doors to the rooms open.

But as I sat down to sign the final document, I was plagued by the realization that for four years as an undergraduate I had tried unsuccessfully to get a girl into my room, and there I was setting all this aside with a stroke of the pen. I sure hoped someone was studying!

A DAY IN THE LIFE OF A
COLLEGE PRESIDENT

With the fall semester of 1970 well underway, the Board of Trustees in executive session (that always lends an air of mystery) announced to the presidents of the respective state colleges and universities that it would like each president to submit a written report of his activities. What with President Kingman Brewster of Yale coming out with his statement that a president's leadership and effectiveness should be reviewed every five or six years and a decision made as to the desirability of his reappointment, I wondered if the members of our Board had not been reading too many eastern newspapers.

The obvious growth data are always readily available. I could overwhelm them with statistics like in the five—going on six—years I had been at Idaho State, the student body had grown from 4,080 to 8,415. Or, I could mention all that detail that fills biennial reports and is circulated to all state officials before being stuffed unread into some musty file—millions of dollars of construction completed, square feet of buildings added, acres acquired, new academic programs introduced, research published. I could even throw in two unique features—the world's first mini-dome on a college campus and the first four pillars of a Greek Parthenon on Red Hill.

But the particular dilemma that arises in evaluating leadership (one's own or that of others), is that the judge often never really knows whether these events happened because a particular president was in office at this time, or whether they would have occurred regardless of who presided over the affairs of the institution. This reflects Dr. Sidney Hook's comment in his book, *The Hero in History*, when he states: "There is a natural tendency to associate the leader with the results achieved under his leadership even when these achievements, good or bad, have resulted despite his leadership rather than because of it."[1]

[1]Sidney Hook, *The Hero in History*, Beacon Press, Boston, Mass., 1934, p. 4.

Some presidential critics on our faculty, for example, would argue that the chief barrier to ISU's becoming a "great" university over the past six years was a continuing lack of leadership on the administrative level—that they were provided an anchor rather than a compass, a shallow after-dinner speaker rather than a learned statesman. They not only cite the deficiencies, they propose the solution—turn the administration over to the faculty.

Of course, this would come into conflict with those agitating for "student power," whose goal is to turn the administration over to the students. (This is hardly a new concept, but reflects back on medieval times when students set up and ran *their own universities,* employed and fired the faculty, played fast and loose with the town authorities, and, when things got too hot for them, packed up their university and carried it off like itinerant peddlers and set it down again where they pleased. Of course, the enthusiasm wanes when it is pointed out that a completely "free" student controlled university in the medieval sense means that they would be free from the use of any campus facilities or the nucleus of a "hired" faculty subsidized by the state.)

Perhaps the true measure of leadership is the ability (or lack of it) on the part of a president to create and maintain a working partnership between governing board, administration, faculty, students, and the people of the state and community (who support the institution) necessary to move the university forward. Lacking excellence in leadership in any one of these important areas for any length of time, failure or mediocrity is almost a certainty.

But whether the president's decisions actually change the institution or whether he merely rides the crest of the times, he, nonetheless, is the man out front, the spokesman for the institution. His is the glamour and the public exposure, for good or bad.

On the good side (from the president's point of view) there is an exhilaration in working with not only the talented and enthusiastic representatives of the academic community, but also with the key political and civic leaders of the state. Speaking appearances before university or public groups average between two and three hundred a year.

Such exposure can spoil one in a hurry, all that sitting at head tables, being accorded the courtesies of a dignitary with people hanging onto your every word. It is easy to get trapped into thinking you should say something profound every time you open your mouth, because that often is the expectation of the audience and the press. But the pragmatic president knows how ridiculous this is. Faced by a time factor that has allowed only limited preparation for a major address, I well know the near panic of sitting at a banquet table desperately trying to pull together a coherent message while carrying on a vague conversation with the lady on my right and the lady on my left. In such cases I always pray that my wife is seated next to me so I can ignore at least one dinner partner with impunity. (I am amused, however, when sitting in an audience awaiting some other speaker's profound words to see him staring mystically at his plate while others are eating frantically. I know full well that it isn't his appetite that is bothering him, just his speech.)

But there is another side to public exposure for the college president. While I have been accorded the courtesies and honors that accompany the office, I also have been the recipient of heated personal attacks, harassment via obscene phone calls, bomb threats to my office and campus buildings, and whiskey bottles through the windows of my home. I have been blasted by the conservatives for being too permissive with students on campus, and by liberals for being repressive in opposing obscene words in the student newspaper or terminating a "sit-in" with summary suspensions.

Perhaps this vehement castigation is but par for the times. Where once the college president resided in a place of respect and honor, somewhat removed and isolated from the brickbats of public ire and criticism, today he finds himself smack-dab in the middle of not only the academic arena with all its internal intrigues and power struggles, but the political arena as well.

The position is tenuous and without any guaranteed tenure. While the president is appointed by a governing board and is vested with all the powers and authority and responsibility to administer a multi-million dollar operation which the board expects to be managed with a business-like efficiency, he also is governing by consent of the governed in a community which prides itself on the free-wheeling exchange of ideas (and where strong and conflicting opinions and debate are regarded as symbols of true academic freedom). If by his actions the president alienates himself from any one of several important constituencies—students, faculty, governing board, state legislature, alumni the general public—his effectiveness is greatly diminished. He walks a tight rope, carefully balancing the potential impact and importance of literally thousands of decisions, most of which are acceptable and accepted. A few, however, are bitterly contested and passionately aired. I am sure that there are moments when every college president feels himself in the middle of a no-man's land where the contesting factions are lobbing hand grenades back and forth.

In such an atmosphere, the necessity for perspective and balance, and sometimes even a sense of humor, seems imperative. But while perspective, balance, and humor are relatively easy for a college president living with the day-to-day issues and problems, I often wonder if they are as apparent to those who make sporadic or spontaneous judgments.

Just for fun, I would like to expose them to a typical day in the life of a college president such as I experienced on a routine day in the early fall.

I arrived at the office on a Wednesday morning geared up to face those twin terrors of tranquility, the morning mail and a jangling phone (always a moment of nervous anticipation.)

The first letter I opened charged that I was turning the campus into another Berkeley because of a change in key privileges in the women's dorms. (Somehow when people in Idaho wish to make an invidious comparison, they tend to choose Berkeley. And I have a hunch they aren't referring to that institution's distinguished academic program or its prestige as one of the acknowledged centers of excellence in higher education.)

A memorandum from one of the residence halls informed me that my dictatorial policies in denying the dorm students open visitation were puritanical and neo-fascist.

The phone rang and a leading local Republican complained because I introduced the Democratic candidate for governor at the dedication of the Mini-Dome. (I also introduced the Republican governor.) I hung up and it rang again. This time it was a local Democrat protesting because I didn't introduce the whole slate of Democratic candidates.

A businessman called to convey his disappointment in not being invited to sit in the president's box at the football game. I then picked up a letter from a businessman who did sit in the box, but whose named had been inadvertently omitted from the list of donors to the academic scholarship drive which had appeared in the football program.

I picked up the student newspaper, the newly-named *Speculum* (which I later discovered that, among other definitions, was a medical instrument used by gynecologists). The *Speculum* took strong exception to the fact that I introduced anyone at all, and particularly leaders in the business community, while ignoring the student body except for several elected student officers and assorted campus queens. It also accused me of returning to my days of football glory by kicking off the football in the dedication ceremonies. (I thought about replying to the effect that it wasn't a *return* to glory, that I had never kicked off in a game, and that this might be my first and last chance. But I decided to let this one lie.)

At that moment, a Board member called to ask why I was permitting the parachute club to jump onto our campus after a sister institution had had an unfortunate accident when a jumper's chute collapsed above their new football stadium. I didn't know anything about this, but quickly passed the word, "No parachute drops on campus."

With the mail and urgent phone calls out of the way, I started on the round of appointments. The Dean of Medical Arts had a financial crisis. At the Allied Health Conference banquet the preceding Friday, one hundred had bought tickets and one hundred and fifty showed up.

Next on the agenda was an honor student who wanted to apply for a Rhodes scholarship and needed a recommendation. He had discovered that the Library was missing some key documents in the recommended reading list on Oxford, so I placed an order.

The Academic Vice President came in. A faculty member was irate because he had to pick up his material for advising freshman on September 4, when his contract was not effective until September 5. Another had chased a student across campus with a jack handle because the latter had parked in his reserved spot. Clearly, the parking policy needed overhauling again, and this one was only two weeks old.

The Student Body President dropped by to register a protest that even though the students were strongly represented on the Stadium Control Board, they resented the fact that the Minidome manager (a former student body president) chaired the board. The immediate criticism seemed to revolve around the fact that a local high school team had exceeded the time limit allocated for its practice, thus delaying a series of scheduled intramural touch football games in the Minidome the previous night.

By then, it was time to go to a Chamber of Commerce luncheon meeting. These gentlemen had read the *Speculum* and its criticism of the business community and wondered why, with all their support and advertising, the students didn't like them.

In the afternoon I finalized the agenda for the upcoming weekend meeting with the Trustees, reviewed the proposed curriculums for the Doctor of Arts programs, approved 25 travel forms banishing the English department to Sun Valley where ISU was hosting the Western Modern Language Association Meeting, agreed to make some opening remarks at the same meeting, and signed five grant requests I had to accept on good faith because the deadline for submitting them was midnight that night. (I flinched as I recalled the last time I had signed something without reading it, 37 faculty members had been listed for a 33 per cent increase in pay.)

Having a few idle moments, I called up the football coach to congratulate him on his 64 to 34 win the previous Saturday. His feelings were hurt because the wife of the athletic director had suggested that his pass defense left something to be desired. I told him to cheer up and not worry about the coming game with the University of Idaho—that it was strictly a no-pressure contest. His chuckle sounded like a death rattle. He not only was losing his hair, but also his sense of humor.

I threw some homework into my briefcase and prepared to leave when the phone rang again. I had forgotten to introduce Miss Rodeo Idaho at last Saturday's game.

I went to the gym and changed clothes in preparation for the practice session for the Administration-Student Senate touch football game scheduled for the next Sunday. As if I didn't have enough on my mind, our star halfback, Jarring Jay Jensen, the Dean of Students, pulled a thigh muscle and had to be placed on the waiver list.

Arriving home at 6:15, I sat down to supper. The phone rang. It was the Chairman of the Legislative Finance Committee wanting an extra ticket for the Idaho game. We were sold out, but I wasn't about to tell that to one of the most esteemed state representatives. I was willing to make almost any sacrifice. I offered him my wife's ticket.

At 7:00 we had a meeting of the ISU Development Foundation which lasted until 10:00. From there I rushed over to Turner House, one of the women's dorms, where I talked to the girls from the lower four floors about the University. At 11:00, I made the same talk to the girls from the upper four floors. I was glowing in the warm reception and informal discussion when a young lady in the corner raised her hand and asked, "Why is the University building all these buildings when it should be putting money into faculty salaries?"

About midnight, I arrived home, took off my clothes, brushed my teeth, and flopped in bed. I was just about asleep when my wife poked me in the ribs. "You didn't kiss me goodnight," she said. "What's the matter? Don't you love me anymore?"

And so it goes—the trivial and the serious. And this was a day without any *real* crisis.

259

FROM QUICK KICKS TO QUICK QUIPS

As a football coach and later as a college president, I have lived in two different worlds. From time to time, however, these unlikely and dissimilar backgrounds have overlapped, and there have been variations on themes that have woven in and out of both professions. So, I work hard at keeping the two roles separated for fear that in the confusion of a crisis, I might come flying off the bench. Apprehension about such confusion is shared by others.

This apprehension began early in my administrative career. Following my appointment as President of Idaho State University in 1965, I was warned that certain academic types had lapsed into a state of shock upon discovering that I had once been a college football coach. Then they read my won-loss record at the University of Colorado (2 wins—8 losses), noted the brevity of my tenure as head coach (six months), and relaxed. With credentials like that, there was not much danger of overemphasis. In fact, some hardy souls endowed with the gambling spirit were making book I wouldn't last the year.

But, one of the many lessons gleaned from coaching is a primitive instinct for survival and a cat-like knack of landing on your feet when flipped head over teakettle by a threshing machine. And in the eye of the threshing machine that characterizes the life of an administrator on the turbulent college campus today, I figure a president can well afford a little combat experience.

Prominent in the coach's survival kit is maintaining a sense of humor. He learns that the quick quip is often better than a quick kick in softening the blow of irate criticism.

For example, when a highly-touted team has had a catastrophic season, the coach can muse: "I can't honestly say any one player caused this. It truly was a team effort." The president can use the same comeback in reviewing the causes of a campus riot.

Or, when a beleaguered coach is asked if a complicated new play he is diagraming for the Booster Club would win for his team, he replies, "No, but it is one with which we can lose with dignity." The president can follow the same line in his budget presentation to the legislature.

Both the coach and the president learn to treasure togetherness. Take the case of the confused coach who called a bonehead play in the heat of the game. Disgustedly, he asked himself, "Now, why did I call a play like that?" He looked in the stands and realized that 40,000 people were wondering the same thing. It was a great feeling of togetherness.

The same thought must run through the mind of the college president as he floats through the air after deciding to ignore a threat from dissident factions that the administration building had been bombed.

This leads into that old coaching axiom of giving credit where credit is due. I like the sentiment expressed by Michigan State's Duffy Daugherty when, at the end of a great season culminating in a Rose Bowl victory, he stated: "I should like to give all the credit to my fine staff of assistants. After all, had we suffered through a miserable year, I fully expected to give them all the blame."

This has its parallels in the academic world. The president can state that when a student comes to the campus and conducts himself like a gentleman, provides effective leadership within the student body, and achieves a fine academic record, credit should go where credit is due—to his family, his high school, his church, and his community. Likewise, when he comes to the campus and just plain raises hell and makes a darned fool of himself, credit should also go where credit is due.

When humor fails, the coach knows he had better get up off the floor and fight again. In one of the low points of my brief coaching career at Colorado, my team had just been massacred by Oklahoma, 62 to 0. I received a kindly note from Jacob Van Ek, the Dean Emeritus of the College of Arts and Sciences. He called to my attention the Scotch hero, Johnny Armstrong, who said to his men after a hard day's battle:

> Fight on, fight on, my merry men all.
> I'm hurt a little, but I am not slain.
> I'll lay me down and bleed awhile;
> Then I'll arise and fight again.

I read this to my bloodied troops just prior to the next game, which was against the University of Missouri. Our brave lads got out there and fought again, and this time the score was only

57 to 0. (Another moral here might be: "If you can get five points worth of inspiration from poetry, take it!")

Both coaches and presidents can do with a little humility at times. After that morrendous game with Missouri, the CU President called me in and asked, "What do you have to say about Saturday's score?"

I replied, "Thank God we were up for the game."

The coach and the president have other things in common, like anxiety about keeping their jobs. A football coach hit hard by graduation was asked by a persistent sports writer, "Coach, who would you most like to see back next year?" The coach eagerly replied, "Me!"

I understand this sentiment. Recently, when learning of the violent and unceremonious manner in which a college president had been separated from his job, the thought ran through my mind, "Good grief! They treated him like a *losing* coach."

Like the coach, the president is not always a noncombatant. This sometimes is a matter of choice. As an ex-jock, for example, I still relish the rigorous contact of the playing field. Carried away by such nostalgia, I once accepted an invitation to play in the Varsity-Alumni game that marked the conclusion of spring football practice at ISU.

It was rigged that I should catch the opening kick-off, hand it quickly to another back, and get out of the way and out of the game. As the session wore on, however, I pulled rank and coerced an assistant coach into letting me go in as a tight end in a punting situation.

I rushed onto the field, dashed from the huddle, and took my offensive stance. Assuming my most ferocious grimace and posture, I glared at the big tackle on the opposite side of the line. He recognized me and broke down laughing.

The ball was snapped, and I ripped him with a lethal forearm. He retaliated by picking me up and throwing me into the path of the kicker.

When I recovered, the head coach pleaded with me not to play in any more games, arguing that it completely destroyed the decorum of the occasion. At that point, I formally retired, or so I thought.

My next experience as a combatant occurred at the Weber State game. Now, some schools experience anxiety and trepidation at playing Notre Dame or Ohio State or Southern Cal. In our Big Sky Confernce, however, the bugaboo is Weber State. Rumor has it that they have one big, ugly tackle who is so mean that he got kicked out of the Marine Corps for unnecessary roughness. So when Weber State comes to town, everyone tightens his pucker string.

The 1969 game with Weber was a blood battle all the way. Just before half-time, some of our ISU heroes in the stands took exception to a Weber banner that proclaimed, "Bomb the Bengals." In the closing minutes of the second quarter, they stole the banner, touching off a brawl that would do justice to the Green Bay Packers and the Chicago Bears.

Thinking my personal presence might restore some dignity to the donneybrook, I walked smack into the middle of the altercation. It took a punch in the nose to remind me that there is no such thing as an innocent bystander.

On another occasion, I learned that I couldn't be an innocent bystander even in the safety of the stands. In a crucial game, our team was holding a 14 to 12 lead with thirty seconds left to play. ISU broke from the huddle and, to the amazement of all, our quarterback faded back to pass.

He rifled the ball down the middle, where it was deflected into the air. A halfback on the opposing team caught it in full stride and ran seventy yards for the winning touchdown.

Later, amidst the rubbage and debris of a dejected locker room, an enterprising reporter found the coach. "Who called that pass?" the reporter inquired.

The coach glared at him and replied, "Pesident Davis."

With my background in coaching, I have to keep reassuring the coach that he is under no pressure. I carefully explain that when we entertain our sister institutions, the University of Idaho or Boise State College, in our fabulous four and one-half acre covered football arena, we don't have to win. But the time we don't, he'll be separating the big potatoes from the small ones in the grandest potato cellar in the whole Northwest.

Admittedly, there are times that the flak gets thick, and emissaries representing both friend and foe fervently suggest that I forget about being a college president and return to coaching football. But I just laugh and say, "No thanks. I've been gone too long. Nobody runs the single wing anymore."

Besides, I *like* being a college president—so much so that I have resolved never to be among those who complain about the long hours, the impossible demands, the ungrateful faculty, the oppressive board, the restless students, or the recalcitrant alumni. As my old grandmother once told me, "You knew all that when you hired out for the job." And in terms of pressures and hardships, I well appreciate what it's like to be out of the uncertainty of coaching college football and into the relative serene and tranquil life as a college president. Mostly it has been great fun. Not always—but, again, harking back to my former coaching career, I have learned that you can't lose 'em all.

While never intending to belittle or demean the many serious aspects of being a college president, nor the appropriate demands on sincerity or dignity, nonetheless, I find that it often helps to step back and laugh at yourself or find some humor or good times to relish in the sometimes hectic tumult. So, come what may in the way of daily disaster, when someone asks how things are going on campus, I smile and reply, "Just great!" This can give a big lift to one's supporters and confound one's enemies. And if, in times of crisis, you can come up grinning, those around you never really know whether you have all the answers or just something devious up your sleeve.

SWEET LITTLE GLADIATOR

Well, it fiinally happened! After years of waiting, my onliest son, Doug, arrived at that age when he finally could go out for Little League football. At ten and a half years, he was more than ready. Each autumn he had participated in the ritual of tagging along with the family to every high school and college football game in the area. And, for countless gorgeous Sunday afternoons he had tolerated his old man hiding in the den watching the Green Bay Packers or Chicago Bears go at it. With his dad having been a former coach and his two elder sisters active in high school cheer-leading and drill teams, football had long been a part of family life. So, with all this build up, he was eager to change from spectator to participant.

Frustration and humility he learned early. When reporting for the initial practices, he was a gentleman when the kids lined up to receive their equipment. No pushing or shoving for him— he patiently waited his turn at the end of the line. By the time the coach got to him, *all* the helmets and jerseys had been issued. Nonetheless, he saw the bright side of the picture, he at least had shoulder pads and pants.

The family survived that crisis by scrounging up an old helmet (painted a bright orange in contrast to the team colors of white and green), so he could participate in the scrimmages. His attitude toward having no jersey was optimistic and cheerful: "Coach says *if* I ever get in a game I can borrow someone else's jersey."

The following day he brought home from practice a soggy, crumbled form indicating he had to pay a five dollar fee, submit a certification of health from his doctor, and be equipped with a mouth piece and an athletic supporter. The latter put his mother in shock—the stark reality that her son was experiencing the first initiation rites of manhood was somehow symbolized in his first "jock-strap." I had to laugh. A wide rubber band would have served the actual purpose just as well.

That team play required subordination of personal aspirations was an early lesson he learned. Since he could first catch a football, Doug had envisioned himself as a split end. Our workouts in the yard had consisted of slant patterns, hooks, down-and-outs, and his very favorite, the "long bomb." (The "long bomb" was limited to the length of the yard and the fading potency of my throwing arm and usually ended with the ball bouncing off Doug's nose into the rose bushes.) But he had to put all this behind him when the position assigned him was defensive tackle.

Actually, I accepted this decision with the rationalization that the coach had the perceptiveness to observe that Doug was not endowed with a gift of natural speed—an inherited trait direct from his father who could run all day in a cigar box. Defensive tackle probably suited him well. Around the house we became accustomed to his getting down into a four-point stance, grimacing appropriately, growling menacingly, and crashing into the nearest chair with a forearm lift.

Likewise, we adjusted the family routine to conform to his practice schedules, which meant Doug didn't arrive home for dinner until about seven o'clock each night.

He was ebulient about the team's offense, and described it thusly: "We have a quick opener right, a quick opener left, an end run right, an end run left, and an end-around-double-reverse to score the touchdowns." That was simple enough. The pass offense was more picturesque in description than it was in execution, namely: "Quick slant to the end hook." But Doug went on to inform me that they didn't use this play much because something bad might happen if their quarterback ever threw the ball. Obviously, his team was going to rely upon three yards and a cloud of dust.

At long last came the night of his first big game—a moment I had been anticipating since the day he was born. We had an early dinner so we could get him dressed and off in style. Doug was too excited to eat and rushed from the table to dress. When he presented himself properly attired for combat, I noted he had omitted his orange helmet. He brushed that aside, commenting that he would borrow one at the appropriate time.

About the only advice I could give him as we drove across town was that as a non-starting substitute, he should stay close to the coach, be right under his feet. Then, when the coach reached out to grab a substitute, he would be conspicuous and ready. Doug had his mind on other things. He wondered if it would be all right to get a hot dog at the half.

Arriving at the field, we underwent the first crisis of the evening. Doug had misplaced his mouthpiece. I left him with his team and hurried madly back downtown to buy another mouthpiece before the sporting goods store closed. I just made it. When I returned, I found that Doug had already borrowed a mouthpiece from his buddy, Elwood. He also had borrowed Elwood's jersey and helmet. (Elwood wasn't playing because in his own words, he had a "slightly sprained toe." Elwood's bad toe was Doug's good fortune!)

Doug's team, the Holiday Inns, was very colorful, what with its jerseys of gold with red numbers and white helmets with green trim. Doug was number 13, which must have had some symbolic connotation. The opponents, McDonald's Hamburgers, looked formidable and organized, warming up for more than an hour before the kickoff while two other Little League teams concluded their game. Doug's team merely stood around and watched, obviously husbanding the big effort for the action to come.

I joined my wife in the breezy bleachers for the long awaited kickoff. It went ten yards and hit a lineman on the noseguard, at which time there occurred the grand-daddy of all dog-piles and confusion. Doug's team came up with the ball, and after three fumbles and three off-side penalties, had the ball "fourth and infinity" deep in its own territory.

I, naturally, expected a punt. But, no, such things like kicking on fourth down are disdained in Little League football. Something bad might happen, such as the center not getting the ball back to the kicker or the kicker not catching the ball or not kicking it if he got it.

Audaciously, the Holiday Inns lined up in a full-house T, and on their "quick opener right" popped the fullback up the middle for a sixty yard touchdown. Now that someone had scored and the game was in the bag, I began to look for Doug.

I moaned when I saw Elwood and a friend huddled under a blanket far across the field down near the goal line. I foresook the comfort of the stands to give my son a little fatherly support and advice. Much to my relief, the other body shivering beneath Elwood's blanket was not Doug. I found him dutifully squatting right under the coach where the latter could hardly move without stumbling over him.

As I approached, the coach was admonishing his defensive linemen to stay low and hit hard. I can't vouch for how hard they were hitting, but on the subsequent play they were so low they served more as a floor-mat than a road-block to the hungry McDonald's Hamburgers. But all ended well because the long gain was nullified by a backfield-in-motion penalty.

Players shuttled in and off the field in wild abandon and once the starting lineups were altered, chaos reigned. Plays were started with nine men on a team, or thirteen, or such odd assortments as four linemen and six backs. The wild-eyed look in the eyes of the contestants was not so much the fervor of action as it was blank confusion and bewilderment. Other fathers also prowled the sideline, yelling encouragement and instructions and admonitions that could never be heard amidst the din.

Frantically, the poor coach would grab number 33 and tell him to get in there for 26. Number 33 dutifully would rush on the field and chase 26 off without learning just where 26 was playing. The team would rush from the huddle and the quarterback would turn to hand off the ball to the fullback (number 33), who in the meantime had turned to the sidelines to find out what position he was playing. Number 26, however, was running back on the field with the precious information, the quarterback was getting mauled, and the referee was throwing his red flag. But the whole disaster was nullified because the other team also had twelve men on the field. And so it went.

Doug didn't play that first half. I swallowed my disappointment and moved toward him to console him about this oversight and tragedy. To my amazement, he was grinning from ear to ear, happy and content that *his* team was ahead. I backed off.

Toward the end of the third quarter, the coach stumbled over Doug for what must have been the fiftieth time. Grabbing him by the shoulder pad, the coach said, "Doug, get in there for Number 22!"

What magical, mystical, electrifying words! The millennium had arrived. Doug raced on the field and gave the bad news to 22. Number 22 didn't want to come out. Finally, his father went out and got him by the nap of the neck and the seat of the pants and carried him off.

Doug positioned himself somewhere in the middle of the line and got down into his most ferocious four-point stance. But just before the snap of the ball, he backed off, raised up, and turned toward the bleachers on the far side of the field. Lifting his hand chest high, he waved to his mother in the stands. Then he was buried as the play came smack-dab over his position.

Despite the trimmings and trapping of combative warfare, here, clearly, was no gladiator—just a sweet little kid taking another step into the unknowns of manhood, waving to his mother.

Was it goodbye?

EPILOGUE

I end these ramblings of an itinerant educator with Doug waving goodbye. Somehow it is symbolic of the concluding of a chapter with the full realization that others will yet unfold. Within the next month or so I shall be announcing my resignation or leave of absence as President of Idaho State University to become a candidate for the United States Senate.

Debbie, at this writing, is a freshman at the University of Idaho, home of the vaunted Vandals and arch-rivals of ISU. We sent her there as a spy.

Becky is completing her junior year at Poky High, where she is still majoring in cheer-leading and boys.

Bonnie and Brooke have just turned two. So far, all they have learned to climb out of is their training pants. As they wander about the house with bare fannies exposed, I keep hoping this is just a stage they are passing through.

Polly, meanwhile, is striving valiantly, against odds, to keep our home life organized. If she succeeds, there must be hope for the United Nations.

And, as usual, the announced intent of a possible change in careers has met with mixed reactions. There had been rumors and talk and name-dropping in political circles, but no real tangible manifestations until I took a trip to Washington in November, 1971. While in the nation's capitol, I had lunch with Chris Carlson, a former ISU student, who was writing for a string of several northwest newspapers. He asked if I would mind a little tourist item like I was in town for a meeting with the National Advisory Committee on R.O.T.C. Affairs. I replied, "Of course not."

On the way back to Idaho, I stopped in Denver for three days to attend another meeting. Later, still enroute home, I was delayed by missing a plane connection in Salt Lake City. I called Polly to explain and got Doug on the line. I told him I wanted to speak to his mother. There was a long silence, then Doug came back to proclaim, "Mother just read the evening paper and says to tell you she isn't speaking to you any more."

Upon my arrival at the old homestead, I received a chilly welcome as my wife waved the front page of the *Idaho State Journal* in my face. I flinched as it announced that Davis was considering running for the U.S. Senate as a Democrat.

I shrugged sheepishly as her eyes flashed.

"You could have told me before you announced it to the whole world!" she exclaimed with appropriate wild gestures.

I tried to demure that the *Idaho State Journal*'s circulation didn't exactly include the whole world, but she wasn't listening.

Since that day, I haven't been able to introduce a campus speaker talking on "The Nutrient Offshoots of Vitamin B" without it being interpreted as a political speech.

The news of my political aspirations served to launch an immediate "Dump Davis" campaign on campus. Critics amongst the student body and faculty rushed around furiously scrawling on bulletin boards and painting on garbage cans, "Dump Davis." This created considerable confusion. It wasn't clear whether it meant to dump Davis as President, as a candidate for the Senate, or as quarterback of the Administration-Faculty touch football team (where I had acquired the reputation as the George Blanda of college presidents). The only clear message was that this seemed to be one sure way of getting rid of me.

I really became suspicious when I started receiving inquiries as to who would be on the Search Committee for the new president.

People began to ask what this would do to my non-partisan role in politics—one I had scrupulously cultivated as President. I had been like a eunuch in the legislative harem—close enough to observe the carrying-ons in the political halls, but not really in on the action. In another sense, to many I was viewed as being politically ambidextrous, equally inept with either the far left or far right.

Critics begrudgingly allowed that I did have some qualifications for a candidate. After standing in commencement lines for years, I had mastered the art of the "firm" handshake.

Others acknowledged that I had attempted to span the generation gap, trying to bring together on middle ground the idealism and realism that sometimes chracterized that span between adolescence and senility.

Friends questioned my sanity, wondering why I would leave an exciting and exhilarating job for the rough and tumble of partisan politics. (One of the Board members harrumphed, "I didn't even know you were a Democrat!")

As the days swept by and the time neared when we might be leaving a home and way of life and close friends we had known and loved the past seven years, each pending goodbye was accompanied by a nostalgic tug—a constant reminder—nothing remains simple.

I could only reflect on Theodore Roosevelt's challenge of the larger arena, the drive to compete, and the reluctance to be among those timid souls who tasted neither victory nor defeat.

Nonetheless, there are those times I am tormented by the vision of Polly sitting in the middle of the street in August or November, 1972, with two howling twins and a pail of dirty diapers. I sure hope I can find something humorous for the next chapter in the next book.

Pocatello, Idaho
February, 1972